WITNESS a most remarkable rejuvenation . . .

COME ALONG on a poetic journey through the underworld of a distant planet . . .

DISAPPEAR into the mysterious center of a Black Hole . . .

WATCH a race of vast, godlike creatures who find Earth a very entertaining plaything!

SCIENCE FICTION DISCOVERIES
Edited by Carol and Frederik Pohl

Eight brilliant journeys into the fantastic published for the first time

---

Frederik Pohl, four-time Hugo Award-winner, editor of some thirty science fiction anthologies and author of more than forty books, is an acknowledged master of his field.

Each book that bears the crest "A Frederik Pohl Selection" reflects the taste, integrity and discrimination that have made his own works so highly respected by critics and enjoyed by millions of readers.

Science Fiction Discoveries

Edited by
Carol and Frederick Pohl

BANTAM BOOKS · TORONTO · LONDON · NEW YORK

RLI: VLM 7 (VLR 6–8)
      IL 8–adult

SCIENCE FICTION DISCOVERIES
A Bantam Book / August 1976

ISBN 0-553-08635-9

Published simultaneously in the United States and Canada

Bantam Books are published by Bantam Books, Inc. Its trademark, consisting of the words "Bantam Books" and the portrayal of a bantam, is registered in the United States Patent Office and in other countries. Marca Registrada. Bantam Books, Inc., 666 Fifth Avenue, New York, New York 10019.

PRINTED IN THE UNITED STATES OF AMERICA

Contents

Introduction

(A Dialogue)

CAROL POHL:
This is, let's see, the fourth anthology Fred and I have done together, but it's the first one made up out of original stories. It's also the first one in which I came to the stories cold.

What we had done on the reprint anthologies was for Fred to pick out some stories he had read, liked very much and remembered. They came in the form of musty old stacks of magazines and flaking tearsheets, and he would dump these on me, and I would pick out of the lot the ones that I really enjoyed. We figured that any story he remembered as really good, and I thought very good in reading for the first time, pretty much had to please a lot of readers.

This time, though, the manuscripts were submitted to us by the writers or their agents, and I was the one who read them first.

FREDERIK POHL:
In the long run, we both read everything, but I'm willing to admit Carol had the hard job this time. After she passed them on with her com-

ments I could sometimes skim. She had to read every word.

C.P.: There were times when it seemed that I had to wade through tons of not-very-good, but also not-obviously-very-bad, stories in order to find one that I really liked. I'd hate to be the editor of a magazine. You get the feeling, "I'll *never* find a story I really like, they're *all* going to be halfway passable and we'll be sorry we ever started this thing"—and then something wild and weird, or a funny romp, or a dear and touching story comes up, and you can hope again.

F.P.: When we started, I wondered if Carol would be particularly interested in "woman's angle" science fiction.

C.P.: That's a sexist remark. It is true that two of my favorites in this book are by women, but they're really not specially *about* women.

And I didn't really care whether the authors were women or not. I liked these stories, as stories. There are a lot of good women writers in science fiction today, I'm very happy to say; I like Rosamond Campion and Doris Piserchia very much; and I like Katherine MacLean and Joanna Russ and others, too. But I also like the male authors in this book, along with Lester del Ray, Alfie Bester, William Tenn ... I even like stories by Fred Pohl. Some of them.

F.P.: There were, however, a fair number of stories that I would have bought that Carol just couldn't see.

C.P.: And the other way around, too.

But I think it's true that I have a personal bias. I am not all that in love with technology. There are women who are, MIT-technical types who groove on quasars and time machines. I'm not one.

The way I read most of the stories was to stack them in a pile by my bed, reading a few every night, making notes to pass on, until I felt too sleepy to go on. (Usually when that happened I felt it told me something about the story.) And quite often when there were too many gadgets, too much technical material, I felt my brain beginning to fog over.

But when something came along like "Error Hurled" or "The Age of Libra" or the "Owl Creek" story, I didn't get sleepy. I *cared* about the people, and about what was happening to them.

> F.P.: Altogether—I didn't keep records throughout all of it—I think we read something like four hundred and fifty manuscripts to find these eight that we both agreed we wanted to publish. Most of them were easy decisions; one or two, one of us liked enough to carry the other along, but there were a few stories where we didn't see eye to eye at all. Either I was crazy about it and Carol thought it was appalling, or the other way around. Those we reluctantly returned to the writers, each time explaining that it was the other person who was the villain.
>
> Eight out of four hundred and fifty sounds like a very low proportion. What makes it worse is that nearly all of the authors submitting work were professionals. (Magazine editors probably buy about the same percentage of submitted stories, but they have "slush piles"—stacks of manuscripts from amateurs—to dilute their reading. We had very little of that.)

Of course, what cut the percentage was that two diverse people had to approve. I could have quarried at least one completely different anthology out of the stories we read.

C.P.: So could I.

F.P.: And they both would probably be good anthologies, too. But the stories that pleased both of us—both the old pro (me) and the relative newcomer (Carol)—only amounted to enough to make one book. And this is it.

C.P.: And, frankly, I'm very proud of this anthology—not because of anything I've done, or we've done, but because I think they're great stories.

I hope you'll think so, too!

—CAROL AND FREDERIK POHL

Science Fiction
Discoveries

Starlady

by George R. R. Martin

George R. R. Martin earns his living as a director of chess tournaments. Many people are weekend writers; Martin is a weekend worker, flying to places like Cleveland, Miami, Indianapolis and Los Angeles to supervise the 64-square joustings, and a writer all the rest of his time. He is 25 years old, and already a man to be reckoned with in science fiction.

THIS STORY HAS NO HERO IN IT. It's got Hairy Hal in it, and Golden Boy, and Janey Small and Mayliss, and some other people who lived on Thisrock. Plus Crawney and Stumblecat and the Marquis, who'll do well enough as villains. But it hasn't got a hero . . . well, unless you count Hairy Hal.

On the day it all began, he was out late, wandering far from the Plaza in the dock section near the Up-end of the Concourse. It was night-cycle; the big overhead light-panels had faded to black, and here the wall-lights were few and dim. Elsewhere, just down the Concourse, the Silver Plaza was alive with music; multi-colored strobes were flashing, and joy-smoke was belching from the air ducts. But Hal walked in darkness, through silent halls full of deserted loading trucks, past shadowed stacks of freight. Here, near the docks, Thisrock was much as the Imperials had known it. The corridors near the Plaza were all shops and disfigured plastic; the walls of the Concourse were covered with boasts and slogans and obscenities. But here, here, the only markings on the shining duralloy were the corridor numbers that the men of the Federal Empire had left. Hairy Hal knew the business was elsewhere. But he'd given up on business that night, and he was here.

Which was why he heard the whimper.

Why he followed it is something else again. The starslums were full of whimpers, plus screams and shouts and pleading. Hairy Hal was a child of the starslums, and he knew the rules. But that night he broke them.

In the black of a cross-corridor, up against some crates, he found Crawney and his men, with their victims. One victim was a youth. He stood in shadow, but Hal could make out a slender, graceful body, and his eyes. His eyes were immense. With him was a young woman, or maybe just a girl. She was backed up against the wall, under a yellow wall-light. Her face was pale, scared. And dark hair fell past her shoulders, so clearly she was off-world.

Crawney confronted them, a short slim man with black and red skull stripes and a mouth full of teeth that stuck out too far. He dressed in soft plastic, and he worked for the Marquis. Hal knew him, of course.

Crawney was unarmed. But the pair with him, the silent giants with the heads painted black, each of them carried a dark baton, and they waved them gracefully in front of them. Stingsticks. They kept the victims cornered.

So Hairy Hal, unnoticed, knelt in darkness and watched it all. It was a bleak episode, but one he'd seen before. There were soft threats from Crawney, delivered in a mild slurring voice. There were pleadings from the woman. There was a lightning pass from a stingstick, and a scream from the boy. Then whimpers, as he lay crumpled on the floor. Then another stingstick pass, a touch to the head, and the whimpering stopped.

Finally there were two rapes; Crawney, amused, just watched. Afterwards they took everything, and left her there crying beside the boy.

Hairy Hal waited until they were long gone, until even the echoes of their passage had faded from the corridor. Then he rose and went to the woman. She was naked and vulnerable. When she saw him, she gave a small cry and struggled to get up.

So he smiled at her. That was another of Hal's trademarks; his smile. "Hey now, starlady," he said. "Easy. Hal won't hurt you. Your friend might need help."

Then, while she watched through wide eyes, he knelt down near the boy and rolled him under the wall-light with one hand. The youth was blacked out from pain, but otherwise unhurt. But Hal didn't notice that much. He was staring.

The youth was golden.

He was like no boy Hal had ever seen. His skin was soft cream gold, his hair was a shimmery silver-white. The ears were an elf's, pointed and delicate, the nose small and chiseled, the eyes huge. Human? Hal didn't know. But he knew it didn't matter. Beauty was all that mattered, beauty and glowing innocence. Hairy Hal had found his Golden Boy.

The woman had dressed, in what Crawney had left of her clothing. Now she stood. "What can you do?" she said. "I'm Janey Small, from Rhiannon. Our ship . . ."

Hal looked up at her. "No, starlady," he said. "No ship no more. Crawney got the name tabs, the Marquis'll sell. Some insider will be Janey Small, from

Rhiannon. See? Happens, well, every day. Starlady should have stayed on the Concourse."

"But," the woman started. "We have to go to someone. I mean, the man with the striped head, he said he'd show us the good stuff. He hired the other two for us, as bodyguards. Can you take us to the police?" Her voice was even, quiet, and the teartracks on her face were dry now. She recovered fast. Hal admired her.

"Starlady landed on Thisrock," he said. "No police here. Nothing. Should've hired a real bodyguard. Crew would give you a steer, usual. Crawney hit, instead. Starlady wasn't Promethean, wasn't insider, wasn't protected, probly four-class passage, right?" He paused, she nodded. "So, right. Crawney wanted tabs, starlady was stupid, easy hit." Hal glanced down at Golden Boy, then up at the woman again. "With you?," he asked.

"Yes. No." She shook her head. "Not precisely. He was on the ship. No one could understand him, and no one seemed to know him, or where he was from. He started following me around. I don't know much about him, but he's good, kind. What's going to happen to us now?"

Hal shrugged. "Help get Golden Boy over Hal's shoulder. Come with, to home."

Hairy Hal's home; a four-room compartment on a cross corridor near the Concourse, just off the Silver Plaza. It was good for trade. The door was heavy duralloy. Inside was a large square chamber, with a low couch along one wall and opposite a built-in kitchen. Above the couch were racks of books and tapes; for a starslummer, Hal was an intellectual. A big plastic table filled most of the room, and closed doors led off to the bedrooms and the waste cube. A glowing globe sat in the center of the table, sending pink reflections scuttling across the walls as it pulsed.

Hairy Hal dumped Golden Boy, still out, on the

4

couch, then sat down at the table. He pointed to a second chair, and Janey sat too. And then, before either of them could say anything, a bedroom door opened and Mayliss entered.

Mayliss was very tall, very regal; sleek legs and big breasts and a hard, hard face with small green eyes. She painted her head bright red to let people know what she was. What she was was one of Hal's girls. At the moment, she was his only girl.

She stopped in the door to her bedroom, studied Janey and Golden Boy, then looked at Hal. "Spin," she said.

So Hairy Hal spun it. "Starlady got hit," he told her. "Crawney did a bodyguard grabtab, threw in rip an' rape." He shrugged.

Her face grew harder. "Hairy Hal scoped it all, right? Did nothing." She sighed. "So?"

"Seal it, Mayliss," Hal told her. He turned back to Janey Small, smiled his smile. "Starlady know what comes now?" he asked.

Janey wet her lip, hesitated. Finally she spoke. "If there really are no police, I guess we're stuck here for a while."

Hal shook his head. "For good. Better face that, or you'll get hurt. Easy to get hurt on Thisrock, starlady, not like Rhiannon. Look." With that, his left hand reached across his body, grabbed a corner of his heavy green cape, and flipped it back over his shoulder. Then he took his right arm by the wrist, and lifted it onto the table.

Janey Small did not gasp; she was a tough woman, Janey Small. She just looked. Hairy Hal's right arm wasn't really much of an arm. It bent and twisted in a half-dozen places where an arm ought not to bend, and it was matchstick-thin. The skin was a reddish black, the hand a shriveled claw. Hal clenched his fist as it lay there, and the arm trembled violently.

Finally, when she'd looked enough, he reached

over again with his left hand, and took it off the table.

Then he smiled at her. "Easy to get hurt," he repeated.

She chewed her lip. "Can't you get it replaced?"

He laughed. "Probly, starlady, on Rhiannon. Probly Prometheans could, too. But Hal's here, and Thisrock forgot a lot during the Collapse. No. Not even if Hal was an insider, an' Hal is no insider. Hairy Hal is a starslum pimp."

Janey's eyes widened. "I don't care," she said. "You're better than those others. You helped us."

Behind him, Mayliss laughed. Hal ignored her. "Hey now, starlady," he said, smiling. "Listen and learn, an' learn quick. Starslummers don't help anyone, less they get a slice. Hal is no hero, he didn't even try to stop that rip an' rape, right? But Hal is offering you good, and straight, so listen to him spin. Starlady and Golden Boy can stay here till day-cycle. When the lights come on, they got to pick. One, go out and take their chances, and good luck. Two—" he cocked his head questioningly—"they stay, and work for Hal."

He lifted his right arm then, struggling and trembling, without using his left. It hit the table with a thump. Mayliss was laughing again. "Hairy Hal was good with a no-knife," he said, patting his arm with his good hand. "Still, this. Pick."

Well, I told you he wasn't a hero.

Janey's face went baffled at first, as she listened to Hal's words. Then, despite herself, she began to cry. Mayliss kept on laughing, but Hal's smile faded then. He shrugged, and shook his head, and went to bed.

The tears stopped in time, and Janey sat alone, watching pink shadows race across the room. After a long time, her gaze wandered to Golden Boy asleep on the couch, and she went to him and curled up on the floor so her face was close to his. She stroked his silvery hair, and smiled at him, and thought.

But, of course, she had no choice. When day-cycle came Janey told Hal what she must.

He gave her a smile. He did not get one back.

"You'll work the Silver Plaza," he told her, as he stood across the table and buckled a plastic belt. "Starlady's fresh, an' young, an' she smells of stars, an' that's all good for trade. Mayliss'll take the Concourse. Hal will take you round today, an' spin out all the rules. Listen."

She looked at the couch. "What about the boy?"

"*Mayliss!*" Hal bellowed. When she came, glaring, he gestured. "Stay an' feed the Golden Boy, spin him soft when he blinks, an' don't let him fly. Hal's got plans for Golden Boy." He went back into his bedroom.

Mayliss watched his door shut with a sullen expression, then turned on Janey. "Why don't you run, ship girl?" she said. "Run back to your ship. You don't click here, and Hairy Hal don't click so good himself. Scope him smart before you root, he isn't all that much. You and Golden Boy will get shoved up an air duct if you believe *his* wobbly spin."

Hal emerged from the bedroom, dressed in a black swoopshirt and his cape. "Seal it, redhead," he told Mayliss. Then, to Janey: "First lesson, listen now." He reached across his body, beneath his cape, and his hand came out holding a finger-sized rod of black metal.

"No-knife," he said. He did something with his thumb, and suddenly there was a humming, and a foot-long blue haze that stuck out from his fist. "They make them, well, not here. They come on ships. The force-blade'll cut anything, cept durloy, an' it's clean an' quick. Hal was good once, now not so good, but still he's better than most. This is your protection, starlady. This is why you don't get hit no more. Today Hal's parading you round the Plaza, an' the word gets out. Tomorrow no one touches you."

"Cept Marquis," Mayliss said. Her tone was cutting. "Cept Marquis and Crawney and Stumblecat, and any other blackskull who wants you. They get you free, starlady, and they do anything they want with you, and Hal don't do a thing. Right, Hairy Hal? Spin that at her."

Hairy Hal made a palming motion; the ghost blade blinked out and the black rod vanished beneath his cape. "Dress, starlady," he told Janey. "Take something from Mayliss, anything you like, an' cut it to size."

"Hey now," Mayliss started, but Hal raised his voice and bulled right over her.

"You pick, you get, starlady," he said. "Keep your hair, so they know you work for Hal. But tie something red round your head, so they know you work."

Afterwards, they left Mayliss and Golden Boy alone, and went out into the corridor, down to the Concourse, out towards the Plaza. Janey Small wore a red headband and a gossamer yellow clinger and a cool, pale face. She did not talk. Hal did all the talking, Hal in black and green, who smiled and kept his arm around her.

The Concourse, already, was jammed. Hal pulled Janey to a food stall, nodded to the man behind the counter, and they both ate crusty brown breadsticks and cubes of cheese. Janey put her elbows up on the counter. Hal put his arm around her, rubbed her shoulder, and pointed at people with his eyes.

That one's a thief, he told her, and that one pushes dreams, and the other with the wide eyes and the drools, well, he's that buys them. And there's another pimp, but his girls are old and baggy, and there's Bad Tanks who owns a stall out near the Plaza. Don't ever eat there, though, cause he laces his sticks with dust to bring in more new dreamers. French is a joy-smoke merchant, he's quick but you can trust him, but Gallis don't sell nothing but a spin.

They started down the Concourse together, past the grimy plastic walls and the countless shops, past fat, half-naked women with shaved red skulls who glared at them resentfully, past swaggering youths with stingsticks who gave Hal a wide berth. All the time Janey Small walked in silence, while Hal kept on his lessons.

The place with the blue curtains is Augusty's, he told her; he rents you bodyguards that you can trust. But never, never get a guard from Lorreg, worse than Crawney, only half the brains. That fat man with the green stars on his head? He's a pimp, a straight one, if someone gets to me, you go to him. Dark Edward pimps too, yes, but don't go near him, he used to be much bigger than he is. Over there you've got yourself religion, if you're the kind who likes to mumble in the dark. The guy in the silver swoopsuit, he don't have long to live, he talks too loud and he's going to get a stingstick up his ass.

They reached the Silver Plaza; a huge open place at the end of the Concourse, a ceiling far above that spilled down silver lights, tiers of balconies and shops, welling music all around them, a troupe of dancers whirling in the street. Hal pushed his way toward them, Janey followed. He watched, smiling. One of the women, a blur in scarlet veils, spun up against him, stopped, and grinned. He reached under his cape and pressed something into her palm. She grinned again, and danced away.

"What did you give her?" Janey asked, curious despite herself, after they'd elbowed free.

"A coin," Hal said, shrugging. "The dancing clicks for Hal, starlady. Probly that's another lesson for you. You won't get hit cause you're with Hal, right? But you don't hit no one, see? Hal spins straight; the ship men give steers to pimps who serve up girls without the stingsticks."

Suddenly his arm tightened on her shoulder. "An' there," he said, pointing with his chin. "There's two more lessons for starlady, walking right together."

She looked in the direction he'd indicated. A man

and a woman were making their way across the Plaza slowly. The man was broad-shouldered and blond, dressed in a dark floor-length cloak with heavy gold embroidering. The woman was brown-skinned, with kinky black hair and a pale green uniform.

Janey was still looking when she heard the voice from behind her. "The man is one of the leading citizens of Thisrock," the voice said, in a mellow, purring tone. "We call his kind insiders. The woman is an officer from a Promethean starship, of course; I expect that you knew that, dear. And your lesson, I'd guess, was to be that both insiders and Prometheans are to be treated with deference. They are powerful people."

They turned. The speaker was wearing a Promethean uniform, too; but unlike the woman's his was thin and patched. He had nothing else in common with the starship officer, or with anyone else in the crowd. Instead of being hairless, his face and hands were both completely covered by a soft grey fur. His ears were pointed, his nose was black, his eyes feline. He was, in fact, a man-cat.

"Hello, Hal," he said, in the oddly gentle voice that mocked the stingstick swinging from his belt. Then he smiled at Janey. "Right now you're full of questions," he said. "I know them all. First, I don't talk like the others because I'm not from Thisrock, and I have an education. I don't look like the others because I was genetically altered. A game they play with the low-born on Prometheus, you know. My alterations were not satisfactory, though, so I wound up here. Some of them work, however. I heard Hal's last comment from quite a distance. Now, yes, that should cover it." He smiled. His teeth were very sharp.

Hal did not smile back. "Janey Small," he said, pointing. "Stumblecat."

Stumblecat nodded. Janey stood frozen.

"You're clearly a star-born," Stumblecat said in his

10

cultured tones. "How ever did you wind up with Hal?"

"Starlady was passing through," Hairy Hal said sharply. "She hired the wrong bodyguard. Listened to Crawney spin, an' wound up raped and ripped. Now she's with Hal."

"You always were one to take advantage of a ripe situation, Hal," Stumblecat said. He laughed. "Well, I'll keep the starlady in mind the next time I'm looking. She might be an interesting change."

Hairy Hal was not amused, but he kept from showing it. He shrugged. "Yours anytime, Stumblecat."

"For a spin and a smile, Hal?"

Hal's face was dark. "For a spin and a smile, Stumblecat," he said slowly.

Stumblecat laughed, stroked Janey with a soft furred hand, then turned and left.

And Janey, hot eyes glaring, turned on Hairy Hal. "I agreed to work for you, because you gave me no choice. I don't like it, but I recognize the situation I'm in. There was nothing said about you giving me away to your friends."

Hal frowned hard. "An' nothing done, either. Listen to the biggest rule, starlady. Insiders, Prometheans, well, you scope them good, an' give them room, an' let them be customers. Nobody gets you free, cept black skulls. *Yes*, starlady. Like the ones who raped you up, don't look so white. For them, you do anything, be nice, charge nothing less they offer to pay. An' also for the blackskull bosses. Like the Marquis, who Hal will tell about. Like Crawney, who hit you. An' Stumblecat.

"Hey now, starlady, you look shocked. Why? Mayliss spun you straight, you knew it. Probly you thought Stumblecat was a good guy, right? Cause he talks like you, only better. Well, starlady just did another stupid. First she hums to Crawney, now to

11

Stumblecat. Next thing you'll be cuddling the Marquis himself; you already got both his leetenants."

His good hand was pinching her shoulder painfully as he spoke, and people in the crowd were throwing quick looks their way. Janey, furious, spun free.

"What about all that *protection?*" she shouted. "If I don't even get *that* much, why should I wear *this?*" She tore off her headband, thrust it at him.

Hairy Hal stood there, looking down at it. When he spoke, his voice was low. "Maybe you shouldn't," he said, shrugging. "Up to you, starlady. Hal doesn't force no one." He smiled. "But he's better than them."

Janey stared at him, saying nothing, holding the red rag out in her hand. Hal looked at the ground and scratched his head. And, in the awkward silence, a third man approached.

He was short, heavy, off-world; his clothes were rich. And his eyes moved constantly in a nervous scramble to see if anyone he knew was around. "Excuse me," he said. Quickly, quickly. "I—that is—the man on my ship told me to look for a man with a green cape and, well, ah, hair." He waited expectantly.

Hairy Hal looked at him, then at Janey. He said nothing.

Her hand fell. She stared at Hal's face, then at the ground, then—finally—at the off-worlder.

"Come on," she said at last.

Somewhere along the line, her name got lost. Janey Small of Rhiannon was gone, flown away on a ship hardly remembered. She was Starlady, and she did a thriving trade.

It wasn't the off-worlders so much; after the first, they came to her no more than any other. It was the starslummers who gave her business, the kids with the hand-me-down stingsticks and the whooping swoopsuits who caught the scent of stars. They'd grown up with shaved-skull hard-eyed redheads, and they wanted hair and dreams and maybe innocence. They hummed to Starlady. They came to Starlady.

And she learned, yes yes, she learned.

There was a night-cycle near the docks, when a corridor club got ahold of her. The queen of the club was a blue-skulled dreamer, and the man she hummed to had gone to Starlady. So she stared and smiled and drooled while her three underboys stripped their catch and started to play with their stingsticks. Ah, but then Hairy Hal was there! Starlady had friends all along the Concourse, and the friends had seen the grab, and they got to Hal, and he knew the dock section where the club called home. Such a short fight. An underboy swung his stingstick, Hal lifted his humming blue ghost blade, the baton sheared neatly in two, and the club ran.

And she learned, yes yes, she learned.

There was an afternoon at Hal's in the third bedroom, the special one with the canceller that wiped out Thisrock's gravity grid. But the customer wanted more than free-fall fun; he had a nervelash, which is like a stingstick, only worse. She screamed, and Hal was there, kicking off and floating fast and graceful, bringing his no-knife up and around. Afterwards they had to turn off the canceller, to ground all the droplets of blood.

And she learned, yes yes, she learned.

There was a conference at Hal's one night, and she met Dark Edward with his hot red eyes and his double stingstick and his plans for being emperor again, plus Fat Mollie who ran a stable of boys. They wanted Hairy Hal to join them. "It's a straight spin, Hal," Dark Edward said in a ponderous voice. "We can hit him good, and I'll make you my leetenant." He talked and talked and talked, but Hal just shook his head and threw them out. Afterwards he and Mayliss fought for hours.

But there came a silver morning two weeks later,

when Crawney and Stumblecat dragged Dark Edward screaming to the center of the Plaza. At first Janey just watched Stumblecat, in all his soft-furred clumsiness, and noted the lack of feline grace that Hal had told her of, the curious lack that made him a reject from Prometheus and gave him his curious name. Then she saw the Marquis, and she knew what was going to happen.

The Marquis had all of Stumblecat's stolen grace. He wore black boots and the robes of an insider, but he was very silent. His skull was silver; it shone in the Plaza light. Around it, covering his eyes, was a solid ring of tinted blueblack plastic.

While Janey watched, while hundreds watched, he took Dark Edward's double stingstick and turned it on. Crawney and Stumblecat held the victim. The Marquis played for hours.

And she never saw Fat Mollie after that day, either.

Oh yes, she learned, and soon she knew the rules. She was Starlady, and Hairy Hal was her protection, and she was safer than most around her. The blackskulls never bothered her. She was beneath them.

"The Marquis is a stupid," Hal told her after Dark Edward's death, when she came home early from the Plaza. "Dark Edward, well, he was worse, but still. Listen, the dreamboss clicks, right? The dust comes in on ships an' his men get it quiet an' sell it quiet an' no one knows the dreamboss an' no one knows how to touch him. Lametta tried, got hit. *Hard!* Probly the dreamboss will buy himself inside someday, the way he clicks. See?

"But Marquis, he doesn't click. Too *loud*. Everybody knows the Marquis, everybody chills to him, only he won't *never* buy his way down inside. The insiders don't want him marching round the Ivory Halls, less he's got an exotic for them and a quick exit-pass.

"He started with exotics, starlady. Alters like Stumblecat, an' a couple Hrangans, green gushies, Fyndii

14

mindmutes, that kind. Got all the exotics on Thisrock, right? The insiders, well, some of them hum sick, but they want to hum bad, an' they want to hum quiet, an' they pay a lot. Prometheans come too. The Marquis hums sick himself, but different; he hums to pain, an' power probly, but mostly pain. Good with a stingstick, though, an' he got the exotics. After that he got a lot of other things, joysmoke and grabtabs and ripping, all his now. Exotics are still a big slice, the Marquis has them all.

"Only, well, he's so loud, an' it'll kill him. Someday he'll try to hit the dreamboss, or squeeze an insider for quiet-money, or *something*. Maybe Stumblecat will take him. Stumblecat spins quieter, starlady, an' Hal knows he don't like seconds. Hitting Dark Edward in the Plaza was just a *stupid*. The Marquis wants to chill everybody, cept it won't click."

He was sitting at his table eating as he spoke, his cape thrown back, his claw-like right hand clutching the plate as his left cut and speared with a kitchen knife. Janey sat across from him. In the corner of the room, regarding them both with immense blue eyes, Golden Boy sat on the couch.

Golden Boy had an easier time of it than Janey. Hairy Hal had run boys before, he said, but he wasn't running Golden Boy, not yet. He just kept saying that he had plans. The youth sat around the compartment all day, eating and staring at people, never saying a word. Somehow he seemed to know what was required of him, whenever something was. Mayliss, after mothering him for a week, had finally gotten tired of the way he shrank away in fear whenever she came near him. She clawed him badly with sharpened nails, then ignored him after Hairy Hal promised her a taste of no-knife if she did it again. "Golden Boy's got to stay *pretty*," he told her, with his ghost-blade in his good hand. She'd been backed up against her bedroom door, looking terrified but oddly ecstatic. That night she and Hal had slept together; the only time since Janey Small and Golden Boy had arrived.

Most times Hal slept alone. That first night, he'd tried to sleep with Janey, but she'd pulled away and glared at him. "I did it for you all day, and you've got the money," she said. "I'm not going to do it *with* you too."

And he'd let her go, and shrugged. "Starlady, you're a strange one," he said. Then he went to his room, by himself. Janey sat by Golden Boy on the couch, looking at his eyes and brushing back his silver hair. Finally they'd gone to sleep together in the free-fall chamber, arms wrapped around each other as they nestled in the sleep-web. Golden Boy simply held her and slept. He knew what was required of him.

It was that way every night. Hairy Hal tried once more, after he'd saved her from the corridor club. Back in the compartment, he'd sat by her on the couch and kept his arm around her until she stopped her trembling. Then he got up and went to his bedroom. He paused at the door, favoring her with a smile and one of his cock-the-head questioning looks. "Janey?"

"No," she said. He shrugged, and gave up trying.

After all, he wanted Janey, and Janey was long gone. She was Starlady, and she had her Golden Boy.

Then one day, when Janey came back from the Silver Plaza, Golden Boy was gone. She looked around the compartment frantically; he'd never left before. But there was no one home but Mayliss and a paunchy off-worlder, afloat in the free-fall room. Mayliss glared at her as she stood in the doorframe, but the man just chuckled and said, "Well, well, c'mon in."

When he'd left finally, Mayliss put on a sheath and came storming and spewing out at her. "I'll chill you

16

down good, starlady, and if Hal don't like it I'll cut off his crottled arm. What's the big spin?"

"Golden Boy is gone."

"So? Hal's out selling him, little girl. Grow up."

Janey blinked. *"What?"*

Mayliss snorted in disgust, and put her hands on her hips. "I spun you straight. Why'd you think Hairy Hal let Golden Boy sit round here all day and powder his ass with dreamdust like he was an insider or something? Cause Hal clicks right, is that what you figured? So, wrong. Hal was waiting for a big sell. He spun it all out to me. With all those fun boys coming through here every day, sooner or later word's probly going to get down inside, that's where Hal wanted it, see? Lots of insiders like little boys, and he knew they'd pay big for a little *golden* boy with pointy ears and big ears and silver hair. Only Hal couldn't zactly parade round the Ivory Halls giving out handbills, right?"

"He won't do it," Janey said stubbornly. "Golden Boy won't do it!"

Mayliss laughed. "You warm me, starlady, you're such a *stupid*. Listen good, cause I'm going to spin you right. Golden Boy will do zactly what Hal says. You think you learned a lot, but you don't know *nothing*. Stead of a clear skull, you got a head full of hair and stars. I think you hum to Golden Boy, you know, and that's so warm it's *boiling*."

"I love him," Janey said, with storms flashing across her face. "He's kind and gentle and he's never done anyone any harm, and he's a hell of a lot better than anyone else on Thisrock."

But Mayliss only laughed again. "You'll learn, starlady. Hal don't click, but at least he clicks better'n Golden Boy. Listen, I used to hum to Hal once. I had to learn."

"What? That he uses people? Well, I learned *that* fast enough," Janey said. She turned and went to the couch and sat down.

Mayliss followed her. "No, starlady, you got it spun up all wobbly and tangled. I thought Hairy Hal was a big hero. He was faster with his no-knife than *anybody*, and he looked good, and he spun big about how he was going to click. Yes, and little Mayliss believed it all. Cept one night, after Hal'd been doing too good, there was this knock on the door, right? Crawney. Back then, Hal had me and two other girls and a couple boys and some exotics, plus he had some 'sticks working for him, and he was spinning about a slice of joy-smoke. Well, Crawney came to chill him down. The Marquis wanted joy-smoke, you see, and the Marquis didn't like Hal having exotics.

"Well, Hairy Hal just laughed at Crawney, and I hummed to that. It was a long time ago, right, and the Marquis wasn't so big and Hal wasn't so small, and Lametta was even still round. Hal had plans.

"Cept Crawney didn't like being laughed at. A couple cycles later, the blackskulls grabbed Hal and me and took us down by the docks. Crawney was there, and Stumblecat, and the Marquis. They made me watch, while the blackskulls broke his arm all up, again and again until he was screaming. Right? Then the Marquis just smiled and said, 'Hey, Hal's arm is broken, he needs a splint,' and they splinted it with a *stingstick*, and just stood there and watched him on the floor.

"Afterward, all the nerves were crottled or something, and Hal wasn't nothing with his no-knife. Everybody left him; his 'sticks, his girls, everybody. The Marquis took his exotics. Hairy Hal had nothing cept *me*. Little stupid Mayliss, she still hummed to him, and I stayed. I helped him use his other hand, and I thought once he was good again, he'd take his no-knife and go *after* the Marquis, right?

"Well, wrong. That's where my spin went wobbly on me, and I learned. Hairy Hal was scared, and he still is. He's never dared to get big again cause the Marquis gives him big chills. Every once in a while one of the blackskulls'll come by to have me, and they never pay, and Hal never does anything. They'll do it to you, too, watch. You'll learn, starlady. You're a *stupid* if you hum to *anyone*, or buy anybody's spin, or do anything for anyone but *you!*"

Janey waited until the outburst had passed. Then, very quietly, she said, "If you gave up on Hal, then why are you still here?"

Before Mayliss could answer the door opened, and Hairy Hal and Golden Boy were back. Hal was smiling broadly. He reached under his cape, pulled out a packet, and tossed it on the table. Mayliss looked at it, grinned, and whistled.

"Golden Boy clicked *good* down in the Ivory Halls," Hal said. Then, startled, he stopped and looked at Janey. She'd gone to Golden Boy and wrapped her arms around him and now she was fighting not to cry.

So things began to click.

Down inside, in the Ivory Halls and the Velvet Corridors, in the great cool compartments around the Central Square, the word was loose. And the customers came; sleek blond men in woven robes, matrons in dragon dresses, adventurous girls in soft plastic. Others sent for Golden Boy, and Hairy Hal took him to them, walking the streets inside as if he were born to them. He handled things quiet and smooth, and he sold Golden Boy only for big money. No starslum fun-boys got their hands on him; Hal had his wide-eyed gold mine reserved for men of taste.

And Golden Boy went, and did what was required of him. He never spoke, but he seemed to understand, sometimes even without Hal telling him. It was almost like he knew what he was doing.

Sometimes the insiders would buy him for a night, and Janey would float in her sleep-web alone.

On one of those nights, Hal returned from inside by himself, carrying a heavy book under his good arm. He was sitting at the table, poring over the pages, when Janey and a customer returned from the Silver Plaza. He ignored them and kept poring.

When the man had gone, Janey came out and looked at him sullenly. "What's that?" she asked.

Hal glanced up, smiled. "Hey, starlady. Come an' look. Hal got it for Golden Boy tonight, from an insider. It's old, you know, pre-Collapse. Straight spin!"

Janey walked around behind him to peer over his shoulder. The pages were big, glossy, full of closely packed text and bright holostrations of strange creatures in colorful costumes.

"There's something here, look here, about a race that might be Golden Boy's. Where, ah there, see. Bashii, you ever hear of them? Look at that picture, starlady, the same, only the hair is the wrong color. Still. They were a Hrangan slave-race before the war or the Collapse. So, probly Golden Boy is a little Bashii. Unless . . ." He riffled some more pages. "Here, this part about genetic alteration experiments an' cloning an' that stuff. The Earth Imperials were trying to clone their best pilots an' such, duplicate them. An' you had alters, like Stumblecat cept he's a defect. See starlady, it has this bit about *esthetic* alters on Old Earth, pretty boys, being worked up. So. Maybe he's one of those. From Old Earth, what a spin! Thisrock hasn't heard from that far in, well, long time. It chills you, right Janey?"

His enthusiasm was a flood; Janey felt herself smiling at him. "I don't think he's from Old Earth," she said. "If he were, he could talk to us. He's probably a Bashii. But I really don't care what he is. He's just Golden Boy."

"*Just!* Janey, you're positively warm. Listen, he's clicking for us, starlady. They hum to him down there, they hum high an' hot, an' probly they're going to want him down there more, right? But he won't do it right less Hal wants it, *an'* Janey, of course. In a while, starlady, we can buy down inside, all of us, cause Golden Boy is Golden Boy. An' cause Hairy Hal is quiet, right?"

"Not quiet enough, Hal," the voice said from the doorway. Stumblecat stood there, smiling, his hand on his stingstick. "Not quite quiet enough."

He sauntered in with the clumsy ease that was uniquely his. Crawney followed, pushing Mayliss ahead of him. She stumbled up against the table, reeled, then pulled away towards the bedrooms.

"They want to see you," she said, looking apprehensively at Crawney and Stumblecat. "They found me on the Concourse and took my keyplate."

Hairy Hal closed his book and stood. "Spin it," he said. His face was a guarded blank.

"You know it all already, Hal," Stumblecat said. Such a soft voice he had, such a civilized purr. "You've known it all along. We told you long ago that we bear you no grudge. You can pimp all you like, girls, boys, anything. But exotics, well, you know. The Marquis has a sentimental attachment to exotics. He collects them, you might say."

"You been spinning us wobbly," Crawney put in, grinning at Hal and showing off all his teeth. "But you can straighten out. Just give us your exotic."

"Golden Boy, I believe he's called," said Stumblecat.

"Yes," Hal said. "Only Golden Boy isn't an exotic. Would Hal spin you wobbly, eh? He's just human, an alter, look at the book." He tapped it, offering.

"I'm not interested in any books, Hal," Stumblecat said. "An alter is exotic enough for the Marquis. And even if you were right, well, the sad fact is we'd still want him. That much inside business is too tempting."

"You want to get your other arm crottled?" Crawney said. "Wrong? Then you better hum to us, Hal."

Hal did not move. But Mayliss did. She came around the table, grabbed him, shoved him towards them. *"Hal!"* she shrieked. "Hey, this is your *chance!*

Only two of them, and Crawney never carries nothing, and Stumblecat is a clumsy stupid with his stick.
Take them!" She pushed him again from behind.

And he hesitated, then whirled and slapped her
hard. "You want to spin me cold, redhead," he said.
"There might be more outside."

Mayliss pulled back, said nothing. Stumblecat and
Crawney just watched and smiled. Janey frowned.
"Hal," she said. "You can't give Golden Boy to the
Marquis. You can't do that. Hal, she's right."

But Hal ignored her. "Golden Boy's gone now," he
said, turning back to the two men. "He'll be back,
straight spin! You can have him."

"We'll wait," Crawney said.

"Yes," said Stumblecat. "And Hal, you haven't
treated us very hospitably, you know."

Hal's lip trembled. "I—no, Hal will set you right.
Drinks?"

"Later," said Stumblecat. "That wasn't what I had
in mind." He walked over to Janey, reached out and
stroked her hair. She shivered.

Hal looked at her. "Janey?" he said. "My starlady?
Will you . . . ?" But she was already gone, with Stumblecat, to the bedroom.

Crawney, not to be left out, took Mayliss.

They watched pink shadows run as the globe
pulsed.

Two of them.

Alone together.

The insider had brought Golden Boy back at last,
and the blackskulls who'd been outside had taken
him. Mayliss had left too, packing all her things in
silence. Now there was Hairy Hal and Starlady.

She sat there, calm, cold, and watched him and the
shadows. This time Hal was crying.

"I can't, Janey," he said, over and over, in a broken
voice. "I *can't*. He chills me, starlady, and I've seen
him with his stick. The no-knife, yes, it's a better

weapon, quicker, cleaner. But *him*, the Marquis, he's too *good*. Probly Hairy Hal could've taken him, he thought he could've, one on one, no-knife against stingstick. No chance, though. An' now, Hal's all crottled. Marquis'll never face him alone anyhow."

"You're Hairy Hal," Janey said evenly. "If he could take Marquis once, you can take him now. You can't leave Golden Boy with him. You *can't*. I love Golden Boy."

Hal looked up, wincing. "Hey, starlady," he said. "I'm spinning you straight. You want Hal cold?"

"If you won't do anything," she said. "Yes."

He shrugged. "I hum to you, Janey," he said suddenly, staring at her with something that was almost fear.

"Wonderful. But you'll never see me again." She stood up. "Give me your no-knife, Hal. If you won't try, I will."

"They'll kill you starlady, or worse. Root down an' listen. You won't even find the Marquis."

"Yes I will. And he'll face me one on one, too. You told me how, Hal. The Marquis is loud, remember? Well, me too. I'll stand in the middle of the Silver Plaza and shout for him until he comes. He can hardly have his blackskulls gang up on me then. If he did, who'd ever get chilled again? Will you give me the no-knife?"

"No," he said, stubborn. "You're wobbly."

"All right," she replied, leaving.

Night-cycle in the Plaza, and the silver-shining overheads were out. The wall-lights provided a different illumination, winking through their color-phases, alternately dyeing the faces of the revellers blue or red or green or violet. The dancers were out in force, music was everywhere, and the air was thick with the sweet gaiety of joy-smoke.

On the polished stairway that curved up towards

the second tier of shops, Starlady took her stand and began to spin.

"Hey," she called to the throngs below her, to the people pushing by, "hey, stop and listen to me spin. You won't soon have the chance. The Marquis is going to kill me."

Below the off-worlders paused, curious, admiring. Whispers were exchanged. Prometheans shook their heads and grinned. And the swaggers in their swoop-suits, the redheads out to sell, the drooling dreamers and the men who doled out dreams, the pimps, the bodyguards, the dancers and the thieves—well, they knew what was going on. A show was coming. They stopped to watch.

And Starlady spun, Starlady with the shiny dark hair, in a suit of milky nightwhite that took the colors of the lights, Starlady with a black rod in her hand.

"Marquis took my lover," she shouted to the gathering crowd. "He chilled down Hal and stole the Golden Boy, but he hasn't chilled down me." And now the no-knife in her hand was alive, its ghost blade flickering strangely in the violet light. And Starlady was sheathed in purple, her face stained grim and somber.

"I'll kill him if he comes," she said, as they drew away around her, leaving her alone on the stairs. "Me, Starlady, and I've never used a no-knife in my life." The Plaza was growing quiet; tension spread outward like ripples in a pool. Here the talking stopped, there the dancers ceased to whirl, over in the corner a joy-man killed his smoke machine. "But he won't come, not Marquis, and I'll tell you why. He's chilled."

And now the light clicked over, and Starlady was a vision in green, the ghost blade a writhing bluish shadow. "You've seen him kill, starslummers," she said, with a shake of emerald dark hair. "And you've heard the wobbly spins, right? Marquis, who hums to pain. Marquis, Thisrock's top 'stick." She threw back

24

her head and laughed. Over on the far side of the Plaza, they were muting their music and drifting her way. "Well, think now, have you ever seen him *fight?* Without his blackskulls? Without Crawney—" she pointed, and a man with a shiny striped skull straightened and glared and rushed towards the nearest corridor—"and Stumblecat—" she whirled the other way and picked him out lounging against a food stall, and Stumblecat smiled and lifted his stingstick and waved—"to hold the arms of his victim?"

The light clicked again, and she was bright blue and glowing, and the no-knife was suddenly invisible. Now the Plaza was dead, still, captive to the Starlady. "No," she shouted, "you haven't, no one has. Straight spin! Remember what you see tonight, watch when the blackskulls come and take me, watch how they hold my arms when Marquis kills me, and remember how he was too chilled to come alone!"

A murmur went through the throng, and eyes lifted. And Starlady turned and smiled. Two blackskulls were coming down the stairs behind her, their faces hard chalk blue. "See?" she told the crowd. "I spun you straight!"

Only then someone bounded out of the audience below, a yellow-faced youth with sparkling circles on his head and a glittery gold-flake swoopsuit. He took the stairs three at a time, past her, and a stingstick was in his fist. He waved it at the blackskulls. "No, no," he shouted, grinning. "No grabs, soursticks. I'm humming to a show."

The blackskulls drew their own sticks and prepared to take him. But then another swagger joined him, all aglow in dazzlesilk. And then a third, and a fourth with a wicked white nervelash. And others came running down behind them, sticks drawn.

Out in the plains of the Plaza, a dozen other blackskulls found themselves surrounded. The mob wanted Marquis.

And Starlady, shining crimson, stood and waited,

and when she moved the red reflections flashed in her hair like liquid fire. Till another voice challenged hers.

"You spin a wobbly spin, starlady," Hairy Hal said from the foot of the stairs. They'd gone for him, of course. By now the news had rippled far beyond the Silver Plaza. "Probly little Janey Small of Rhiannon hasn't seen the Marquis kill, but Hairy Hal has. He's *good*, redhead, an' Hal is going to watch while he teaches you how to scream."

Heads turned, people murmured. Hairy Hal, well, wasn't he her lover? No, the answers came, she never hummed to him, so maybe his hum's gone sour.

"There's Hairy Hal," Starlady called from her perch, "Hairy Hal the quiet pimp, but you ought to call him Chilly Hal. Ask Mayliss, and she'll tell you. Ask me, too, about Golden Boy and Hal."

Stumblecat, his stingstick sheathed, pushed his way forward and stood next to Hal. "Hal's just smart, Janey," he said, smiling. "You, sadly, are not. Though you *are* pretty. Maybe the Marquis will let you live, and rent you out to nervelash freaks."

Hal laughed, coarsely. "Yes. Hal could hum to that."

Her eyes flashed at him, as the red light flicked to gold. Then Marquis came.

He walked easily, gracefully, swinging his stingstick and smiling. His eyes were lost behind their dark ring. Crawney scrambled beside him, trying to keep up.

As if on signal, Stumblecat drew his stick and gestured. People pulled back, leaving a clear circle at the base of the stairway. A wall formed to keep onlookers out; blackskulls and Starlady's swaggers, working together.

Starlady descended, golden.

The ring closed around her. Inside was only Crawney, Stumblecat, the Marquis, and Hairy Hal. Plus her, plus Starlady. Or was it Janey Small, from Rhiannon?

The light went violet again. The Marquis smiled darkly, and Janey Small suddenly looked small indeed. She shifted her no-knife nervously from one hand to another, then back again.

As they advanced, Stumblecat sidled up to Hairy Hal. He grinned, and lifted his stingstick, and jabbed Hal very lightly in the chest. Pain sparkwheeled out, and Hal winced.

"Your no-knife, Hal," Stumblecat said. "On the ground."

"Hey, sure, Hal's on your side," he said. His good hand reached under the cape, came out again, and dropped a dead knife to the floor. "Straight spin, Stumblecat! Starlady needs a stinging, she never learned the rules, right?"

Stumblecat just smiled. "Maybe," he said. "Maybe that's what you think." He eyed Hal speculatively. His stingstick wandered under the corner of the cape, began to lift it. Then, suddenly, he glanced over at the Marquis, laughed, and changed his mind. Stumblecat put the stick away.

"They all saw me disarm you, Hal," he said, nodding.

Meanwhile Janey circled, holding her no-knife out clumsily, trying to keep the Marquis at bay. He hadn't moved yet. He just grinned at her, and waved his stick, like a snake preparing for the strike.

When the light clicked from purple to green, she jumped, bringing the ghost blade down at his baton. One touch, cut it in half, and he was hers. She'd seen Hal do it oh, so often.

But the Marquis just flicked his stick back, blinking-quick, and her no-knife severed air. Then it whirled forward again, to brush her wrist. Janey screamed, and pulled back. The no-knife rang upon the floor.

She backed away. The Marquis followed. "Not over, silly ship girl," he said to her softly, as she clutched her wrist. "I'm going to chill you good, and hurt you, and teach you how things work. Come to me, starlady."

And he darted at her, his stick brushing one cheek. She screamed again, as an angry flush appeared. The Marquis had his stick set on maximum.

He was cornering her, advancing towards her, herding her towards the ring of stingsticks that kept the crowd away. As he drifted in, oh so slowly, the watchers pushed and shoved for better position, while inside the ring, Crawney and Stumblecat and Hairy Hal followed behind him.

Janey took one step too far backwards, came up against a stick, yelped, jumped forward again. The Marquis stroked her lovingly down her side, and heard another scream.

She rushed at him then, tried to grab the stick, screamed again as she finally caught it and had to let it go. He gave her another swat as she rushed past, past him and Hal and Stumblecat, towards the fallen no-knife.

Marquis swiveled and started to follow. But Hal stepped beside him, then, and the Marquis shoved up against his cape.

And cried a gurgling cry.

And fell.

It was quite an ordinary kitchen knife sticking through Hal's cape. Beneath, clutching it and trembling, a crottled blackened hand.

By then, Janey had recovered her no-knife. She finished the Marquis as he lay there bleeding.

There were loud noises from the crowd. Stumblecat snarled and gestured, and suddenly the ring broke, the blackskulls began swinging their sticks, and people shouted and shrieked and scattered. A few swaggers fought briefly before running. And Crawney was still standing open-mouthed while Stumblecat picked up Hal's no-knife, moved in behind him, and neatly slit his throat. There was only room for one emperor at a time.

In the center of chaos, Hal stood smiling. Janey knelt by the Marquis. "Hey, starlady," Hal said. "We did it. I did it. Now we can get back an' buy our way down, an' . . ."

"I still don't have Golden Boy," she said, coldly.

Stumblecat walked over and smiled down at her. "Ah, but you do. He doesn't seem to understand us. I think he had some sort of empathic link with you, or Hal, or both. Join us, starlady, and you'll have him every night."

"*Hey!*" Hal said, angrily.

"All right," said Janey.

He looked at her shocked. "*Janey*," he said. "You're spinning wobbly. I killed him for you, starlady, my starlady. Like you wanted."

"That's what Mayliss wanted, Hal," she said, standing. "I just wanted Golden Boy. And I'm going to have him. He's not like the rest of you. He's still clean, and kind, and I love him." She smiled.

"But," said Hal. "But, starlady, Hal hums—I *love*, you. What about me?"

"What about you?" Starlady said.

And she went off with Stumblecat, to find her Golden Boy.

In the end, some of them were dead. The rest survived.

The Never-Ending Western Movie
by Robert Sheckley

*Robert Sheckley burst like a meteor in the sky
of science fiction 20-odd years ago and achieved
in his first few months of published writing a
standing he has maintained ever since at the
very top. His story "The Seventh Victim" was
made into a film starring Ursula Andress called,
for reasons known best to film makers, The
Tenth Victim. He makes his home in the
Balearic Isles with his new wife and even newer
daughter.*

THE NAME IS WASHBURN: just plain Washburn to my
friends, Mister Washburn to enemies and strangers.
Saying that, I've said everything, because you've seen
me a thousand times, on the big screen in your neighborhood theater or on the little pay-TV screen in your
living room, riding through Cholla cactus and short
grass, my famous derby pulled down over my eyes,
my famous Colt .44 with the 7½-inch barrel strapped
down to my right leg. But just now I'm riding in a
big air-conditioned Cadillac, sitting between my
agent-manager Gordon Simms, and my wife, Consuela. We've turned off State Highway 101 and we're

bouncing along a rutted dirt road which will end presently at the Wells Fargo Station that marks one of the entrances to The Set. Simms is talking rapidly and rubbing the back of my neck like I was a fighter about to enter the ring, which is more or less the situation. Consuela is quiet. Her English isn't too good yet. She's the prettiest little thing imaginable, my wife of less than two months, a former Miss Chile, a former actress in various gaucho dramas filmed in Buenos Aires and Montevideo. This entire scene is supposed to be off-camera. It's the part they never show you: the return of the famous gunfighter, all the way from Bel Aire in the jolly jittery year of 2031 to the Old West of the mid-nineteen hundreds.

Simms is jabbering away about some investment he wants me to come in on, some new seabed mining operation, another of Simms's get-richer-quick schemes, because Simms is already a wealthy man, as who wouldn't be with a thirty percent bite on my earnings throughout my ten biggest years as a star? Simms is my friend, too, but I can't think about investments now because we're coming to The Set.

Consuela, sitting on my right, shivers as the famous weatherbeaten old station comes into view. She's never really understood The Never-Ending Western Movie. In South America they still make their movies in the old-fashioned way, everything staged, everything faked, and the guns fire only blanks. She can't understand why America's famous Movie has to be done for real when you could contrive all the effects and nobody would get killed. I've tried to explain it to her, but it sounds ridiculous in Spanish.

It's different for me this time, of course: I'm coming out of retirement to make a cameo appearance. I'm on a no-kill contract—famous gunman to do comedy bit with Old Jeff Mangles and Natchez Parker. There's no script, of course: there never is in The Movie. We'll improvise around any situation that comes up—we, the commedia dell'arte players of the

Old West. Consuela doesn't understand any of this. She's heard about contracts to kill, but a no-kill contract is something new in her experience.

And now we've arrived. The car stops in front of a low, unpainted pinewood building. Everything on this side of it is twenty-first century America in all its recycled and reprocessed glory. On the other side is the million-acre expanse of prairie, mountains and desert, with its thousands of concealed cameras and microphones, that is The Set for The Never-Ending Movie.

I'm in costume already—blue jeans, blue and white checked shirt, boots, derby, rawhide jacket, and 3.2 pounds of revolver. A horse is waiting for me at the hitching post on the other side of the station, with all my gear tied aboard in a neat blanket roll. An assistant director checks me over and finds me in order: no wristwatch or other anachronisms for the cameras to find. "All right, Mr. Washburn," he says, "you can go through whenever you're ready."

Simms gives his main-event boy a final rub on the back. He's bouncing up and down on his toes, excited, envying me, wishing he were the one to be riding out into the desert, a tall, slow-moving man with mild manners and sudden death always near his right hand. But Simms is short and fat and nearly bald and he would never do, certainly not for a heroic gunman's role, so he lives it vicariously. I am Simms's manhood, and he and I have ridden the danger trail many times, and our trusty .44 has cleared out all opposition until we reigned supreme, the absolute best gunslinger in the West, the one who finally retired when all the opposition was dead or laying low ... Poor Simms, he always wanted us to play that last big scene, the final definitive walkdown on some dusty Main Street. He wanted us to go out high, wide and handsome, not for the money—we've got too much of that as it is, but just for the glory, retiring from The Movie in a blaze of gunfire at the top of our form. I wanted it that way myself, but the opposition got cautious, and Washburn spent a final ridiculous year in The Movie, riding around looking for something to do, six-shooter ready, but never finding anyone who wanted to shoot it out with him. And even this cameo appearance—for Simms it is a mockery of all that we have stood for, and I suppose it's that way for me, too. (It is difficult to know where I start and where Simms ends, difficult to separate what I want and what Simms wants, difficult to face this, the end of our great years in The Movie.)

Simms shakes my hand and grips me hard on the shoulder and says nothing in that manly Western style he's picked up through the years of associating with me, being me. Consuela hugs me, there are tears in her eyes, she kisses me, she tells me to come back to her soon. Ah, those incredible first months with a new wife! The splendor of it, before the dreary old reality sets in! Consuela is number four. I've ridden down a lot of trails in my time, most of them the same, and now the director checks me again for lipstick smears, nods OK, and I turn away from Consuela and Simms, throw them the little two-finger salute I'm famous for, and stride across the creaking floor of the Wells Fargo Office and out the other side, into the blazing sunshine and the world of The Never-Ending Western Movie.

From far away the camera picks up a lone rider, moving ant-like between brilliantly striped canyon walls. We see him in successive shots against an unfolding panorama of desert scenery. Here he is in the evening, silhouetted against a flaming sky, derby cocked jauntily on the back of his head, cooking over a little fire. Now he is asleep, rolled in his blanket, as the embers of his fire fade to ash. Before dawn the rider is up again, making coffee, preparing for the day's ride. Sunrise finds him mounted and moving, shielding his eyes from the sun, leaning back long in the stirrups, letting his horse pick its own way over the rocky slopes.

I am also the audience watching me the actor, as well as the actor watching me the audience. It is the dream of childhood come true: to play a part and also watch ourselves play it. I know now that we never stop acting, never stop watching ourselves act. It is merely an irony of fate that the heroic images I see coincide with what you, sitting in front of your little screen, also see.

Now the rider has climbed to a high saddleback between two mountains. It is cold up here, a high wind is blowing, the rider's coat collar is turned up and his derby is tied in place with a bright wool scarf. Looking over the man's shoulder, far below, we see a settlement, tiny and lost in the immensity of the landscape. We follow as the rider clucks to his tired horse and begins the journey down to the settlement.

The derbied rider is walking his horse through the settlement of Comanche. There is one street—Main Street—with its saloon, boarding house, livery stable, blacksmith's, general store, all as quaint and stark as a Civil War daguerreotype. The desert wind blows unceasingly through the town, and a fine dust is settled over everything.

The rider is recognized. Loungers in front of the general store say: "Hey, it's Washburn!"

I dismount stiffly in front of the livery stable—a tall, travel-stained man, gun belt worn low and strapped down, the cracked, horn-faced gun butt standing out easy to reach, easy to see. I turn and rub my face—the famous, long, sorrowful face, the puckered scar along one cheekbone, the narrow unblinking gray eyes. It is the face of a tough, dangerous, unpredictable man; yet a sympathetic one. It is me watching you watching me.

I come out of the livery stable, and there to greet me is Sheriff Ben Watson, an old friend, hard tanned face and black handlebar moustache, tin star gleaming on his worsted vest.

"Heard you might be coming through," Watson says. "Heard you been to Californee for a spell."

"Californee" is our own special codeword for retirement.

"That's so," I say. "How's everything around here?"

"So so," Watson tells me. "I don't suppose you heard about Old Jeff Mangles?"

I wait. The sheriff says, "Happened just yesterday. Old Jeff got thrown, out on the desert. We figure his horse shied at a rattler—Christ knows I told him to sell that big, skittery, walleyed brute. But you know Old Jeff—"

"What happened to him?" I ask.

"Well, like I say, he got thrown and dragged. He was dead before Jimmy Conners found him."

Long silence. I push the derby to the back of my head. Finally I say, "Okay, Ben, what else do you want to tell me?"

The sheriff is ill at ease. He fidgets, shifting from one foot to the other. I wait. Jeff Mangles dead; that blows the scene I was hired to play. What other development is coming up?

Watson says, "You must be thirsty. What say we put down a beer—"

"Just tell me the news."

"Well ... You ever hear of a cowpuncher from the Panhandle name of Little Joe Potter?"

I shake my head.

"He came drifting up this way a while ago, bringing with him quite a reputation as a fast gun. Didn't you hear about the shootout down at Twin Peaks?"

Now that he mentions it, I do remember hearing something about it. But I've been out to Californee doing other things, and shootouts just didn't interest me much until right now.

"This Little Joe Potter," Watson goes on, "he went

up against four X-Bar riders in a dispute over some woman. They say it was quite a fight. The result was that Little Joe blew them four riders all to hell, and he picked himself up quite a reputation thereby."

"So what?" I ask.

"Well, some time after that, Little Joe was in a poker game with some of the boys down Gila Bend way ..." Watson stops, uncomfortable. "Washburn, maybe you better get the story from Charlie Gibbs, since he spoke to a man who was actually present at that game. Yeah, you better hear it from Charlie. See you later, Washburn."

The sheriff moves away, following the Movie dictum of keeping the talk-scenes short and letting other people have a piece of the action.

I walk to the saloon. There is someone following me, a kid, no more than eighteen or nineteen, a gangling snub-nosed freckled kid in too-short overalls and cracked boots. He wears a gun. What does he want of me? What everyone else wants, I suppose.

I enter the saloon, my spurs clattering on the plank floor. Charlie Gibbs is drinking at the bar, a fat sloppy man all grin and crinkle, not wearing a gun because Charlie Gibbs is a comic character and therefore does not kill or get killed. Charlie is also our local Screen Actor's Guild representative.

I buy him a drink and ask him about Little Joe Potter's famous poker game.

"I heard about it from Texas Jim Claire. You remember Texas Jim, don't you, Washburn? Good old boy who works for the Donaldson outfit as a wrangler? Well, sir, Texas Jim was in this poker game over by way of Gila Bend. The action commenced to get hot. There was this one big jackpot at the end, and Doc Dailey bet a thousand dollars Mex on his hand. Little Joe was right fond of the cards he was holding, but he didn't have no more money to back hisself with. Doc said he'd take collateral, if Little Joe could think of any. Little Joe thought about it for a while, and then he said, 'How much would you give me for Mr. Washburn's derby?' There was a silence then, because nobody just walks up and takes away Mr. Washburn's derby, not without first killing the man underneath it. But on the other hand, Little Joe was not known as a braggart, and he'd handled hisself well during that shootout with the X-Bar riders. So Doc, he thought about it a while, then he said, 'Sure, Joe, I'll allow you a thousand for Washburn's derby, and I'd gladly pay another thousand for a ringside seat when you go to take it off him.' 'You can have that ringside seat for nothing,' says Little Joe, 'if I lose this hand, which I'm not fixing to do.' So the bet is accepted and they show down. Little Joe's four eights lose to Doc's four Jacks. Little Joe rises and stretches, and says, 'Well, Doc, looks like you're going to get your ringside seat after all.'"

Charlie finishes off his drink and looks at me with bright, malicious eyes. I nod, finish my own drink and go out back to the outhouse.

The outhouse is a designated off-camera area. We use it for talks which are necessary, but are out of our Western context. Charlie Gibbs comes out a few minutes later. He turns on the hidden air conditioning, takes a pack of cigarettes from behind a beam, lights up, sits down and makes himself comfortable. As SAG representative, Charlie spends a fair amount of time out here listening to gripes and grievances. This is his office, and he's tried to make it pleasant for himself.

Charlie says, "I suppose you want to know what's going on?"

"Damned right I do," I tell him. "What is this crap about Joe Potter coming to take away my derby?"

"Don't get excited," Charlie says, "everything is in order. Potter is a new star on his way up. After Jeff Mangles got killed, it was natural to match up you and him. Potter went along with it. Your agent was approached yesterday and he renegotiated your contract. You're getting a hell of a bonus for this shootout appearance."

"Simms renegotiated my contract? Without asking me first?"

"You weren't available then. Simms said it would be fine with you. He gave a statement to the newspapers about how you and he had talked about this many times, and that it had always been your desire to leave the Movie big, at the top of your form, in one last shootout. He said he didn't have to discuss it with you because you and he had talked it over many times and you and he were closer than brothers. He said he was glad this chance had come up, and he knew you would be glad, too."

"Christ! That simple-minded Simms!"

"Was he setting you up?" Charlie asks.

"No, it's not like that at all. We did talk a lot about a final showdown. I did tell him that I'd like to end big—"

"But it was just talk?" Charlie suggests.

"Not exactly." But it's one thing to talk about a shootout when you're retired and safe in your house in Bel-Air. It's another to suddenly find yourself involved in a fight without preparation. "Simms didn't set me up; but he did involve me in something that I'd want to make up my own mind about."

"So the situation is," Charlie says, "that you were a fool for shooting off your mouth about wanting a final match, and your agent was a fool for taking you at your word."

"That's the way it looks."

"So what are you going to do about it?"

"I'll tell you," I say, "as long as I'm talking to my old buddy Charlie, and not to Gibbs the SAG representative."

"Sure," Charlie says.

"I'm going to waltz on out of here," I say. "I'm thirty-seven years old and I haven't practiced gunplay for a year. I've got a new wife—"

"You don't have to go into all that," Gibbs says. "Life is sweet, that says it all. As your friend, I approve. As your SAG representative, I can tell you that the Guild won't back you up if you break a valid contract made by your legally appointed representative. If The Company sues you, you're all alone on your lonesome."

"Better all alone than underground with company," I tell him. "How good is this Little Joe?"

"He's good. But not as good as you are, Washburn. You're the best I ever seen. You thinking about meeting him?"

"Nope. Just asking."

"Keep it that way," Charlie says. "As your friend, I advise you to get out and stay out. You've already taken everything that can be gotten out of The Movie: You're a hero, you're rich, and you've got a pretty young wife. You've won everything in sight. Now don't hang around and wait for someone to take it off you."

"I'm not fixing to," I tell him. But I find that my hand has come to rest on my gun butt.

I go back into the saloon. I sit alone at a table, a shotglass of whiskey in front of me, a thin black Mexican cigar between my teeth. I am thinking about the situation. Little Joe is riding up from the south. He'll probably figure to find me here in Comanche. But I don't figure to be here. Safest way would be for me to ride back the way I came, back to the Wells Fargo station and out into the world again. But I'm not going to do it that way. I'm going out of The Set by the way of Brimstone in the extreme northeastern corner, thus making a complete tour of The Territory. Let them figure that one out . . .

Suddenly a long shadow falls across the table, a figure has moved between me and the light, and without a thought I roll out of my chair, gun already drawn, hammer back, forefinger tightening on the trigger. A boy's frightened, high-pitched voice says, "Oh! Excuse me, Mr. Washburn!" It's that snub-nosed freckle-faced kid I saw watching me earlier, now gaping at the end of my gun, scared, as he damned well should be having just startled me out of a year's growth.

I thumb down the hammer of my .44. I get up, holster the gun, dust myself off, pick up my chair and sit down on it. Curly the bartender brings me another drink. I say to the kid, "Kid, don't you know better than to move up sudden on a man like that? I should have blown you to hell just on the off-chance."

"I'm sorry, Mr. Washburn," he says. "I'm new out here, I didn't realize . . . I just wanted to tell you how much I admire you."

He was new, all right; he looked fresh out of The Company's School of Western Skills which we must all graduate from before we're even allowed on The Set. I had been just as raw as him during my first weeks in The Movie.

"Someday," he tells me, "I'm going to be like you. I thought maybe you could give me a few pointers. I got this old gun here—"

The kid draws, and once again I react without thinking, slap the gun out of his hand, chop him down with a fist to the ear.

"Goddamn you!" I shout, "haven't you got no sense at all? You just don't up and draw like that unless you're meaning to use it."

"I just wanted to show you my gun," he says, not getting up yet.

"If you want someone to look at your gun," I tell him, "take it out of your holster slow and easy, keeping your fingers outside the trigger guard. And first announce what you're going to do."

"Mr. Washburn," he says, "I don't know what to say."

"Don't say anything," I tell him. "Just get out of

here. You look like bad luck to me. Go show someone else your goddamned gun."

"Shall I show it to Joe Potter?" he asks, getting up and dusting himself off.

He looks at me. I haven't said a word. He gulps, he knows he's put his foot in it again.

I stand up slow. "Would you care to explain that remark?"

"I didn't mean nothing by it."

"You sure of that?"

"Real sure, Mr. Washburn. I'm sorry!"

"Get out of here," I say, and the kid scrams fast.

I go over to the bar. Curly has the whiskey bottle out, but I wave it away and he draws me a beer. "Curly," I say, "I know they can't help being young, but isn't there something they can do about being so stupid?"

"I reckon not, Mr. Washburn," Curly says.

We are silent for a few moments. Then Curly says, "Natchez Parker sent word he'd like to see you."

"All right," I tell him.

Dissolve to: a ranch on the edge of the desert. In the chuckhouse, the Chinese cook is sharpening his knives. Bud Farrell, one of the hands, is sitting on a crate peeling potatoes. He is singing as he works, his long horse face bent over the spuds. The cook, oblivious to him, looks out the window, says, "Rider comes."

Bud Farrell gets up, looks, scratches his hayseed head, looks again: "That's something more than just a *rider*, you heathen Chinee. That's *Mister Washburn*, sure as God made little green apples!"

Bud Farrell gets up, walks to the front of the main house, calls, "Hey, Mr. Parker! Mr. Washburn is riding up here!"

Washburn and Parker are sitting together at a small wooden table over steaming mugs of coffee in Natchez Parker's sitting room. Parker is a huge moustachioed man sitting in a straight-back wooden chair, an Indian blanket over his withered legs. He is paralyzed from the waist down because of an old bullet crease in the spine.

"Well, Washburn," says Parker, "I heard about you and Little Joe Potter, just like everyone else in The Territory. Ought to be one hell of a meeting. Wish I could see it."

I say, "I wouldn't mind seeing it myself."

"Where is it going to take place?"

"In hell, I guess."

Parker leans forward. "What does that mean?"

"It means that I'm not meeting Little Joe. I'm riding for Brimstone, and then straight on, away from Little Joe and the whole damned West."

Parker leans forward and vigorously rubs his shock of gray hair. His big face puckers together like he had bitten into a rotten apple.

"You're running?" he asks.

"That's it," Washburn says.

The old man grimaces, hawks, spits on the floor. He says, "I never thought to hear you of all people say a thing like that. I never thought to see you go against the values you've always lived by."

"Natchez, those were never my values. They came ready-made with the role. Now I'm through with the role, and I'm turning in the values, too."

The old man chewed that over for a while. Then he said, "What in hell is the matter with you? Got too much to live for all of a sudden? Or just gone yellow?"

"Call it what you like," I tell him. "I came by to tell you. I owe you that."

"Well, wasn't that nice of you?" says Parker. "You owed me something and it was on your way anyhow, so you figured the least you could do was come by and tell me you was running away from a jumped-up baby gunslinger with one fight under his belt."

"Get off my back."

"Tom," he says, "listen to me."

I look up. Parker is the only man in The Territory who ever calls me by my first name. He doesn't do it often.

"Now look," he says, "I am not one for fancy speeches. But you simply can't run away like this, Tom. Not on account of anything but yourself. You've got to live with yourself, no matter where you go."

"I'll manage that just fine," I tell him.

Parker shakes his head. "Damn it all, what do you think this thing is all about? They let us dress up in fancy clothes and strut our stuff like we owned the whole damned world. They pay us plenty just to be men. But there's a price for that. We gotta keep on being men. Not just when it's easy, like at the beginning. We gotta stay men right straight through to the end, no matter what the end is. We don't just act these parts, Tom; we live them, we stake our lives on them, we *are* these parts. Christ, anybody can dress up in a cowboy outfit and swagger down Main Street. But not everyone can wear a gun and use it."

I say, "That's a beautiful speech, Parker, and you're such a pro that you've blown this scene. Get back in character and let's get on with it."

"Goddamn you," Parker says, "I don't give a damn for the scene or The Movie or any of it. I'm talking to you straight now, Tom Washburn. We've been closer than kin ever since you came into The Territory, a frightened tanglefoot kid who made a place for himself on sheer guts. I'm not going to let you run away now."

"I'm finishing this coffee," I tell him, "and riding on."

Natchez suddenly twists in his chair, grabs a handful of my shirt and pulls my face close to his. In his other hand I see a knife.

"Get out your knife, Tom. I'd rather kill you myself than let you ride away a coward."

Parker's face is close to mine, glaring at me, the old

man's breath sour in my face. I brace my left foot on the floor, plant my right foot on the edge of Parker's chair and push hard. Parker's chair topples over and I see the look of shock on the old man's face as he falls to the floor. I draw my gun and take aim between his eyes.

"Christ, Tom," he says.

I thumb back the hammer. "You stupid old bastard," I say, "what do you think this is, some kind of a game? You've gotten sorta heavy-handed and long-winded ever since that bullet creased your spine. You think there are special rules, and you know all about them. But there aren't any rules. You don't tell me what to do and I don't tell you. You're a crippled old man, but if you pick a fight with me I'm going to fight my own way, not yours, and I'm going to put you down any way I can."

I take up slack on the trigger. Old Parker's eyes bulge, his mouth starts trembling, he tries to control himself but he can't. He screams, not loud, but high-pitched, like a frightened girl.

I thumb down the hammer and put my gun away. "Okay," I say, "maybe now you can wake up and remember how it really is."

I lift him up and slide the chair under him. "Sorry it's gotta be this way, Natchez. I'm going now."

I stop at the door and look back. Parker is grinning at me. "Glad to see you're feeling better, Tom. I should have remembered that you got nerves. All of the good ones have nerves. But you'll be fine at the showdown."

"You old idiot, there's not going to be any show-down. I told you before, I'm riding out of here."

"Good luck, Tom. Give 'em hell!"

"Idiot!" I got out of there.

A horseman crosses a high ridge and lets his horse pick its own way down the other side to the desert floor. There is a soft hiss of wind, glitter of mica, sand gathered into long wavering windrows.

The noon sun beats down as the rider passes through gigantic rock formations carved by the wind into fantastic shapes. At evening, the rider dismounts and inspects his horse's hooves. He whistles tunelessly to himself, pours water from his canteen into his derby, waters his horse, puts the hat back on and drinks sparingly himself. He hobbles the horse and makes camp on the desert. He sits by a little fire and watches the swollen desert sun go down. He is a tall, lean man, with a battered derby on his head and a horn-handled .44 strapped down on his right leg.

Brimstone: a desolate mining settlement on the northeastern edge of The Territory. Rising above the town is the natural rock formation of Devil's Highway—a broad, gently sloping rock bridge. The far end, out of sight from here, is firmly anchored just outside The Set, two hundred yards and 150 years away.

I come in on a limping horse. There aren't many people around, but I do spot one familiar face: it's that damned freckle-faced kid. He must have ridden pretty hard to get here before me. I pass him by without a word.

I sit my horse for a while and admire The Devil's Highway. Five minutes' ride to the other side and I'll be out of the West for good, finished with it all, the good times and the bad, the fear and the laughter, the long slow days and the dull, dangerous nights. In a few hours I'll be with Consuela, I'll be reading the newspapers and watching TV . . .

Now I'm going to put down one last shot of redeye and then sashay out of here.

I pull up my horse at the saloon. A few more people are on the street now, watching me. I walk into the saloon.

* * *

There is one man drinking alone at the bar. He's short and stocky, wearing a black leather vest and a Mountain Man's buffalo hat. He turns; he carries one unholstered gun high in his belt. I never saw him before, but I know who he is.

"Howdy, Mr. Washburn," he says.

"Howdy, Little Joe," I reply.

He holds the bottle out questioningly. I nod. He reaches behind the bar, finds another shotglass, fills it up for me. We sip quietly.

After a while I say, "Hope you didn't have too much trouble finding me."

"Not too much," Little Joe says. He's older than I had expected, nearly thirty. He's got a tough, craggy face, high cheekbones, a black handlebar moustache. He sips his drink, then says to me, very gently, "Mr. Washburn, I heard a rumor which I don't believe. The rumor said that you were leaving this territory in sort of a hurry."

"That's right," I tell him.

"The rumor also said that you wasn't planning to stay around long enough to give me the time of day."

"That's also true, Little Joe. I didn't figure I had no time for you. But here you are anyhow."

"Indeed I am," Little Joe says. He rubs down the ends of his moustache and pulls hard at his nose. "Frankly, Mr. Washburn, I simply can't believe that you're not planning to waltz around with me. I know all about you, Mr. Washburn, and I just can't believe that."

"Better believe it, Joe," I say to him. "I'm finishing this drink, and then I'm walking out this door and getting on my horse and riding over Devil's Highway."

Little Joe tugs at his nose again, frowns, pushes back his hat. "I never thought to hear this."

"I never thought to say it."

"You're really not going to face me?"

I finish my drink and set the shotglass down on the

bar. "Take care of yourself, Little Joe." I start toward the door.

Little Joe says, "There's just one last thing."

I turn. Little Joe is standing away from the bar, both hands visible. "I can't force you into a show-down, Mr. Washburn. But I did make a little bet concerning that derby of yours."

"So I heard."

"And so, although it pains me more than you can know, I'll have to have it."

I stand, facing him, not answering.

Little Joe says, "Look, Washburn, no sense you just standing there glaring at me. Give me the hat or make your play."

I take off the derby. I smooth it on my sleeve, then sail it to him. He picks it up, never taking his eyes from me. He says, "Well, I'll be."

"Take care of yourself, Little Joe." I walk out of the saloon.

A crowd has assembled opposite the saloon. They wait and watch, talking in hushed voices. The saloon doors swing and a tall thin bareheaded man comes through. He is beginning to bald. He carries a .44 strapped down on his right leg, and he looks like he knows how to use it. But the fact is, he hasn't used it.

Under the watchful eyes of the crowd, Washburn unties his horse, mounts it, and sets it at a walk toward the bridge.

The saloon doors swing again. A short, stocky hard-faced man comes through, holding a battered derby. He watches the horseman ride away.

Washburn spurs his horse, which hesitates a moment, then mounts the stone bridge. It takes constant urging to keep the horse going, picking its way across the sloping pebble-clad surface, to the center. Here Washburn stops the horse, or allows it to stop. He sits at the highest point of the bridge's curve, astride the joint between two worlds, but looking at neither. He reaches up to tug at his hat's brim and is mildly surprised to find himself bareheaded. He scratches his forehead lazily, a man with all the time in the world. Then he turns his horse around and starts back down the bridge to Brimstone.

The crowd watches as Washburn rides toward them. They are motionless, silent. Then, realizing what is about to happen, they scatter for the shelter of wagons, duck down behind water troughs, crouch behind grain sacks.

Only Little Joe Potter remains in the dusty street. He watches while Washburn dismounts, shoos his horse out of the line of fire, walks slowly toward him.

Little Joe calls out, "Hey, Washburn! Come back for your hat?"

Washburn grins, shakes his head. "No, Little Joe, I came back because it's our dance."

They both laugh, it is all some ridiculous joke. Then, suddenly, both men draw. The heavy bark of their .44s crashes through the town. Smoke and dust obscure the fighters.

The smoke blows away. Both men are still standing. Little Joe's gun is pointed down. He twirls it, and watches it fall from his hand. Then he collapses.

Washburn holsters his gun, walks over to Little Joe, kneels, lifts his head out of the dirt.

"Goddamn," Little Joe says, "that was one short dance, huh, Washburn?"

"Too short," Washburn says. "Joe, I'm sorry . . ."

But Little Joe doesn't hear this. His eyes have gone blank and unfocused, his body is limp. Blood trickles out of two holes in his chest, blood stains the dust from the large exit wounds in his back.

Washburn gets to his feet, finds his derby in the dust, wipes it off, puts it on. He walks over to his horse. People are coming out now, there is a buzz of conversation. Washburn sets one foot in the stirrup, begins to mount.

At that moment a wavering, high-pitched voice calls out, "Okay, Washburn, draw!"

Washburn's face contorts as he whirls, trying to get his gun-hand clear, trying to spin out of the line of fire. Even in that cramped and impossible posture he manages to get the .44 drawn, spins to see the freckle-faced kid ten yards away with gun drawn and aimed, firing.

Sunlight explodes in Washburn's head, he hears his horse scream, he is falling through the dusty floors of the world, falling as the bullets thud into him with a sound like a butcher's cleaver swung flat against a side of beef. The world is coming apart, the picture-making machine is smashed, his eyes are a broken lens that reflects the sudden destruction of the world. A red light flashes a final warning and the world goes to black.

The viewer, audience and actor, looks for a while at the darkened screen, stirs in his easy chair, rubs his chin. He seems to be in some distress. Then, at last, he belches, and reaches out and turns off the screen.

The Age of Libra
by Scott Edelstein

Scott Edelstein says, "I feel a work of art should stand completely on its own. Hence, I prefer to remain in the background and let the story do the telling.

"I will say, however, that 'The Age of Libra' is the best short story I have written, to date."

HOMA STOOD AT THE TOP of the wooded hill, gazing down at the village below. The buildings blended with the surrounding trees, forming a mosaic that defied his vision to distinguish details. Thin smoke rose from a corner of the village, where the power plant was located.

The afternoon was cool; the sky held a sprinkling of clouds. Homa could feel the intermittent sunlight pressing lightly on his head and back. He was barefoot; the dry grass and clover brushed softly against his feet.

He searched the path to the village with his eyes. He did not see anyone approaching. He squatted, preparing to wait, then stood and walked over the crest of the hill and down, away from the village.

At the bottom of the hill was a small stream. He knelt and drank, relishing the taste and the cold of the water. He settled down nearby, beneath a big pine tree on a small mat he kept there.

He closed his eyes and attempted to meditate, but his mind would not empty.

Her facial muscles were taut, her lips pursed. "You're drunk again," she said.

Homa felt a rush of anger, could feel for a moment his heartbeat quicken. "You're always accusing me of something. I'm not drunk. I've made my decision and I'm going to stick to it. There's nothing to argue about."

She persisted. "So you're twenty years old and you've decided there's nothing for you in life; why shouldn't I argue with you? Do you think we raised you so you could live in a village? So you could throw your life away?"

"I've already signed the papers. I have to report within seven days. You can scream at me without stopping for the whole week and the papers aren't going to unsign themselves." He felt the tenseness in his throat; his voice threatened to turn to a squeak.

She rushed toward him, and for a moment Homa thought she would strike him. He took a step back, then checked himself. At the age of twenty he was still frightened by his own mother. She did not strike him, or touch him at all, but walked jerkily across the room and collapsed into a chair. She was silent and Homa turned away, hoping the incident had ended and wondering what to do next. Then he heard sobbing behind him. He whirled. "Look, you can't change what's already happened," he said. Her sobbing continued.

He turned and stared out the window at the city, a mass of concrete and metal and bodies and filth that stretched far past his own gaze. He had assumed that his decision to live in a village would have been a turning point in his relationship with his parents. He had hoped it would have provided him with some sort of revelation about his own personality. But nothing had changed; it was as if he had not signed the papers, had not make a commitment; except that he would have to report to a retirement center in seven days.

Behind him, his mother was speaking hysterically into the telephone, pausing to sob or wipe her eyes and nose with a tissue. She looked ludicrous to Homa, standing there, speaking into a shiny black object in her hand, as if that object could offer her some sort of solace.

Staring at her, and then staring back out of the grimy window at the concrete and metal shells, he felt only a vague confusion. There was not even a loneliness to nurse, just a slippery sensation that something was happening behind his back that he could never glimpse.

His mother hung up the telephone. He waited, expecting an announcement.

"Your father's on his way home right now," she said, "to talk to you."

"I won't be here." His own words dissatisfied him; they held no distinction. He searched his mind for a sentence that was uniquely his, for words that embodied his own personality. He found nothing. "I'm going out."

"No, you're not."

"Don't order me around. I'm not your servant. I'm going out. I'll be back later on. I'll talk to you both then."

"Where are you going?"

"I don't know. What does it matter?"

"I don't want you going out and smoking that marijuana or getting drunk."

"I don't want you crying," he said. "Is that going to stop you from doing it?"

"You're such a big-mouth," she said, the last words

53

turning into a shriek. She ran to him and struck him
with clumsy blows; he reeled backward, stunned.

Homa opened his eyes and stared into the creek.
He could change his environment, but his past clung
to him like an infant to its mother.

He rose, and drank again from the stream. The
water did not refresh him. He strode further into the
woods. He kept walking until he could see the fence
at the edge of the woods, and the farmland beyond;
then he stopped, gazing into the distance, trying to
clear his mind of thoughts. He could not do it. He
walked to the fence, glanced at the sign which said
DANGER: HIGH VOLTAGE.

He seated himself, crossed his legs, and placed his
palms on his knees. He closed his eyes, then thought,
I'm still expecting something to happen, hoping to get
some sort of vision.

A maintenance tractor was approaching, its
scanners seeking malfunctions or breaks in the fence.
The tractor driver sat hunched over his controls, staring straight ahead.

"Good afternoon," Homa shouted at the man as the
tractor approached. "How's the wife and kids?"

The driver did not respond; he concentrated on his
driving.

"Hey," Homa yelled at him, raising his voice further, "Want to stop a while and have a talk? Listen,
I'm not going to do anything; they don't sell weapons
in the village, you know. At least look at me, will
you? Damn it, will you at least look my way?"

The driver's gaze did not waver.

"I'm going to die tomorrow," Homa shouted. "Today's my last day on this Earth. I've been here almost
one full year. Tomorrow I meet my maker. What do
you think of that?" Homa jumped up and trotted
along the length of the fence, keeping up with the
tractor. "Your fly's open; hadn't you better zip it up?
Hey, watch it, there's this huge hornet on your ear."
Homa gave up, slowed to a walk.

He turned away from the fence and walked back up the hill.

His father wore a perpetual scowl on his face. Homa thought the scowl was grimmer than usual; he thought there was a hint of desperation in his father's eyes.

"Look, Dad, what am I supposed to do, build a time machine and go back and relive the day over again? I signed up for retirement; whether or not it was a stupid thing to do doesn't matter anymore. So can we please just drop of the abject? I'll be around for another week; let's live that happily, at least, okay?"

"But you haven't answered me—why? Why? What would make you want to retire, at the age of twenty? Think of all the things you haven't seen, the things you haven't done." *The arguments were always the same, a string of accusations and demands and incredulous questions, repeated over and over and over.* "I didn't raise you to throw your life away at the first opportunity."

"What else is there to see? It's nothing but eat and drink and breathe filth every day of your life, living in a box in the middle of millions of other boxes just like it, working all day at dulling your brain and your senses, and then dying. Ending with one year of happiness, one goddamned year of freedom. And by that time your mind and body are all so ruined that that year doesn't mean anything—you're dead already. It's a slow process; every year you die a little bit more, until by the time they finally put you to sleep you hardly feel it. If I can have one good year of my life, I want it now; do you understand?"

"No, I don't understand." *His father drew nearer, put his hand on Homa's shoulder and pressed down.* "Let me tell you something. What you don't think about is us, your mother and I. You think we enjoy living the way we do? You think we had any reason to live? Well, we did, Dave—it was you. And now you're taking our whole lives away from us. There was nothing we could have done for ourselves, but we wanted you to be something. You could have been someone famous, someone important."

"You've told me that all my life. Will you please get it through your skull that I just can't be this 'somebody important' you keep talking about? Sure, there's still hope for a few; how many—one out of a hundred thousand? The geniuses, the top athletes, the kids who are born rich or who inherit a fortune, they get something more out of life besides another breath of filthy air. I'm not one of them; I've known it all along. You've just been afraid to admit it to yourself. And now it's too late, do you hear me, too late for you, or Mom, or me, to do anything."

The hand fell off Homa's shoulder. "You snotty kid," his father said. "You did it all for spite. You always want your own way. Always Dave first, Dave before anybody else."

"It doesn't matter, it doesn't matter," Homa found himself shouting. He felt the first wash of tears coming to his eyes. He blinked, focused his eyes on his mother, who sat quietly in a straightbacked chair, rubbing her hands together nervously, crying.

"Nothing matters to you."

Homa suddenly found that the situation was totally out of his control: ironically, he felt as if a huge burden had been taken from him. "Fuck it, fuck it, fuck you all," he found himself saying, and abruptly he was at the front door, pulling it open. His father was behind him, barking orders; his mother sobbed in the background. He began shaking his head and stumbled outside, slamming the door behind him. Too angered to wait for an elevator, he bolted down seven flights of stairs, through the lobby, and out the door of the apartment building.

He stood on the sidewalk, catching his breath. The buildings loomed around him. The sky was gray.

Amanda was waiting for him just over the crest of

the hill. She lay on her stomach, idly brushing her hair off her forehead and moving one foot back and forth against the ground in a slow rhythm. A paper bag was beside her on the grass.

She saw him as he approached, and she raised herself to her knees, still brushing the hair out of her eye. He kissed her lightly and knelt beside her. They stroked each other's hair.

"You're very late," she said.

"No, you were," he said, smiling. "I waited for a while and then went down by the creek."

She patted the paper sack. "You weren't at lunch, so I got something for you. It's some quiche and some grapes."

He lay down beside her, kissed her gently again. Her tongue gently skimmed the surface of his teeth. "I'm not really hungry," he said, although he was.

Sometime later he discovered that they had removed their clothing and were making love. Homa tried to recall the previous minutes but could not; his mind had the habit of going off on its own for minutes, sometimes hours at a time. Sex, once one of his major preoccupations, could no longer keep his attention. Even as he worked his body against Amanda's and struggled to hold onto his awareness, he felt his movements becoming automatic. He concentrated all his energy on making love.

But he forced himself, and afterward Amanda kissed his eyelids and offered to massage him. She kissed the tip of his nose and said, "You're tense. All over."

He raised himself on his elbows and felt something building inside of him. He waited, and the pressure remained but neither lessened nor broke. He tried to force it to break and failed. He pressed his mouth on Amanda's. They embraced, and for a moment he hoped that they would make love once again, but they both soon drifted into sleep.

He had walked the streets of the city for half an hour, hunched against the wind and the grime. With each step his course of action became more obvious. He tried to find a phone booth with a working phone, but could not. Finally he stopped inside a crowded, hot lunchroom and called his parents from a pay phone there. His mother answered.

"Hello; Mom?"

"Dave? Where are you?"..

"I'm calling from a restaurant, Mother. I just wanted to tell you that I'm going to the retirement center now. I decided there wasn't any point in waiting out the week. Take the money out of my savings; it's yours." *He paused, uncertain how to continue, waiting for a response.*

"What? Did you say you were retiring this minute? Wait a minute, Dave, you come home and we'll discuss this."

"No, Mom."

"You'd better listen, young man. You come right home and we can discuss this over dinner." *She was stern and insistent, but her voice had broken; Homa could hear her crying softly.*

"I'm your flesh and blood, so I guess I'm your slave, too, is that it? Look, Mom, don't wait up for me, okay?" *He paused again, expecting her tone of insistence to change to sorrow.*

"Listen to me, David—"

"Goodbye, Mom."

id Scott Homa 1977–1998 David Scott Homa 1977–1998 David Scott Homa 1977–19

The retirement center had an unassuming exterior; outside hung a single large sign, in gold and green, which said USDRS RETIREMENT CENTER. *Inside, the center could have been mistaken for the waiting room of a very expensive doctor.*

The waiting room was empty except for the receptionist. Homa strode to her desk and stared at her. "My name's David Homa," *he said.* "I signed up earlier today. I'd like to retire right now; I'm waiving my seven day extension."

She smiled professionally, and ran her finger down a list of names on the desk beside her. "All right, sir, if you'll wait just a moment I'll get things arranged for you. Are there any personal articles you wish to take with you?"

He shook his head. "Just what I have on me. I was told I'd be issued clothing and so forth at the village."

"Yes, sir, a selection of clothing is available." She pushed a button and, bending forward slightly, said into a microphone Homa could not see, "Ten-ninety, Waiver, Homa, David Scott." There was a loud buzz, and a door behind the desk swung open. "Right through the door, please," she said to him, still smiling. "Just go around in back of my desk."

He smiled back at her, walked through the door, and heard it shut behind him. As an experiment, he tried to turn the doorknob. It would not turn.

He was in a tiny cubicle about the size of a passenger elevator. The walls were imitation wood-paneled. Set into the wall opposite him was a large television screen.

Abruptly, another door slid shut over the first one, and he felt the room move downward. He realized that he was indeed in an elevator. The television screen lit up with an image of a man's smiling face. There was a faint hum, and the man began to speak. "Welcome to the United States Retirement Program, sponsored by the U.S. Department of Retirement Services. Every year, the population of the nation increases by over ten million. To help keep this increase to a minimum, the United States sponsors sixteen hundred and forty-five retirement villages throughout the nation." The man's face was replaced with an aerial view of a large cluster of buildings set in a wooded mountain valley. The buildings were painted in shades of brown and green. "Each of these villages houses twenty-nine hundred residents, who stay, free of charge, for a period of one year. During this final year of their lives, they are supplied with com-

fortable living quarters, meals, clothing, toilet articles, cleaning and laundering services, and two hundred dollars per month to spend in village stores. A wide variety of entertainment is offered, and the large and highly trained staff of your village will do their best to meet your personal needs, whatever they may be." The voice fell silent, and the picture changed to that of a slightly larger cluster of buildings, also surrounded by woodland. The woods here were hilly rather than mountainous. A woman's voice replaced the man's. *"This is Redwood Village,"* the voice said, *"in northern California. This is a resort village designed for single members of your own age group. The residents of Redwood Village range in age from eighteen to thirty. Redwood Village is one-half male, one-half female."* The elevator stopped its descent, but the doors behind Homa did not open. *"This is the entrance to an underground railway car which will take you to Redwood Village,"* the voice said. The television screen grew dark, and the elevator doors opened behind him. Homa turned and saw yet another set of closed doors. *"When the doors open,"* the voice continued, *"please step inside and strap yourself into the seat. The train travels at very high speeds; therefore, it is not safe to move about the cabin while the car is in motion. The trip will take about twenty minutes. The United States Government would like to thank you for making your important contribution to the welfare of the nation, and hopes your stay at Redwood Village will be a pleasant one."* The last set of doors opened, and Homa entered the tiny curved chamber, sat down in the single padded chair.

Homa awoke when he felt Amanda stirring beside him. He opened his eyes, slowly rolled toward her. The sun was setting; her face was outlined in a pale glow. She was on her knees, buttoning her blouse hurriedly. He reached out, touched her elbow. She turned her head quickly to him.

"You're leaving," he said sleepily. "You wanted to be gone when I woke up."

She looked at him, and he tried to see directly into her eyes, but they were lost in the shadows. "It hurts so much less this way," she said. Abruptly, she took his head in her hands and kissed him: Then she was running away from him, down the hill, toward the village.

Homa stood, watching her run down the hillside, occasionally losing sight of her against the brightness of the setting sun. He thought of running after her, and of returning to the creek and meditating, but neither seemed to make much sense. Finally, he stretched himself out on the cool grass and, once again, slept.

The car slowed; Homa was pressed back into the padded seat. "You are approaching Redwood Village," a low female voice said from somewhere behind him. "Your living quarters have been prepared for you and are ready for occupancy. When the car comes to a complete stop, please enter the elevator. It will take you to the public square, where you will find the New Arrivals Office. A representative from New Arrivals will be waiting for you when you disembark from the elevator. You will be given your identification card, which operates the lock to your apartment door, and two hundred dollars spending money for the coming month. The representative will be able to answer whatever questions about Redwood Village you may have."

The car stopped; two sets of doors slid open. Homa undid the restraining straps on his seat, stood, and stepped inside the elevator.

Everybody I meet, he thought, will be dead before the year is out. I'll outlive every one of them.

The doors closed behind him and the elevator ascended.

He awakened to the sight of a sky peppered with stars. The moon was full, and it lit the hillside dimly.

He lay still for several minutes, staring at the sky, trying to determine the time by the position of the moon. He wondered if the patrol would come for him immediately after midnight, then gave up on the thought.

He found the food Amanda had brought him and ate slowly, silently, savoring its taste and texture. Then he walked slowly back to the village.

Nobody but Amanda knew that this was his last day; it was an unwritten law that no one made public the date of his or her own execution.

He strode through the brightly-lit streets of the village. On a street corner half a dozen people were smoking marijuana and drinking liquor, and singing loudly. Homa joined them, asked for some marijuana, was passed a joint. He toked on it idly for a few minutes, then passed back the roach and walked on. He was restless.

He walked through the shopping arcade, where all the stores were open all night. A thought struck him and he went into the hallucinogen dispensary.

The shopkeeper, a thin, short, balding man, looked up from a book he was reading when Homa walked in. "Can I help you, sir?" he said.

"Do you know what time it is?"

The man glanced at his wristwatch. "It's just past eleven."

"You work here," Homa said. "You don't live here. Where do you live?"

The man's face registered surprise. "In Elyria, about twenty miles away."

Homa said, "I never saw a retirement village in my life until I came here. You can't reach them at all, or even see them, unless you live there or work there. What made you take a job here?"

"Sir," the man said, polite but insistent, "this is a dispensary. I'm authorized to give out drugs for your personal enjoyment, not personal information. I'm not permitted to, even if I wanted to."

"Have you ever heard of the year-gods?" Homa asked.

"No. Should I have? Is it a new movie?"

Homa turned and walked out the door. "No," he said.

He and Amanda stood on the street corner near the shopping arcade, eating ice cream from plastic cups. They were stoned, and were talking and laughing wildly. She got mad at something he said and threw her ice cream at him. It struck him in the face, and they both stood there, giggling hysterically like small children.

They heard a commotion behind them, and they turned. A man was running past them frantically, shrieking. Four men dressed in dark green uniforms ran behind him. From around a corner three more patrolmen appeared, cutting the fleeing man off. He screamed again and stumbled, finally falling to his stomach on the red tiled floor, sobbing. "Please," he mumbled through streaming tears as the patrolmen picked him up, held him. "Please, I made a mistake. I didn't really want to come here; I'm only twenty-three years old. I didn't know any better. It was all a mistake." His words turned into a hysterical babble; the patrolmen dragged him away, down the tiled street.

Homa found Amanda hugging him, pressing her chest and thighs against him.

ates Government would like to thank you for making your important contribu

are of the nation, and hopes your stay at Redwood Village will be a pleasa

He was reading a novel in his living room when the call came.

"David Homa?" the unfamiliar voice on the telephone said. "Long distance call from your parents."

"From whom?" he heard himself ask, tossing the novel on the floor behind him.

"Your mother and father. Do you want us to connect the outside extension?"

"Wait a minute. I thought there was a rule about no outside influence. No visitors, no communications from the outside, no letters or packages in or out."

"There is one exceptional situation," the strange voice said. "Shall I complete the connection?"

Homa mumbled an affirmative.

"Dave? How are you, Dave?" It was his mother's voice.

He found himself empty of response; the absurdity of the situation was draining him of all thought.

"Just fine, Mom," he said.

"That's good. Your father and I are both glad you're happy." If there was sarcasm in her voice, Homa could not detect it.

"How are you and Dad?"

His father's voice answered him. "That's what we're calling about. We're going in for retirement ourselves, next Tuesday."

Homa felt a physical jolt; he sank down into a chair. His head reeled. "But why? You could have lived for a long time. Retirement wouldn't have been mandatory for you for another ten years."

"Five years," his mother said. "They lowered the age."

There was a pause. "Well," his father said, "we really are getting on in years. I've gotten tired of my work; we just haven't got the energy we used to. Besides, it'll be nice, to have our cooking and cleaning and everything done for us for a year. And I'm sure we'll meet a lot of nice people."

"Are you enjoying it, David?" his mother asked. "Don't you think we'll like it?"

"Oh, I like it a lot," he said hastily. "I think you'll enjoy it. I don't know what the country'll be like where you're going, but around here it's beautiful. And the people are nice. Of course, it'll be different

*for you; I mean, you'll be living with people your
own age, and with other married couples."*

There was another pause. Finally his father said,
*"That's another part of it. Sarah and I are separating;
we're going to go to villages for singles, separate
ones."*

Homa's hand began to tremble. *"Why?"* he could
not help but demand.

"We just thought it would be better, that's all."

"One of your friends called us the other day," his
mother said. *"He asked us how you were."*

"Tell him I'm fine." The trembling worsened. *"Give
him my regards."*

"We will." Another pause. *"David?"* his father said.

"Yes?"

"Take care."

"I will."

His mother said, *"Goodbye, David."*

"Goodbye, Mom. Goodbye, Dad."

"Goodbye."

He had wandered through the streets all night,
waiting for the patrol. He did not return to his apartment, although the night was cold and he wanted its
warmth and quiet; he knew the patrol was almost
certainly waiting for him there.

His legs felt sore, and his head ached. As the sun
rose above the hills outside the village, he found himself walking away from the buildings, toward the
woods.

His awareness vanished then, and the next thing he
was conscious of was drinking from the brook near
the big pine tree. He drank well past the point where
his thirst was quenched, then sat down cross-legged
on his meditation mat and closed his eyes.

When he opened them again the sun was high in
the sky. He felt refreshed, cleansed, aware. His arms
and legs tingled. He stood and took in deep breaths
of air.

He heard a rustling behind him. He turned and

saw three men in dark green coming toward him. They wore dark visors over their heads and faces; only their jaws were visible. He stood still, watching them, until two of them took his arms gently and led him back toward Redwood Village. He did not struggle. The third man walked silently behind.

"How much money do you earn doing this?" Homa asked mildly.

To his real surprise, the man behind him said politely, "Twenty-five thousand a year. Of course, you have to go through plenty of training and have the right kind of mental outlook. I mean, you can't take pleasure in what you do, and you can't let it get to you either."

Homa tried to stop and turn around to look at the man, but the pressure on his arms, though gentle, was insistent.

"You're allowed to talk, then?" Homa asked, stumbling over the words.

All three of the men uttered small chuckles, and the one on Homa's right said, "God, if we weren't, it'd get to be hell in no time. It's just that the villagers never talk to *us*."

They emerged into the clearing on top of the hill. The sun was hot and bright; the village in the valley below gleamed in the light.

"I feel like all my life I've been waiting for something," Homa said. "When I was young, I waited to grow up; when I was in school I waited for something to happen, and nothing did, so I dropped out. At my job I would wait for the working day to be over, and when I went home I waited for the next day to begin. I moved away from home and waited to be free, but I didn't feel any different, so I moved back in with my parents. I waited for something to change in me, and nothing did. Now here I am again, waiting for my own execution. It's like I've never really done anything, just walked around in circles with my hands in my pockets. I don't even know what I was looking for all this time."

"To get laid," one of the men said, giggling. The other two patrolmen laughed politely.

They were approaching Redwood Village. A crowd of people were laughing and talking near the village's entrance; when they saw Homa and the patrolmen approaching they quieted, stared at them for a moment, then tried to resume their conversation. A few of the people crept away silently. Homa deliberately looked away, hoping none of the people were those he knew.

"Where are you taking me?" he asked.

"Underground. You go by railcar to a place about a half mile outside of the village."

They turned a corner; Homa caught a glimpse of a retreating form he thought was Amanda. He could not be sure, however, and he did not look back at her. He opened his mouth to shout her name, then stopped himself.

"How is it done?" he said.

"They attach electrodes to your brain. Very simple, very quick. They gas you first in the train car to make you unconscious. You don't feel anything."

"How are the electrodes attached? By men, or by machine?"

"I don't know," said two of the patrolmen together.

They neared the elevator tube leading to the railroad, set in one corner of the public square. The man holding Homa's left arm pressed his palm against a plastic panel, and the doors to the elevator opened. He led Homa inside; the other two men remained outside. The elevator doors closed and the car descended.

"How old are you?" Homa asked.

"I have fifteen years left," the patrolman said.

"Does this place scare you?"

The elevator slowed, stopped. The doors opened into a small compartment with rounded walls and a single passenger seat. Automatically, Homa stepped inside and seated himself.

"It terrifies me." The man lifted his visor. He had large features and huge brown eyes. He stared into Homa's face. "But I'd kill myself before I'd let them put me to sleep. But if I'm lucky, they'll never get me; I'm working on a plan."

"Good luck," Homa said. The man grunted. The doors closed and the car began to move.

To Mark the Year on Azlaroc

by Fred Saberhagen

Fred Saberhagen has worked as an encyclopedia editor and in electronics, but for the past 14 years he has spent as much of his time as possible writing science fiction, and now he has no time for encyclopedias or electronics. He is best known for his famous "Berserker" series of science-fiction stories, which has been widely enjoyed and even more widely imitated.

THEY HAD BEEN QUARRELING in the ship, and were still at it when they disembarked and left its sprawling metal complexities behind them. Ailanna snapped at Hagen: "So what if I misplaced your camera! What does it matter if you have one more picture of the stars? You can take a dozen when we depart." And when it turned out that they had missed the ground transport machine that was taking the other passengers across the smooth undulations of the golden plain toward the city, Hagen was almost expecting her to physically attack him.

"Son of a nobody!" Ailanna hissed. "Where are we to stay if you have made no reservations?" A kilometer away was the only real city on the star, and

Hagen realized that to one coming to Azlaroc for the first time, the city must look quite small. On the surface there appeared only a few fairyland towers, and little evidence of the many chambers and passageways dug out beneath the plain.

"I haven't made up my mind where to stay." He turned away from her and began to walk after the transport machine.

She followed. "You can never make up your mind about anything." It was an old, intermittent quarrel. If the reservations had been in perfect order, there would have been something else to quarrel about.

She nagged him for a hundred meters across the plain, and then the scenery began to come through to her. The enormous golden-yellow land was humped here and there by paraboloid hills and studded with balanced spheres of matter. The surface looked more like something man-made than like soil, and it stretched in places up to the low, yellowish, sunless sky, in asymptotic spires that broke off in radiant glory at an altitude of a few hundred meters, at the upper edge of the region of gravity inversion.

"What's that?" Her voice was no longer angry. She was looking toward the top of a golden sphere which loomed over the distanceless horizon, at right angles to the way they were walking. The sphere reminded Hagen of a large planet rising, as seen from some close-in satellite, but this sphere was entirely beneath the low, peculiar sky.

"Only part of the topography." He remained calm, as usual, taking her bickering in stride.

When they had gotten under-surface in the city, and arranged for lodgings, and were on their way to them through one of the smaller side passageways, Hagen saw some man or woman of a long-past year approaching through the passage from the other direction. Had there been three or four people of the present year or of recent years in the same part of the corridor just then, the passage of such an old one would have been almost unnoticeable. The old one did not appear as a plain solid human figure. Only a disturbance in the air and along the wall, a mound of shadows and moire patterns that throbbed with the beat of the pulsar somewhere beneath their feet. The disturbance occupied hardly any space in this year's corridor, and Ailanna at first was not aware of it at all.

Hagen reached out a hand and took her by the upper arm and forced her, strong woman that she was, into three almost-dancing steps that left her facing in the proper way to see. "Look. One of the early settlers."

With a small intake of breath Ailanna fixed her eyes on the figure. She watched it out of sight around a corner, then turned her elfin face to Hagen. Her eyes had been enlarged, and her naturally small chin further diminished, in accordance with the fashion dictates of the time, even as Hagen's dark eyebrows had been grown into a ring of hair that crossed above his nose and went down by its sides to meld with his moustache. She said: "Perhaps one of the very first? An explorer?"

"No." He looked about the ordinary overhead lights, the smooth walls of the yellowish rock-like substance of the star. "I remember that this corridor was not cut by the explorers, not perhaps until '120 or '130. So no settler in it can be older than that, of course."

"I don't understand, Hagen. Why didn't you tell me more about this place before you brought me here?"

"This way it will all come as a wonderful surprise."

They met others in the corridor as they proceeded. Here came a couple of evidently ten or fifteen local years ago, walking in the nudity that had been acceptable as fashion then, draped with ten or fifteen of the sealing veils of Azlaroc so that their bodies shimmered slightly as they moved, giving off small diamond-sparkles of light. The veils of only ten or fifteen years were not enough to warp a settler out of phase

71

with this year's visitors, so the four people meeting in the passage had to give way a little on both sides, as if they were in a full sense contemporaries, and like contemporaries they excused themselves with vacant little social smiles.

Numbers, glowing softly from the corridor walls, guided Hagen and Ailanna to their rooms. "Hagen, what is this other sign that one sees on the walls?" It was a red hollow circle with a small pie-cut wedge of its interior filled with red also.

"The amount of red inside shows the estimated fraction of a year remaining until the next veil falls."

"Then there is not much of the year left, for sightseeing. Here, this must be our door. I would say we have come at a poor time."

Opening the door, he did not reply. Their baggage had already been deposited inside.

"I wouldn't want to be trapped here, Hagen. Well, the apartment's not bad ... now what's the matter? What have I said?" She had learned to know at once when something really bothered him, which her inconsequential bickering rarely seemed to do.

"Nothing. Ample warning is always given so the tourists can get away, you needn't worry."

She was in the bedroom unpacking when something came in through the illusory window that seemed to give upon the golden plain. Where a sawtooth range of diminishing pyramids marched in from the horizon there came a shimmer and a sliding distortion that was in the room with her before she knew it, that passed on harmless through her own flesh, and went its way. She gave a yelp of fear.

Hagen was in the doorway, smiling faintly. "Didn't I mention that we might be sharing our apartment here?"

"Sharing—of course not. Oh. You mean with settlers, folk of other years. That's what it was, then. But—through the wall?"

"That wall was evidently an open passage in their time. Ignore them, as they will us. Looking up through their veils they can see us—differently, too. While diving I have asked them to describe how we look to them, but their answers are hard to understand."

"Tell me about diving," she said, when they had finished settling in and were coming out of doors again.

"Better than that, I'll show you. But I'll tell you first, of course." As they walked out onto the plain, Hagen could hear the pulsar component of the triple system beating as sound, the sound coming now from overhead, thick and soft and at one third the speed of a calm human heart. It came through all the strangenesses of space that lay between him and the invisible pulsar that locked its orbit intricately with those of a small black hole and of the world called Azlaroc.

He said: "What is called diving, on Azlaroc, is a means of approaching the people and things that lie under the veils of the years. Nothing can pierce the veils, of course. But diving stretches them, lets one get near enough to the people of the past to see them more clearly and make photographs." And more than that, more than that, oh Gods of Space, but Hagen said no more.

On the plain other tourists were also walking, in this year's fashion of scanty garments each of a hundred colors. In the mild, calm air, under the vague, yellowish sky that was not really a sky, and bathed in sunless light, Hagen had almost the feeling of being still indoors. He was heading for a divers' shop that he remembered. He meant to waste no time in beginning his private search in earnest.

Ailanna walked beside him, no longer quarrelsome, and increasingly interested in the world around them. "You say nothing at all can pierce the veils, once they have fallen in and wrapped themselves about this planet?"

"No matter can pierce them. And this is not a planet. I suppose 'star' is the best term for a layperson to use, though the scientists might wince at it. There's the divers' shop ahead, see that sign beside the cave?" The cave was in the side of a sharp-angled rhombic hill.

Inside the shop they were greeted by the proprietor, a settler swathed in more than a hundred veils, who needed electronic amplifiers to converse with customers. After brief negotiation he began to take their measurements.

"Ailanna, when we dive, what would you like to see?"

Now she was cheerful. "Things of beauty. Also I would like to meet one of those first, stranded explorers."

"The beauty will be all about. There are signals and machines to guide the tourist to exceptional sights. As for the explorer, we can try. When I was last here it was still possible to dive near enough to them to see their faces and converse. Maybe now, when a hundred and thirty more veils have been added, it is possible no longer."

They were fitted with diving gear, each a carapace and helm of glass and metal that flowed like water over their upper bodies.

"Hagen, if nothing can pierce the fallen veils of the years, how are these underground rooms dug out?"

Now his diver's suit had firmed into place. Where Hagen's face had been she saw only a distorting mirror, that gave an eerie semblance of her own face back to her. But his voice was familiar and reassuring. "Digging is possible because there are two kinds of matter, of physical reality, here coexisting. The stuff of the landscape, all those mathematical shapes and the plain they rise from, is comparatively common matter. Its atoms are docile and workable, at least here in this region of mild gravity and pressure. The explorers realized from the star that this mild region needed only air and water and food, to provide men with more habitable surface than a planet ... there, your diver's gear is stabilized about you. Let's walk to Old Town, where we may find an explorer."

Sometimes above ground and sometimes below, they walked, armored in the strange suits and connected to the year of their own visit by umbilical cables as fine and flexible and unbreakable as artists' lines on paper. Adjusting his gear for maximum admittance, Hagen nervously scanned the faces of all passing settlers. Now some features were discernible in even the oldest of them.

"And the other kind of matter, Hagen, the other physical reality. What about the veils?"

"Ah, yes. The material between the stars, gathered up as this triple system advances through space. What is not sucked into the black hole is sieved through nets of the pulsar's radiation, squeezed by the black hole's hundred billion gravities, shattered and transformed in all its particles as it falls toward Azlaroc through the belts of space that starships must avoid. Once every systemic year conditions are right and a veil falls. What falls is no longer matter that men can work with, any more than they can work in the heart of a black hole. Ailanna, are you tuned to maximum? Look just ahead."

They were out on the surface again. A human figure that even with the help of diver's gear appeared no more than a wavery half-image had just separated itself from an equally insubstantial dwelling. A hundred and thirty years before, someone had pointed out a similar half-visible structure to Hagen as an explorer's house. He had never spoken to an explorer, but he was ready now to try. He began to run. The gear he wore was only a slight hindrance.

Close ahead now was the horizon, with just beyond it the golden globe they had earlier observed. No telling how far away it was, a thousand meters or perhaps ten times that distance. Amid glowing dunes —here the color of the land was changing, from yellow to a pink so subtle that it was effectively a new color —Hagen thought that he had lost the explorer, but then suddenly the wavery stick-figure was in his path. Almost, he ran through or collided with it. He regained his balance and tried to speak casually.

"Honorable person, we do not wish to be discourteous, and we will leave you if our inquiries are bothersome, but we would like to know if you are one of the original explorers."

Eyes that one moment looked like skeletal sockets, and the next as large and human as Ailanna's own, regarded Hagen. Or were they eyes at all? Working with the controls of his sensory input he gained for one instant a glimpse of a face, human but doubtfully either male or female, squinting and intense, hair blown about it as if in a terrible wind. It faced Hagen and tried to speak, but whatever words came seemed to be blown away. A moment later the figure was gone, only walking somewhere nearby, but so out of focus that it might as well have flown behind the golden sphere somewhere.

Question or answer, Hagen? Which had it offered you?

Ailanna's hands clamped on his arm. "Hagen, I saw—it was terrible."

"No, it wasn't. Only a man or a woman. What lies between us and them, that can be terrible sometimes."

Ailanna was dialing her admittance down, going out of focus in a different way. Hagen adjusted his controls to return fully with her to their own year. Very little of the land around them seemed to change as they did so. A chain of small pink hills, hyperbolic paraboloid saddles precisely separating members, seemed to grow up out of nothing in the middle distance. That was all.

"Hagen, that was an explorer, that must have been. I wish he had talked to us, even though he frightened me. Are they still sane?"

He looked around, out over the uninhabited region toward which they had been walking, then back toward the city. In the city was where he would have to search.

He said: "The first veil that men ever saw falling here caught them totally by surprise. They described it as looking like a fine net settling toward them from an exploding sky. It settled over the first explorers and bound itself to the atoms of their bodies. They are all here yet, as you know. Soon it was realized that the trapped people were continuing to lead reasonable human lives, and that they were now protected against aging far better than we on the outside. There's nothing so terrible about life here. Why shouldn't they be sane? Many others have come here voluntarily to settle."

"Nothing I have seen so far would lead me to do that." Her voice was growing petulant again.

"Ailanna, maybe it will be better if we separate for a time. This world is as safe as any. Wander and surprise yourself."

"And you, Hagen?"

"I will wander too."

He had been separated from Ailanna for a quarter of a day, and searching steadily all the time, before he finally found her.

Mira.

He came upon her in a place that he knew she frequented, or had frequented a hundred and thirty years before. It was one of the lower subterranean corridors, leading to a huge pool in which real water-diving, swimming, and other splashy sports were practiced. He was approaching her from the rear in the corridor when she suddenly stopped walking and turned her head, as if she knew he was there even before she saw him.

"I knew you would be back, Hagen," she said as he came up.

"Mira," he said, and then was silent for a time. Then he said: "You are still as beautiful as ever."

"Of course." They both smiled, knowing that here she could not age, and that change from any sort of accident was most unlikely.

He said: "I knew that, but now I see it for myself." Even without his diving gear he could have seen enough through one hundred and thirty veils to reassure himself of that. But with his gear on it was almost as if he were really in her world. The two of them might hold hands, or kiss, or embrace in the old old way that men and women still used as in the time when the race was born of women's bodies. But at the same time it was impossible to forget that the silken and impermeable veils of a hundred and thirty years would always lie between them, and that never again in this world or any other would they touch.

"I knew you would come back. But why did you stay away so long?"

"A few years make but little difference in how close I can come to you."

She put out her hands and held him by the upper arms, and stroked his arms. He could feel her touch as if through layers of the finest ancient silk. "But each year made a difference to me. I thought you had forgotten me. Remember the vows about eternity that we once made?"

"I thought I might forget, but I did not. I found I couldn't."

A hundred and thirty years ago he and Mira had quarreled, while visiting Azlaroc as tourists. Angry, Hagen had gone offstar without telling her; when an alarm sounded that the yearly veil was falling early, she had been sure that he was still somewhere on the surface, and had remained on it herself, searching for him. By the time he came back, meaning to patch up the quarrel, the veil had already fallen.

She had not changed, and yet seeing her again was not all that he had expected it to be.

The reaction to his coming back was growing in her. "Hagen, Hagen, it *is* you. Really you."

He felt embarrassed. "Can you forgive me for what happened?"

"Of course I can, darling. Come, walk with me. Tell me of yourself and what you've done."

"I ... later I will try to tell you." How could he relate in a moment or two the history of a hundred and thirty years? "What have you done here, Mira? How is it with you?"

"How would it be?" She gestured in an old, remembered way, with a little sensuous, unconscious movement of her shoulder. "You lived here with me; you know how it is."

"I lived here only a very little time."

"But there are no physical changes worth mentioning. The air my yeargroup breathes and the food we eat are recycled forever, more ours than the rooms we live in are. But still we change and grow, though not in body. We explore the infinite possibilities of each other and of our world. There are only eleven hundred and six in my yeargroup, and we have as much room here as do the billions on a planet."

"I feared that perhaps *you* had forgotten *me*."

"Can I forget where I am, and how I came to be here?" Her eyes grew very wide and luminous—not enlarged eyes like Ailanna's; Mira like most other settlers had kept to the fashions of her year of veiling—and there was a compressed fierceness in her lips. "There was a time when I raged at you—but no longer. There is no point."

He said: "You are going to have to teach me how to be a settler here. How to put up with gawking tourists, and with the physical restrictions on which rooms and passages I may enter, when more of them are dug out in the future. Do you never want to burrow into the rooms and halls of later years, and make them your own?"

"That would just cause destruction and disruption, for the people of later years to try to mend. They could probably retaliate by diving against us, and somehow disarranging our lives. Though I suppose a war between us would be impossible."

"Do I disarrange your life seriously, Mira, by diving to you now?"

"Hagen!" She shook her head reprovingly. "Of course you do. How can you ask?" She looked at him more closely. "Is it really you who has come back, or someone else, with outlandish eyebrows?" Then the wild and daring look he knew and loved came over her, and suddenly the hundred and thirty years were gone. "Come to the pool and the beach, and we will soon see who you really are!"

He ran laughing in pursuit of her. She led him to the vast underground grotto of blackness and fire, where she threw off her garments and plunged into the pool. He followed, lightly burdened with his diver's gear.

It was an old running, diving, swimming game between them, and he had not forgotten how to play. With the gear on, Hagen of course did not need to come to the surface of the pool to breathe, nor was he bothered by the water's cold. But still she beat him, flashing and gliding and sliding away. He was both outmaneuvered and outsped.

Laughing, she swam back to where he had collapsed in gasps and laughter on the black-and-golden beach. "Hagen, have you aged that much? Even wearing the drag and weight of diver's gear myself I could beat you today."

Was he really that much older? Lungs and heart should not wear out so fast, nor had they, he believed. But something else in him had aged and changed. "You have practiced much more than I," he grumbled.

"But you were always the better diver," she told him softly, swimming near, then coming out of the water. Some of the droplets that wet her emerging body were water of her own year, under the silken veils of time that gauzed her skin; other drops, the water of Hagen's time, clung on outside the veils. "And the stronger swimmer. You will soon be beating me again, if you come back."

"I am back already, Mira. You are three times as beautiful as I remembered you."

Mira came to him and he pulled her down on the beach to embrace her with great joy. Why, he thought, oh why did I ever leave?

Why indeed?

He became aware that Ailanna was swimming in the water nearby in her own diver's gear, watching, had perhaps been watching and listening for some time. He turned to speak to her, to offer some explanation and introduction, but she submerged and was gone. Mira gave no sign of having noticed the other woman's presence.

"Do you miss the world outside, Mira?"

"I suppose I drove you away to it, the last time, with my lamenting for it. But no, I do not really miss it now. This world is large enough, and grows no smaller for me, as your world out there grows smaller as you age, for all its galaxies and space. Is it only the fear of time and age and death that has brought you back to me, Hagen?"

"No." He thought his answer was perfectly honest, and the contrast between this perfectly honest statement and some of his earlier ones showed up the earlier ones for what they were. Who had he been trying to fool? Who was it that men always tried to fool?

"And was it," she asked, "my lamenting that drove you off? I lament no longer for my life."

"Nor for the veil that fell between us?"

The true answer was there in her grave eyes, if he could read it through the stretching, subtle, impenetrable veils.

The red circles held narrow dagger-blades of urgent warning on all the walls, and warning voices boomed like thunder across the golden, convoluted plain. The evacuation ship lay like a thick pool of bright and melted-looking metal in the field, with its hundred doors open for quick access, and a hundred machines carrying tourists and their baggage aboard. The veil was falling early again this year. Stretching in a row across the gravity-inversion sky, near one side of the directionless horizon, explosions already raged like an advancing line of silent summer thunderstorms.

Hagen, hurrying out onto the field, stopped a hurrying machine. "My companion, the woman Ailanna, is she aboard the ship?"

"No list of names of those aboard has been compiled, Man." The timbre of the metal voice was meant to be masterly, and reassuring even when the words were not.

Hagen looked around him at the surface of the city, the few spare towers and the multitudinous burrowed entrances. Over the whole nearby landscape more machines were racing to reach the ship with goods or perhaps even tourists who had somehow not gotten the warning in comfortable time, or who were at the last moment changing their minds about becoming settlers. Was not Ailanna frantically looking amid the burrows for Hagen, looking in vain as the last moments fell? It was against logic and sense that she should be, but he could not escape the feeling that she was.

Nevertheless the doors on the ship were closed or

closing now. "Take me aboard," he barked at the machine.

"At once, Man." And they were already flying across the plain.

Aboard ship, Hagen looked out of port as they were hurled into the sky, then warped through the sideward modes of space, twisted out from under the falling veil before it could clamp its immovable knots about the atoms of the ship and passengers and hold them down forever. There was a last glimpse of the yellow plain, and then only strange flickers of light from the abnormal space they were traversing briefly, like a cloud.

"That was exciting!" Out of nowhere Ailanna threw herself against him with a hug. "I was worried there, for a moment, that you'd been left behind." She was ready now to forgive him a flirtation with a girl of a hundred and thirty years ago. It was nice that he was forgiven, and Hagen patted her shoulder; but his eyes were still looking upward and outward, waiting for the stars.

An Occurrence at the
Owl Creek Rest Home
by Arthur Jean Cox

*Arthur Jean Cox is a southern-California writer.
His best known previous science-fiction stories
are "A Collection of Ambroses" and "Straight
Shooters Always Win," and he is widely known
as a literary expert in scholarly and historical
areas.*

1

GEORGE CLAY HAD TOILED for seventy-two years
toward a certain end ... and then, after all his trouble, was informed by an officious clerk that his per-
mission to Terminate had been rescinded.

"But," he protested, "my case is in no way exceptional."

"That's true," agreed the clerk, indifferently toying
with the calendar on his desk. "The Commissioner's
decision is ... ah ... unusual. But of course it is final.
Not subject to review or appeal. Come back in half a
century," he added, not unkindly but casting an im-

patient glance at the door. "Perhaps we can do something for you then. Mind you, we make no promises."

With a weary sigh George turned away . . .

"Father?"

. . . and lay staring at the iron frame at the foot of his familiar iron bed.

He gazed at it for a long moment before he quite realized what it meant: his anxious interview had been a dream.

"Father!"

Now that he was awake, was he any better off? His eyes wandered listlessly, seeing without noting the too-familiar scene about him. Yes . . . he permitted the thought to form: Yes, he was better off. After all, there was an obvious escape from this situation. Sooner or later he would die.

He rolled his head to the right, looked past the two rows of beds and out the windows at the end of the ward. It was afternoon, judging by the shadows. He could see the spacious green lawn that encircled the Owl Creek Rest Home, a black smudge that was of course the paved road or street, and a green haze of trees on the other side of the road. As he watched, a car went by on the road—coming from somewhere and going somewhere. Ah! The scene swam before his eyes.

Good God! what he wouldn't give to be well and strong and out there, moving across the lawn toward that greater outside world, in the fresh air and sunshine. "What he wouldn't give—?" What did he have to give? Nothing. He was seeing now all of that world he would ever see again. He would probably never rise from this bed.

"Father!"

He became aware that he had heard that word several times now, each time becoming more peremptory. He lolled his head to the left and saw, without any great surprise, his daughter sitting in the wooden chair between his bed and the wall at this end of the ward. What did surprise him was that her husband was standing beside her, smiling upon him in a closed-mouth way that was probably meant to be reassuring. His daughter was a trim little woman of forty-five, in a trim little dark suit that matched her hair and black eyes. Hugh was also dressed in black. George couldn't remember having seen Hugh wear that suit before: but then he hadn't seen his son-in-law in—what was it?—some two years now. He was relieved to see that Nurse Mildred Paine was standing just inside the doorway, looking on: it mustn't be quite four yet, if she was still on duty. The sight of her pleasant face (strange that he should ever have thought it too narrow and gaunt) was comforting. It meant he wasn't alone with the Enemy.

He knew what they were seeing: An old, wasted man lying in a bed the size of a grave, the skin stretched so tautly across his skull that it seemed a break in it would show the white bone underneath.

"To what"—his voice came out unexpectedly broken, as if it were part hoot, part croak: both of which sounds were appropriate to Owl Creek. "To what," he began again, "do I owe the honor of this visit?"

"Father, we simply wished to see you," said Edith, in an admonitory tone. Perhaps his question had sounded more ironical than he had intended. "You must know, Father, that you have been ill. *Very* ill. And Hugh and I have come to see you, as an act of attention."

"Oh?" He turned his eyes toward Mildred.

"Yes. You have been sick, George," she said. "You've been unconscious since yesterday noon. You have had a fever. Doctor Murray was going to have you taken to the General if there wasn't any change for the better by this afternoon. But now you won't have to go. Your pulse is normal and strong. You're going to be all right ..."

"... for a while," he appended, wearily. He looked

at his waiting offspring and her spouse with a new understanding. "You may not need those dark clothes for a while, but keep them handy. Who knows? They might not even lose their press before you have to take them out again."

Edith raised an impatient and ironical eyebrow. Hugh pretended not to understand.

"You're looking well, Father," said Edith, with a trace of feeling in her voice that he reluctantly recognized as disapproval. He decided not to be difficult. After all, it was probably impossible for Edith to completely eradicate disapproval from her tone, it was so habitual with her.

"Yes, I seem to feel all right. . . . I'm not quite sure, though." He introspected a bit. "There's something wrong. There's a feeling I can't quite . . . Good God!" he exclaimed, making a discovery. "Good God, yes! I'm *hungry!* Why, I haven't been hungry in years!" He greeted his appetite as an old and dear friend, whom he had never thought to see again. He laughed with pleasure, which caused his other visitors to exchange a diagnostic glance. "You didn't bring me any candy, did you?" he asked the two. "No? Well—" eyeing the half dozen roses on the windowsill—"I'm so hungry I could almost eat them."

"I'll get you some food," promised Mildred, and departed for the kitchen.

Edith turned a look of irrational dislike at the retreating white dress. "Paine!" she said, disgustedly. "What a name for a nurse!" She got up from the chair. "But enough of this idle chit-chat. Some of us have work to do, even"—she attempted a smile and a small joke—"even if some of us do just lie around all day. You have to get back to the office, remember, Husband."

She deposited a kiss like ice water on her father's forehead and walked out the door.

Hugh ceremoniously extracted two one-dollar bills from his wallet and dropped them on the broad windowsill which served as George's night table. "There you are, my boy," he said, with his head tilted playfully to one side. "Buy yourself some cigarettes."

"I don't smoke," said George, a trifle testily. "Never have."

"Great! Great! That way you'll live to a ripe old age." And he patted George on his narrow and bony shoulder. He turned to leave but paused in the doorway to look back. "Well, anyway, Dad," he said, "you've led a full life."

2

A full life.

It hadn't seemed so to George. Not that it had been empty, either. He had had a happy childhood and a good education. He had fallen in love, married, raised a family, worked. How he had worked! But he had never gotten to do many of the things he had meant to do. He had wanted to travel, to see Europe, Africa and the Orient, to view the great art treasures of the world (for he was a Sunday painter: one good enough, he had been told, to have painted on the other days of the week, too). That had been his and his wife's lifetime dream. But he had kept putting it off. "Let's wait," he would say to his wife, "until both Edith and Tommy are out of college." Or, later, "Let's wait until I've established Tommy in business." Or, still later, "Let's wait until I've helped Edith's husband over this rough spot; and then, Violet—" turning to his wife, whose dark hair was slowly streaking with gray—"then we'll see the world."

But it hadn't worked out that way. Tommy was always getting into scrapes and having to be helped out of them. Once he forged his father's name to a thousand-dollar check and disappeared. He turned up again two years later, repentant in a sailor suit, so genuinely remorseful that George welcomed him back into his home and his business. Edith's husband had a problem with drink: he couldn't get enough of it. She was constantly calling on her father to set him on his feet again. When that husband got hold of the wrong kind of alcohol, she didn't mourn him long. Six months later she married Hugh Gates, a young fellow in her father's employ.

Things went well enough after that, for a while. That Round-the-World Trip slowly rose up above the horizon into George's view. And then—*debacle!* Tommy again forged his father's name, this time to bigger checks and to company papers, and fled, leaving his Old Man broke. George had to go into bankruptcy and start all over again. He created a new company and, through sheer know-how and industry, made it pay—but not until he had paid his creditors every cent he owed them, just as Sir Walter Scott, his boyhood hero, had done under similar circumstances. He had never seen Tommy again.

In the meantime he had brought the man who had married The Boss's Daughter into a kind of partnership with him. Hugh had none of Tommy's faults. He didn't drink much or gamble at all. He also had none of Tommy's high spirits. A curious thing about Hugh was that he didn't seem to have any interests of any sort. He didn't like sports, movies, or books. He collected nothing and had no hobbies ... Unless the accumulation of capital could be said to be his hobby.

So now George said to Violet: "We have no savings, but that doesn't matter. I'll turn the business over to Hugh so that you and I can travel."

He arranged the matter to his own and Hugh's satisfaction ... and Violet died.

For some months he plunged himself again into work, as a kind of special consultant and spur to Hugh, who was more talented as a salesman than as an executive. Then he fell ill with an "influenza" that lasted for months. He was only sixty-five but, recovering, he found himself an old man. No amount of rest or exercise would restore his strength, and his vision was considerably impaired. The trip was indefinitely postponed. Perhaps, he thought, he would never take it now. That was a great loss, but, really, why should he despair? He still had things to look forward to. He could spend his last years in peace and with enough money to give some graces to his life. He had his home and his family. And he thought, "This house has been silent too long. I'll invite Edith and Hugh to move out of their apartment in the city and come to live with me. It'll be pleasant having company."

The children moved in.

Although he naturally thought that they were living with him, he gradually became aware that he was living with *them.* And it soon became clear that Hugh resented the money George drew from the firm. He was entered on the books as a liability. Hugh took to philosophizing aloud at the dinner table that we must all be producers in this life or fall by the wayside. Edith developed a little habit of referring to her father as The Consumer—which she evidently regarded as a pleasantry. And then one day, when he was very ill, Hugh brought him some papers to sign, and he afterwards found that he had signed away his income.

"Look, Dad, why are you so upset? The company needs that money to meet obligations. It's only temporary. And, besides—" shaking his head sadly—"I told you what you were signing. Your memory's going, Dad."

"You're a liar, Hugh," said George. "You told me lies. And you never will restore that income to me." He retired to his room . . . for he still had the sole use of a room in the house he had built. He explored various avenues in hopes of regaining what was his. They were all dead ends. His old friend and lawyer, Stanley Abrams, had died. He himself was too ill and weak to fight. He was tired . . . so tired. He had turned over everything to his children and now they treated him as an incumbrance and a nuisance. They discarded his paintings in the trash, ignored his questions, shook their heads solemnly at his jokes, and served him his dinner in his room when they had company.

He had repeated the mistake of Lear.

One day Hugh took him for a drive. It wasn't a very long drive, but he never came back from it. It ended in the driveway of the Owl Creek Rest Home.

3

Nurse Mildred Paine came back with food: A clear broth, a small slice of white turkey meat, a five-ounce glass of grapefruit juice, Jello. "This was all I was able to wangle for you, George. The dietician was afraid to give you even this much, after your illness. You may find yourself nauseous."

But he didn't. He gulped the food down, ravenously, and looked around vainly for more.

He usually felt depressed after the youngsters had gone, and certainly their visit had been little joy. But somehow, now, he couldn't remain depressed. His spirits kept lifting—involuntarily, as it were. Maybe it was the meat. Whatever it was, he felt surprisingly good.

But there was a bad sign: His arm itched and, scratching it, he saw the outer skin flake off, almost in a single sheaf, as if he were a snake shedding its skin. In a moment he was itching all over. Mildred put up a screen and gave him a sponge bath and his skin peeled from him in great strips. He saw her concern. It meant that the nutrients weren't reaching the surface of his body, which sometimes occurred in the last stages of deterioration.

But underneath his old skin his new skin glowed pinkly.

Mildred called in Trucky Maoriano to lift him onto his chair while she changed his sheets; but George could almost have clambered onto his chair without assistance. He sat there, exchanging jokes with Trucky, and felt very good. He bobbed like a cork on the waves with elation. But when Mildred put her hand on his forehead, she found no fever.

He lay between the clean sheets, refreshed. Renewed.

When Buena Valdez, the second shift nurse, came on, he slyly neglected to inform her that he had already eaten and was served a dinner along with the rest of the ward. Of course, one of them—Zorbedian, the second bed down on the other side—snitched on him, but when Buena came back to shake her finger at him, like a little girl scolding her dolly, he told her he had already avoided prosecution by swallowing the evidence: the fish, whipped potatoes, peas, roll and butter, custard pudding, and very weak coffee.

That night hunger kept jostling him awake. Finally, George gave up, sat up in bed, and looked around. A rectangle of moonlight lay half on his bed and half on the floor to his right, and regularly spaced rectangles of moonlight overlapped each of the beds on this side of the room. He listened. Silence, except for the habitual night sounds of the ward: sighs, snores, groans, and Horace Hendershot in the next bed muttering a reply to something someone had said to him fifty years ago.

George swung his legs over the side of the bed into the moonlight and looked down. Would he fall if he tried to stand? No, he wouldn't. Or to walk? Again, no. He padded to the door of the ward and looked out.

He was in luck. Nurse Ruth Hoskins was away from her desk, which was an oasis of light in the hall separating the women's ward from the men. A small lamp displayed her blotter and what lay on it: A cup of coffee. And beside it—a sweet roll. With almonds! And maple frosting! He was so hungry he had hardly any control over his actions. He gobbled down the sweet roll and drained off the coffee in a very few seconds; and then, after a moment of reflection, ate all the sugar in the sugar bowl, that being the only other food present. He had tucked the dollar bills Hugh had left him into the breast pocket of his pajamas and he now put one under the empty cup. He felt some small qualms about that, but thought he could bear up under them. After all, she had access to other food and he hadn't. He went back to bed, smiling as he thought of Nurse Hoskins's outrage when she found her snack gone.

"Are we all here now?" asked Nurse Hoskins. She was a large woman with the body of a professional wrestler—and a face that would have been considered ugly even on a wrestler.

"There was a theft here last night," announced Hoskins, looking around the room severely. "Someone took something from my desk and left a mangy dollar bill to pay for it. Well, let me tell you that the thief won't go unpunished. I have taken that dollar bill to the FBI and they are sprinkling it with fingerprint powder right now and they'll tell me whose fingerprints are on it—"

She wouldn't have talked in that fashion to men of her own age; but her presumption seemed to be, always, that anyone who had to be taken care of was childish and of limited understanding. She looked around, perhaps to see if any eye was guiltily averted from hers. Morty, the timid old man who occupied the third bed down on the other side of the room from George, quailed under her glance, his hands fluttering vaguely at his mouth.

"So!" she said, bearing down on him. "I might have known it was you!"

"Just a minute!" called George. He hopped out of bed and strode towards her. "You leave Morty alone. He didn't take your goddam roll and coffee. I did."

Hoskins stared at him with a dropped jaw. Probably what surprised her most was the mere fact of his defiance: compounded by that other fact that recently, up until yesterday, he had been one of the feeblest of the feeble old men here. She recovered, seized his right arm just above and below the elbow, turned him around and walked him back to his own bed, with a threat that turned him pale:

"Just for that, you don't get any breakfast. We're not going to have any overfeeding here."

And so, when the trays were brought in, there wasn't one for him, although he was again terribly hungry. He was ashamed of being so ravenous; and yet, under his shame, was a small trembling pulse of delight. Hunger was so *lively*. It gave him something to look forward to, and he hadn't had that in ... oh, ages!

To his additional delight, when Mildred came on duty at eight, she brought him some orange juice, toast, eggs and cornflakes. It seemed to him the most delicious breakfast he had ever eaten in his life.

4

Looking out the window the next morning, he saw Hugh and Edith coming up the walk. He hopped back into bed, feeling less at a disadvantage there than in his shabby bathrobe.

"This is a pleasure!" he said. "I had hardly expected to see you again so soon."

"You're looking great, Dad," said Hugh. "We phoned and Nurse Hoskins said you were better. She certainly knew what she was talking about."

Edith took her customary place in the chair and Hugh sauntered over to the other side of the bed. There seemed to be something on his mind. George looked at him questioningly.

"Dad, there's something I want to ask you ..."

"Oh? You have something for me to sign?"

"Let's not be childish," advised Edith.

"It's about some money," went on Hugh, faltering a

little. "Is it possible that you, just before the bankruptcy twenty years ago, put aside some money?"

George stared at him. "What do you mean?"

"Well, I have an idea that when you saw the bankruptcy business looming, you put some money aside where the creditors wouldn't get it."

George continued to stare. A chill, almost physical, sank into his heart. "You have an idea . . . ?"

"That's right."

George found words again. "Why, you snivelling ingrate—you mean-spirited worm! Do you think I'd resort to something like *that?* When I turned over my books and accounts to the bankruptcy court, I accounted for every penny I had. I laid everything right on the table. If you think I'm the kind of man who'd cheat his creditors, you still know nothing of me after all these years."

But what was curious was that Hugh, instead of flinching under this scorn as he ordinarily would have done, stood steadfast. "Now take it easy, Dad. No one would blame you if you did keep something aside. It's just what I'd do, myself."

"I'm sure you would!"

"Nevertheless," went on Hugh, determined, "I have it on good authority that you did keep some money aside."

That chilling sensation sank deeper into George's chest as he racked his memory to discover who that authority might be.

"Something," said Hugh carefully, "in the neighborhood of ten thousand dollars."

Ah! So he was talking about Janie's Fund.

Janie Whitmer had been his sister's little girl. When she was a blond and plump two-year-old, he had set up an educational fund for her, amounting to $10,000. He had supposed, quite rightly, that her parents would never be able to afford to send her to college. That had been twenty-two years ago. Two years later Tommy disappeared with the firm's assets and

George was in bankruptcy, but his private misfortunes did not affect Janie's Fund in any way. That money was hers, not his. There was no legal way in which he could have gotten access to it, even if he had wanted to, except if Janie died before she reached college age. That had been a mere formality: he had never expected to see the money again. But six years ago, the gift had returned to the giver. The radiant Janie, on her way home from a high school dance, was killed when the antique automobile in which she and her escort were riding was struck by a train.

He had been in no hurry to touch the money. It held for him too much unhappy feeling. But, gradually, during that last year with Hugh and Edith, he had begun to see that perhaps he had something in reserve worth keeping there. He had never mentioned the fund to Hugh.

Who could have put Hugh and Edith on the track of the money? Surely not the Trust Officer or his old friend Charlie Kincaid, the General Manager, of the Bureford Bank. It was a mystery. But of one thing he was certain: They would never get their hands on that money.

He said, "You're wasting your time, Hugh."

"Dad, this is the way I look at it. That money is never going to do you any good. How can it? So we might as well have it. If you die we would be able to obtain it, I think, but only if we knew where it was. And we need the money now. I've gotten into rather a hole with certain land deals I went into. I fell in with some guys who said they could show me how to make a killing. And they did—only the killing was *me*. Boy, they really buried me! And Nurse Hoskins says you've been doing better lately and ... well, you know ... may be around for some time, and ..."

"I must remember, Hugh, to tell my butler not to admit you again."

"I know I'm not your flesh and blood, but Edith is, and—"

"Goodbye, Hugh."

"Okay, old man," said Hugh, picking up his coat, which he had dropped across George's feet. "You're just being spiteful and you know it! That money can never do you a bit of good. I think you're simply determined that *we* will never get hold of it. Look, I'll tell you what we'll do. Tell us how to get the money and we'll let you have some of it for your personal needs. You can't spend much here, I know, and a few hundred dollars might last you quite a while. You could buy little things, like cigarettes—"

"I don't smoke."

"—and magazines. You like to read."

Hugh fell silent, as if waiting for a reply. Which didn't come. Watching his face, George had the curious impression that he was working himself up to some resolve or sacrifice.

Hugh swallowed, as if forcing down something distasteful. "Look: What with compound interest, over a period of twenty years, that money will be much nearer twenty thousand than ten. And that much money would be more than we'd actually need to make good our losses. What was left over would pay for a personal nurse for you for some time. Nurse Hoskins! We could hire her! That means we could take you home. You could live at home, with us! Wouldn't that be great? Isn't that what you've always wanted?"

"Hugh, you not only shove the knife in, you twist it. But I know you. After you got that money, I wouldn't be with you three months before I was right back here again."

Hugh and Edith exchanged a glance over his bed—and he saw what he had done. He had admitted that the money existed.

"So," said Hugh.

"So," repeated George, laughing in agreement.

"Yes, you're right. The money *does* exist. And you were right about that other matter, too. You will never get your hands on it."

The younger man allowed himself a sneer. "What happened to those high moral principles you were bragging about a moment ago? So you wouldn't cheat your creditors, would you?"

"I'll explain nothing to you, Hugh. All you need to know is this: You've squeezed everything else out of me, by one means or another, but you won't get that money. You have my job and my company—all right. I gave you those. But you also took away my income from the company and my home and even the spot of ground I was to be buried in, and I didn't give you those. I still have a small shred of self-respect left, but I wouldn't keep even that long if I let you sweet-talk, wheedle, nag, trick, or bully the secret of that money out of me. You will never see it. Goodbye."

"Dad," said Hugh bitterly, "you're senile. I'll have you examined and declared *non compos mentis.* You'll be forced to tell what you've done with that money."

George laughed again. "How? By physical torture? Or by withholding my cigarettes? Goodbye."

Hugh made an inarticulate sound of disgust and stalked out the door. Edith rose. "Well, Father, I'm sorry to see you like this. I'll give you some time to think things over and maybe you'll arrive at a better state of mind. I'll come again in a few days ... and I think I'll bring a visitor. A surprise visitor." And she followed her husband ... leaving her father with a good deal to think about.

5

He definitely had his legs.

Sitting on the edge of his bed, he looked down at them. His feet didn't seem so white as they had, and—he lifted his pajama bottoms a little—the skin of his legs had lost that glassy, or porcelain, look. What did it mean? Could it be that his circulation had improved? Well, whatever it meant, he could walk about the ward with a good deal of assurance now and without getting tired. On the contrary, he often felt restless when he lay down and wanted to get up again and be moving about.

As he did now, for instance. He hopped down onto the floor and walked the length of the ward, nodding absently to Morty, Zorbedian, Dumbarton and the other old fellows as he passed them. Odd. Something odd ... What was it? He looked back. Old heads turned suddenly away from him, or looked down at newspapers or at empty hands. They had been watching him. But why? He glanced down at himself. There was nothing odd in his appearance. He was no shabbier than usual. Oh, well, what did it matter? He went to the window at the end of the ward and looked out.

Looked out at the green lawn and the street beyond. On the other side of the street he could see the trees and, here and there, poking their roofs through the greenery, houses. The World Out There. How beautiful! He couldn't seem to see enough of it. His eyes lapped it up, greedily. His gaze soared on over the housetops and trees to some twin towers in the distance—how long had those been there? he'd never noticed them before—and, further, to some blue-gray mountains in the very far distance. How long had *those* been there? Forever, he supposed. And yet, having looked out this window hundreds of times, he had never seen them before. Lord, how clear the air must be today!

After several minutes, he turned away from the window with a wistful sigh. The bed nearest him, Borgman's, was vacant. Someone had dropped a weekly newsmagazine there, open to the medicine section, and the headline of a column caught his eye, partly because someone—the same someone, probably—had drawn a border of black crayon around one of the paragraphs below it. He idly picked up the magazine and read:

OLD USED AS GUINEA PIGS

NYC (Apr. 28) Dr. Bosley Turping charged today, in a speech before the American Medical Ass'n, that aged persons are sometimes used as guinea pigs in this country.

"It is no secret," said Dr. Turping, "that seriously ill persons and terminal patients are sometimes experimentally given drugs whose properties and effects are inadequately understood . . . There is nothing shocking about that; in many cases it is undoubtedly the right thing to do. But it is shocking that elderly men and women in nursing homes without any specific or serious ailments but simply suffering from a general debilitation, from 'old age,' are also sometimes experimentally given substances the effects of which are unknown."

Turping went on to give instances. The paragraph starkly edged in black was one of these:

"The resident physician of a small midwestern nursing home administered various drugs to patients under his care in the hopes of finding a cancer-retarding or regressing drug. As he seldom had a cancer patient (those being taken to the nearby County Hospital and elsewhere), he gave his home-brewed concoctions to inmates who had no sign of cancer. This man, himself very advanced in years and in the opinion of some of his colleagues no longer competent to practice medicine, made the mistake of bragging about his 'researches' to a nurse who informed the local AMA chapter. He is now on 'leave of absence' from the nursing home, while the local board of supervisors, reluctant to undertake any action that might blacken the reputation of a man with decades of public service behind him, is quietly seeking to retire him."

George smiled. Zorbedian. Probably, it was Zorbedian who had marked the paragraph, no doubt thinking that the midwestern nursing home was the Owl Creek Rest Home and that its culpable resident physician was none other than Doctor Ives, who had so unexpectedly taken his sabbatical. And the description did fit rather patly ... but, after all, there were hundreds of such institutions in the midwest, so what were the chances that the item had anything to do with Owl Creek? The pathologically suspicious Zorbedian was always accusing the nurses and staff of putting strange substances in his food and drink, but apparently they didn't think him crazy enough to transfer him to the psychopathic ward at the General.

With the thought, he naturally glanced at Zorbedian, on the other side of the room, and found that the old guy, sitting bolt upright in bed, was glowering at him, his lower lip thrust out as if in surly accusation. George winked at him. He dropped the magazine back onto Borgman's bed and paced the ward back to his own. Again, he was conscious that his fellow inmates were regarding him rather curiously, but when he stopped to look about at them questioningly all dropped their eyes or turned away—except for Zorbedian, who continued to glower at him, as with some undefined suspicion. George shrugged his shoulders and went on. He couldn't let things like that concern him.

But when he was about six feet from his bed, something else made him stop and stare. His hands flew to his eyes.

His spectacles lay on his pillow.

He didn't have his glasses on! He *hadn't* had them on! But ... but then, how had he been able to read that magazine? He hadn't been able to read a page in years without his glasses. And how had he been able to experience that wonderful horizon-scanning vision? Ordinarily, the trees on the other side of the road were to him, without his glasses, a green cloud or haze lying on the ground. My God, his vision had somehow cleared! But how?

He looked about, at his rumpled bed, and at the bare floor. He could see the grain in the wood! It reminded him of his last flight in a plane, years ago: Looking out the window, in the clear sunlight above the clouds, he could see every pinscratch on the metal wing. He shyly, almost surreptitiously, glanced about at the faces of the other old men, his so-diffident companions. How ugly they were! He had never noticed before how very blemished and wrinkled their faces were. *He* wasn't likely to be any handsomer, though, was he? He looked down at his hands. He could see every fine hair on their backs . . . but the age spots, those dark liver spots—he couldn't see those any better than he had been able to before! That was an anomaly. If he didn't know better, he'd swear the spots were fading. And where were the warts on the little finger of his right hand?

One part of his mind was blank, another part buzzed with incoherent speculations, nothing arguable taking shape. He went into the toilet and took a look at himself in the mirror over the washbasin. His eyes looked all right; clear, without redness or film. He was badly in need of a shave, but his face wasn't as blemished as he had anticipated. And it was filling out. If he weren't careful, he'd soon be a fat old man like Hendershot. Was it his imagination, or was his hair fatter, too? He ran his hand through it and it seemed to him more full-bodied than it had been, not quite so wispy.

He went back to his bed. If he continued to wander about restlessly, he'd fret the other old guys. It didn't take much to do that. By way of occupying his mind, and without any more definite purpose, he propped himself up on his pillows and wrote a letter to the Trust Officer at the Bureton Bank, asking for a statement of the exact amount in the Janie Whitmer Trust Fund, and advising that officer that no information concerning the fund was to be released to anyone without his written consent. His hand moved swiftly, legibly, without the slightest tremor, and he gave his signature the old flourish of years past. He had a stamped envelope on hand and, still humoring himself, although it was a pity to waste the stamp, he put the letter into it and addressed the envelope. Which he then posted behind his pillows, as if it were a personal missive to the Sandman.

Staring out the window, he saw his daughter, just passing out of his line of sight and entering the building. There seemed to be someone with her, a figure in brown. Her Surprise Visitor? Something about the figure sent an uneasy thrill through him. A presentiment, but of what, he couldn't have said.

Edith appeared at the narrow door of the ward, crowded by her mysterious companion. "Father," she cried, "look who I've brought you!"

He was a man in his late forties, with a broad face and a wide mouth on which lurked a grin. His eyes were gray and, without being in the least shy or timid—they were very steady—had something vague about them. Perhaps the fact that he seldom blinked them made their steadiness seem unnatural. He looked, thought George, like a carnival barker.

"Hello, Pops," he said, this apparition. "Long time no see."

It had been twenty years, actually.

Tommy, the swindler, embezzler, ingrate, wife-deserter, etc., etc., displayed no sign of guilt in confronting the father he had ruined. He squeezed himself through the door and sauntered over to the one chair.

"As you see," he remarked, "the prodigal son has returned. Please be advised that he expects a fatted calf. No? Well, no matter. He had a late breakfast. You're looking okay, Pops—much better than advertised, which is rare. Only you've apparently lost the power of speech. Too bad. I'd looked forward to a little chat with you.

"One thing is certain," he rattled on, as George, saying nothing, studied him curiously, "and that is that you'll know me if you ever see me again. You may wonder why I came back to these stamping grounds? I can't really say. It must be the Bad Penny principle at work. I hear about you now and then, because I often have dinner with Sis here and her spouse, and there have been times when I was glad to get a square meal, too. Not that I'm complaining. I've been doing all right lately. I'm associated in a very modest way with the Reverend Willie Hardrack. I write some of his radio patter and other advertising copy. 'Keep those dimes and dollars coming in, folks!' Lucrative work it is too, though not for me. The Rev. Willy is a tightfisted old bastard."

"Father," said Edith, "I think you might forgive Brother Tommy. After all, he *is* your son."

"He is," agreed George.

"And you forgave him once for doing the same thing that you're mad at him for."

"And he did it again," said George.

"Well, Pops," said Tommy, trying to put his hands back into his pockets while remaining seated, "that was all a long time ago. Also, you weren't really hurt. You made it all back. Personally, I'm willing to let bygones be bygones . . ."

"Why not? You have nothing to lose by being magnanimous."

"And you, Pops," said Tommy, looking about at the old men and the beds, "what have you got to lose? Which brings me, naturally enough, to the subject of my visit. I have the vaguest memory of your telling me twenty years ago or more—you used to confide in me in those days, you know—that you had done something with ten thousand dollars. I can't quite remember what. And Hugh says that much money hasn't shown up since. I think he'd know. He has an eye for such things. He hinted to me that I might be doing everyone a service, not only you and him but me, if I came here and jogged your memory a bit. After all, I *am* your son—"

"Have you ever been vomited on, Tommy?"

"—and I thought that for old times' sake . . ."

George saw Trucky out on the lawn. He got suddenly out of bed, startling his two offspring by the agility with which he did so. He removed the envelope he had tucked away behind his pillows and, leaning out the window, called Trucky to him. "Would you please mail this letter for me? It's rather urgent."

"I'd hand-deliver it, if you want me to, Mr. Clay," said Trucky.

George got back into bed, hopping up onto it like a boy. He turned to Tommy. "Now, you were saying . . . ?"

Tommy glanced speculatively out the window, as if with some idea of calling the man back and taking a look at the address on that envelope. But, although he dared a good deal, he didn't quite dare to do that: it might mean an unseemly physical struggle with this spry old man. The three of them saw Trucky drop the letter into the red, white and blue mailbox on the distant corner.

"Checkmate, huh, Pops?" asked Tommy. "You've stolen a march on us, I'll bet. You always were a shrewd old buzzard. Well, I guess that's it. I will amble off now into the setting sun. Don't get up. I'm not likely to bother you again . . . unless . . . (I'm still racking my brains, you see) . . . unless I think of something more in connection with that trifling sum: in which case I'll be back. But don't keep a candle burning in the window for me."

He stepped past Edith, saying as he did so, "His eye is not quite so rheumy as you indicated," and went out the door.

"I'm very cross with you," said Edith. "We'd hoped, Husband and I, that Brother Tommy's return would soften you. Of course, Tommy was very flippant. But you know Tommy. You have to make allowances. I'm sure that inside he feels this whole thing very deeply, just as I do."

He surprised himself by letting out a bark of delighted laughter. "Ha! That's beautiful!"

That silenced her for a moment. She glanced around, narrow-eyed, at the old heads turned their way. "You don't need that money," she resumed, in a lower tone. "Brother Tommy and my husband and I do, but all your needs are taken care of here."

"That's right," said George, "you're still out buffeting against the waves of the wide world. You haven't reached this snug harbor."

"I want none of your famous sarcasm, Father. I don't have to take that from you. You think we don't come to see you often enough and then you talk that way. Could you blame me if I don't come back for quite a while?"

He understood her. It was a threat. Well, he thought, it won't work. He took no pleasure in their company and they took none in his.

That night he dreamt he was again in his thirties and at home with his family. It was Christmas Eve. Still another version of *A Christmas Carol* was on the television, the Ghost of Christmas Yet to Come filling the screen at the moment. He and the two children, a blond boy and girl of about seven and eight, were decorating the tree. His pretty blond wife came out of the kitchen with a tray of fudge to which they all, laughing, helped themselves . . .

He awoke, smiling. And yet it seemed to him that there was something slightly wrong with the dream. What was it? It took him a minute or two before he could place it exactly: Violet had had dark hair, as had had both his children from infancy. The laughing woman was not Violet and the children decorating the tree were not Tommy and Edith. The dream was not nostalgic: It took place in the future, not the past. When the woman had come out of the kitchen, he had glimpsed the date on the cloth calendar hanging on the inside of the swinging kitchen door:

1984.

1984? Not Violet . . . ?

He tried to grieve, but couldn't. Despite himself, he felt cheerful. His spirits kept springing up again. He was alert and full of energy. He got out of bed, peeped out into the hallway and saw that Hoskins was asleep at her post, her head slumped forward into her arms. Even the Wicked (as the Reverend Hardrack must have observed at one time or another) sometimes cease from chafing. He tiptoed past her and went down the hall into the recreation room at the rear of the building. A high wind was blowing, rattling the windows vigorously from outside. Guided by the moonlight streaming along the floor, he found his way to the exercycle—a machine not much used by the inmates, heart attack being feared more than flabby leg muscles—and, seating himself, began pedaling away. God, he felt good! He pedaled for what would have been miles, if he had been moving free out there in the wind and through the open world. He pedaled to Bureford. And beyond. And then, tired but happy, he dismounted and made his way back again past the dozing dragon to his bed, where he slept soundly, dreaming of breakfast.

6

George's . . . recovery . . . after this was rapid. He could see well now without glasses and read for hours without tiring his eyes. His hair was darker and fuller; his hairline was creeping forward, stealthily but not unobserved, day by day. His gait changed. His steps these last few years had been short, mincing and rapid, as if he were walking uncertainly down a steep incline. Now he walked easily, as if he were climbing a hill.

He ate voraciously. He consumed three meals a

day, like the other inmates, and in addition cadged candy bars, apples, doughnuts and cups of coffee. He twice raided the kitchen at night, once eating an entire chicken and once a pound of ham. He was ashamed of his gluttony—and yet gluttony looked well on him. He filled out, but no matter how much he ate, his stomach remained flat, perhaps partly because he did stomach-muscle flexing exercises, exercycle pumping, and pushups. He did most of this in secret, one reason being that it alarmed the nurses so when they saw how vigorously he worked out. He exercycled at night, when he could slip past Hoskins. When he couldn't, he would get out of bed to run-in-place or do pushups, hopping back into bed whenever he heard her stirring from her desk. He was up a great part of the night and yet he got plenty of rest. He could sleep as much as he wanted during the day, and this may have been why his steadily-improving appearance didn't excite more comment than it did from habitual visitors to the ward: No one pays much attention to an old man sleeping with the covers pulled up about his ears. Hoskins never saw him during this period.

But of course the marked improvement in his appearance did not escape the notice of his fellows. Few things escaped the observation of those half-blind and half-deaf old men. His one sadness was, in fact, the attitude of the other patients. They were envious and jealous of him, almost as if they felt that he had usurped something rightly belonging to them. What most disappointed him was the attitude of Harry Dumbarton, three beds down on this side of the room. Harry was a taciturn old man with a craggy, weatherbeaten face and white hair like the bristles of a stiff brush. He had been a ship's engineer in the merchant marine most of his life, and George had always found him intelligent and decent, although almost too reticent for conversation. And now Harry's fine impassive face threatened to crumble whenever he looked George's way. His rage—when it did burst out one day—was the more impressive for being so seldom displayed; it was as if he were speaking out at last under some intolerable and prolonged injustice.

He arose from his bed in his nightshirt. He turned, his legs trembling under him, and faced George, who had been restlessly pacing the ward and had stopped to speak to him. Harry must have been a fine man in his day.

"Why *you?*" he cried, as George stared, blankly. "Why not *me?* Are you any better than I am? Where were you when the *Grace de Dieu* went down and everybody was drowning around me? Could you have held Collins afloat in the freezing water for eight hours until we were picked up? Where were you when the boiler exploded—?"

"Harry," said George, as calmly as he could, "Harry, you're not well. I think you should lie down." And, imitating Hoskins's scientific grip above and below the elbow, he wheeled Dumbarton about and placed him back onto his bed. "Don't excite yourself, old man; this is none of my doing."

Harry sank back and lapsed into silence. George turned away, regretting the incident and wondering what in the world he could have meant when he had said, "This is none of my doing."

But the incident wasn't closed yet. The moment he stepped back into the aisle, the others rose against him. If he had been the hero of the encounter with Hoskins, he was the villain of this one. It may be that the taciturn Harry had spoken for them all.

"I know," said Zorbedian, with a good old-fashioned melodramatic sneer, unconsciously imitated from some stage performance he had witnessed as a boy: "I know why you're getting all this preferential treatment. You're Nursie's pet! You're the sweetheart of that Nurse Paine-in-the-ass! You're carrying on an affair with her! That's why they're giving you all the nutritious food and making us eat the wornout scraps with no food value in them!"

"Yes," seconded Bob Burns, wincing as he raised himself on an arthritic elbow, "that's why they're giving you the modern miracle medicines and us aspirin."

And to George's further astonishment, there was a bleat from the prostrate bulk of the huge Hendershot in the bed next to his own: "And that's why they're letting you exercise all hours of the day and night while they make us lie here till our muscles atrophy."

"You fat old slob," shouted George, blazing with anger, "you never exercised in your life! If you want to exercise, get out of bed and do it! Who's stopping you? And you, Zorbedian, if I hear you speaking of Nurse Paine in that way again, I'll wring your scrawny neck like I would a turkey's!"

There was a clamor of voices. The others snapped and snarled at him; all except Dumbarton and the wide-eyed and trembling Morty. But the loudest voice was his own. He outshouted them all. He stalked about the room, roaring with outstretched finger, and sent each of them back to his pillow with a display of energy and resolution that none of them could match, like a trainer in a cage full of raging lions and tigers.

The whole hubbub lasted but a minute. He stood, quivering with anger in the center of the room, looking about him.

Mildred Paine stood just inside the door, looking at him with dismay and wonderment. She had probably heard the last part of the discussion.

She came forward, almost timidly. "I've never seen you like this before, George." Her disapproval was tempered by a small smile. "You're usually so patient and considerate. What's making you so cranky?"

He turned his head away a bit peevishly. "I'm . . . I'm teething."

And so he was: Mildred could see fragments of white thrusting themselves up through his sore and pink gums. The two looked at each other a long moment. Neither spoke, but each understood what the other was thinking. He saw her perplexed and anxious eyes examining his face and knew that she was seeing what she saw when he looked in the bathroom mirror. The wrinkles on his face were disappearing.

Mildred, her face frozen, drew back, as if shrinking from him. But she was a brave girl and she dispelled her feeling, whatever it was, and his answering chill, with a quick smile. "Well ... perhaps I should bring you a teething-ring? Maybe with that you wouldn't be so crabby." He declined that offer, but accepted some camphor to put on his tender gums.

His new teeth grew rapidly. In a short while he was eating with them—fortunately, for he went through a time when they weren't much good as yet but he couldn't use his store-boughten teeth. He had to gum his food, as did some of the other oldsters here. Mildred told various staff members about the new teeth, including the administrator, Pauline Lute; but Mrs. Lute somehow—perhaps because she was preparing for her annual vacation, although it was a curious lapse even so—completely forgot this startling bit of news immediately afterward. The dietician came to peer into George's mouth, after which she sent him frequent glasses of milk, an attention which also aroused the malice of his fellow prisoners. Even those who weren't thirsty resented Mildred and Buena bringing him the white glasses of bone-forming liquid: He was getting something they weren't.

He itched and shed his skin again. And Mildred decided that it was time he had a real bath: it had been more than a year since he had had anything but a sponging. "I think you're strong enough," she told him, "to get in and out of a tub without falling and breaking a leg or drowning yourself. Of course, I'll be there to help you."

He studied her face as she soaped his shoulders, and found it pleasant. She was about fifty years old, but small, slim, trim, well-preserved. Her hair had been blond but was fading into grey. Her face, like her body, was narrow. She had probably been thought pretty as a teenager and—George added a codicil—he would have agreed with that judgment. She smiled under his scrutiny.

"All right, I can dry you now. Here, take my arm. Careful now . . ."

It was while she was drying him with the heavy towel that something happened that hadn't happened in years. He had been feeling for some time a warming, erotic glow, rather pleasant in itself; an incipient stirring; but he hadn't expected his appetite to take on a note of urgency or to manifest itself in any specific or tangible way. But it did.

"Oh, my!" said Mildred, incredulously, staring at it. "Now, don't be childish, George!" He had taken her around the waist and, displaying an unexpected strength, bending his knees, forced her backward to the floor. "George—you'll hurt yourself!"

But he felt quite capable and strong. He got his hand under her skirt and pulled off her panties—fortunately, she wasn't wearing one of those damned body-stockings—and wedged himself into place.

In the tussle that followed she uttered not a sound until, finally, she gave vent to some involuntary ones. She struggled at first. Perhaps from surprise, but after a time ceased to do so, partly because she didn't now want to bring anyone running and partly to lessen the chances of his hurting himself. She waited patiently until he had exhausted himself and then, released, got up; not helping him, for he rose to his feet quite easily.

"Pardon me a minute, George. There's a little thing I have to do. *My!*" she added, as she proceeded to do so. "What's happening to you?" She looked him over seriously, as he—a bit awkwardly but not much—got into his pajamas and robe. "You haven't eaten any monkey-glands, have you? Nothing like this has happened to me before." She smiled. "I don't mean ... well, I was married years ago, you know. I mean, some of the other fellows your age have had that same idea but they've never been able to back it up with anything solid. There's no use denying it, George. You're not just getting well or getting better, you're getting ..." But her voice failed her: she couldn't bring herself to utter that last word. "Anyway, I think that after this you can bathe yourself."

They walked back in silence, arm in arm, to the men's ward. She tucked him into bed and planted a kiss on his firm cheek—a kiss of forgiveness, perhaps, and he didn't know what else. She straightened and stood in her white uniform, looking down at him, her face unreadable in the darkness. He looked back up at her for a long moment. She bent and whispered in his ear:

"I'll soon be too old for you!"

And left.

7

Doctor Murray stopped by one afternoon and sat down on the side of his bed.

"You're looking well, George. Better than I've ever seen you—although of course I've only seen you this past month or so. Dyed your hair, I see. Vanity, vanity, thy name is man! I hear all sorts of wild things about you. If half of them were true, you'd be a phenomenon and I could congratulate myself on my wonderful prowess as a physician. Perhaps I will, anyway."

He looked over some papers he had in a folder: the results, most likely, of the physical examination George had had some five weeks ago, after he had emerged from the coma. "Hmmm ... you *are* in good shape! Heart and lungs good. Blood pressure a little low, but not to worry. Shows what a good clean life will do for you. I see that you don't smoke and of course here you don't drink much. So all we have to watch," he added, with a wink, "is your sex life." George bared his teeth in a smile in which the doctor failed to perceive mockery. "And new choppers, too!" exclaimed Murray, laughing in wonderment. "Well, goodbye, George," he said, closing the folder. "I have an urgent appointment. Have to keep my practice up, you know." And, with another wink, he pantomimed a golf swing.

There was so much talk about George that, inevitably, some of it came to the attention of a wider public. But Owl Creek was such a stagnant backwater that the ripples didn't spread very far. Mildred brought him a copy of the *Owl Creek Weekly*, which had a little story about him.

LOCAL MAN LIVES BACKWARD

OWL CREEK—June 2. Mr. George Clay (72), a patient for the last five years at the Owl Creek Rest Home, may not be there much longer, it is said. He may be discharged on grounds of extreme youth. The patients at the Home are all Senior Citizens and it is rumored that Mr. Clay may soon be too young to be kept on there.

"He looks younger every day," says Nurse Mildred Paine (53). "I wish I could say the same for myself. He is getting stronger. He has new teeth. His hair is darkening and the wrinkles of his face are disappearing. I've never seen anything like it in my life and I've been in this line of work for thirty years."

Dr. Stanley Murray (28), recently appointed staff physician *pro tem* at the Home, replacing Dr. Ives, now on his well-earned sabbatical, has a prosaic explanation for the marvel, however. "It sometimes happens," Dr. Murray tells this reporter, "that a man will look much older than he is after undergoing a particularly debilitating illness. Then, if he recovers and regains his normal appearance, it seems as if he has gotten younger. It is a phenomenon that everyone in the medical profession is familiar with. And I have an idea," adds Dr. Murray, "that George is not quite so old as some people think he is."

But Anthony (Trucky) Maoriano (45), handyman, driver, etc., at the Home, finds that he cannot in good conscience corroborate Dr. Murray's diagnosis. "No, there's no mistake about it," says Trucky. "Mr. Clay is definitely getting younger, not older. I think he's living backwards."

This should worry the staff at the Owl Creek Rest Home. Of course, it wouldn't be the first time they have had a patient who was in his second childhood, but . . . Who knows where this trend will end?

Change your diapers, George?

The story, mused George as he read it, probably wouldn't even come to the attention of his offspring, unless it was picked up by the metropolitan dailies, which was possible. The last few lines raised a problem he had thought of once or twice: Where would this business end? Would he progress—or regress back to infancy? Somehow, he couldn't think so. In his dreams he was always a young man; and his guess was that his body was merely regaining its optimum physical condition, which would naturally be that of a young man. He had bathed unawares in that Fountain of Youth for which Ponce de Leon had been searching. Youth. Not infancy.

He never quarreled with the old men about him now, but bore their little remarks and querulous hints with reserve and fortitude. *Noblesse oblige.* But one thing haunted him and that was Harry Dumbarton's question: "Why *you*—and not me?" Harry, he knew, had spoken for them all. He saw that same question wherever he turned, in every face. "Why *him*—and not me?" He had to admit that they had a real question there. He thought a good deal about it.

Why him? Surely, he wasn't being rewarded with this great gift because he had contributed to charities or helped old ladies across the street. When he hopped back into bed after his exercises, and lay in the dark listening to the others groaning and coughing, muttering and turning in their sleep, he sent up that silent question again and again: *Why me?*

He remembered that suggestive medical item in the newsmagazine; and Tommy's faith-healing Hardrack; and that senile old man, Ambrose, who had bored everyone here silly about a Secret Society of Immortals, until he proved that he wasn't a Member—by dying; and how Floyd, Edith's first husband, had staggered in one day twenty years ago with a bottle someone had sold him, containing, he said, a rejuvenation elixir, and which George found to be mineral water. Nothing was too trivial for him to dredge up. But there was no answer.

Unless ... As he drifted off to sleep in the lengthening hours of the night he wondered: What if he weren't getting younger at all, and all this were an insane delusion? Suppose he were senile and dreaming of his youth? That sounded plausible enough. At such moments, it even seemed likely. It explained the otherwise inexplicable. A man being hanged imagines that the rope breaks, just as the trapdoor of the scaffold opens beneath his feet; and, surely, many another old man, drifting dreamlike on his pillow away from the moorings of reason, had imagined that he was young again? Could it be that he would wake up tomorrow morning and find himself old: his body frail and weak, his vision blurred, his face corrugated, his bowels and bladder unreliable?

But when he awoke in the morning, he found himself even stronger and younger-looking than the night before. It was not youth, but old age and suffering that were fading like a dream.

8

The end was in sight. The end? No, a new beginning. One morning, he walked in the grounds in back of the hospital, arm in arm with Trucky, although actually he needed support no more than Trucky did. He turned his wistful gaze out towards Owl Creek. In his first week here, he had walked away. He had

117

made it as far as the ancient railroad bridge a few hundred yards downstream. But, midway across, he stepped on a loose plank, pitched forward against the guardrail and hung there until an attendant came ("Come on, Pop, that water's too cold to dive into") and took him back to his bungalow.

Yesterday, he had taken a small but fateful step. He had dispatched a letter to the president of the Bureford Bank, Charlie Kincaid, saying that George Clay the Younger would be in shortly to collect the money in Janie's Fund. He was confident that this little stratagem would work. Charlie wouldn't fail to recognize in this young stranger his old friend's features. George had become his own heir. He had stepped into his own shoes.

That is, he would have done so if he had had any to step into. One of the two things that kept him at the Home (Mildred being the other) was that he needed something to walk away in. Bathrobe, pajamas and slippers wouldn't do in the street.

He asked Mildred about the clothes he had worn when he came.

"Why, George, those were given to the Salvation Army years ago. And, besides, they wouldn't fit you now. You really have a fine voice," she went on, laughing a little. "It's gotten deeper and stronger every day. I hate to lose you, you know, but how can anyone keep you? Why don't you wait a few days? Maybe Doctor Murray will discharge you."

He moved restlessly. "I'll wait until tomorrow," he said; and then, "Will you meet me in the Playroom at eleven-thirty?"

She shook her head. But she was there when he looked in.

He was up early the next morning: shaved, bathed, exercised. His release came suddenly.

Supervisor Leland Kapes of the County Board of Hospitals came by on a routine trip of inspection and saw George sitting on the side of his bed. He turned to Mildred.

"What is this man doing here? Has he been occupying that bed?"

Mildred chose her words with care. "He's been sick, but he's well now. He's waiting for Doctor Murray to discharge him."

"Well, for God's sake!" whispered Kapes, as George sat listening. "Get him out of here, will you? Don't wait for Doctor Murray. Do it this afternoon. We've got *old people* waiting for these beds!"

"Yes, sir!" cried Mildred; and Kapes went on to inspect the kitchen.

Mildred reappeared some fifteen minutes later. Her eyes were red, but dry. She carried George's old cane and a suit—not his familiar old brown, but a comparatively new suit, light blue, recently pressed. There was a shirt, a new wide tie, some socks and underwear, polished shoes.

He looked at her questioningly. "They were my brother's," she said. "They'll fit you. And—" reaching into the pocket of her dress—"you'll need money. No, no! It's only fifty dollars. You can send it back to me a year, two years, from now. I know I'll never see you again. I mustn't ever see you again. I know that." Her voice was so low the others could not hear. "But if you will enclose a note when you return the money, I'll know you're all right. Take it. It's insurance that I'll hear from you some day."

He wordlessly accepted the money.

Mildred moved a screen in front of his bed, so that he could dress behind it. Every eye in the room was *riveted* on that screen. Morty sat rigidly upright, staring at the screen with an almost painful suspense. Zorbedian's head was raised from its pillow. Hendershot stared as if he would see through the cloth-covered cardboard, if he could. Even Harry Dumbarton's silent eye revolved in that direction. The television set whispered unattended to in the opposite corner.

The playing cards had dropped from the hands of Burns and Borgman and lay on the counterpane. Parham's newspaper littered the floor by his bed.

A man stepped from behind the screen. He was slightly above the middle height and, in that place, decidedly young: he couldn't possibly be more than forty. His face was slightly pale, his body trim. He carried a cane—unnecessarily, it would seem, as he moved with confidence and ease.

"George," said Mildred, wistfully, "you look like a young Fredric March."

George looked about at Hendershot and at the other old men there. *Old men.* He had been so like them and was now so different. Perhaps some day he would resemble them again, but that was a long way away—almost a lifetime away: he still had some growing young to do before he started back up that long hill. Every pair of eyes in the room returned his solitary gaze; and there was something in this moment that was very terrible to him.

The moment drained away ... and then Morty sent up a thin, quavering cheer. It had not quite died when it was supported and endorsed from across the room by a hearty bull-roar. The stricken Harry Dumbarton, struggling upward from his sheets, sent up a mighty cry of congratulation. It cost him more, perhaps, than those eight hours in the freezing water, but he rose to what was possibly the most selfless act of his long career. His example was irresistible. The others took it up. The vote was unanimous.

"Goodbye!" George called. "Goodbye, Morty, Harry, Virgil, all of you!" He turned away.

Mildred came with him to the door. "Forget me," she said. "Forget all of us, George." And she turned away hastily, toward the back of the building.

He obeyed her. Whirling his cane jauntily, he stepped out onto the porch.

And there coming down the walk towards him was ... Tommy.

He addressed himself to George:

"Say, Buddy, could you tell me where—" He stopped, stared, finished lamely: "—I could find the administrator . . . ?"

They stood facing each other in the clear light of day. Father and son; but it was the father who appeared to be the younger man.

"Turn around," said George, in the tone of one who will be obeyed.

Tommy stared. Then, his face at once anxious and blank, he slowly faced about until his back was to George—who promptly placed a vigorous kick on his rear end. "Deliver that message to Hugh and Edith. Now, git!"

Tommy got. He moved back down the walk to a car parked at the curb. He slumped forward as he walked, his shoulders and arms hanging limply. It was as if George had heaped all his old age and infirmity upon his son.

Pity smote him like a blow.

"Wait, Tommy! Wait!"

The figure froze, its back toward him.

"I forgive you, Tommy," called George. "Tell Hugh and Edith that I forgive them too—and ask them to forgive me. Let there be no guilt! Be happy, Tommy. But be happy away from me!"

The figure at the car slumped forward—then straightened, managed to get the car door open, and sat down behind the steering wheel. George turned away. He heard a car motor start, rise in pitch and fade away . . . and gave it not a thought.

It was a glorious day. The tree-shaded lane, half country road and half city street, stretched before him pleasantly. In the distance he could see the roadside buildings of Owl Creek, gleaming red and white in the sun. A few miles further on was Bureford, where tomorrow morning he would see Charlie Kincaid and arrange to collect his nearly twenty thousand dollars. From Bureford the land stretched south to New Orleans, west to San Francisco, north to bustling Chicago and east to magnetic New York City. Beyond the tall buildings and the restless waters lay London, Paris, Rome, Berlin, all the cities of men—all those places he had always meant to see and which now he would.

> "The world lay all before him,
> Where to choose . . ."

He had time and life and world enough now.

He put his foot upon the black asphalt of the road and strode forward, toward Bureford.

And beyond.

The Force That Through the Circuit Drives the Current

by Roger Zelazny

Roger Zelazny was Guest of Honor at the 1974 World Science-Fiction Convention, a tribute paid only to the most outstanding writers, editors and others in the field. He has received two Hugos and two Nebulas for his previously published science fiction, as well as the French Prix Apollo. Perhaps his most famous short stories are "The Doors of His Face, the Lamps of His Mouth," "He Who Shapes" and "A Rose for Ecclesiastes."

... AND I HAD BEEN OVERRIDDEN by a force greater than my own.

Impression of a submarine canyon: a giant old river bed; a starless, moonless night; fog; a stretch of quicksand; a bright lantern held high in its midst.

I had been moving along the Hudson Canyon, probing the sediment, reaching down through the muck and the sludge, ramming in a corer and yanking it back again. I analyzed and recorded the nature, the density, the distribution of the several layers within my tube; then I would flush it, move to the next likely spot and repeat the performance; if the situation warranted, I would commence digging a hole—

the hard way—and when it was done, I would stand on its bottom and take another core; generally, the situation did not warrant it: there were plenty of ready-made fissures, crevasses, sink holes. Every now and then I would toss a piece of anything handy into the chopper in my middle, where the fusion kiln would burn it to power; every now and then I would stand still and feed the fire and feel the weight of 1,500 fathoms of Atlantic pressing lightly about me; and I would splay brightness, running through the visible spectrum and past, bounce sounds, receive echoes.

Momentarily, I lost my footing. I adjusted and recovered it. Then something struggled within me, and for the thinnest slice of an instant I seemed to split, to be of two minds. I reached out with sensory powers I had never before exercised—a matter of reflex rather than intent—and simultaneous with the arrival of its effects, I pinpointed the disturbance.

As I was swept from the canyon's bed and slammed against the wall of stone that had towered to my left, was shaken and tossed end over end, was carried down and along by the irresistible pressure of muddy water, I located the epicenter of the earthquake as 53 miles to the south-southeast. Addenda to the impression of a submarine canyon: one heavy dust storm; extinguish the lantern.

I could scarcely believe my good fortune. It was fascinating. I was being swept along at well over fifty miles an hour, buried in mud, uncovered, bounced, tossed, spun, reburied, pressed, turned, torn free and borne along once again, on down into the abyssal depths. I recorded everything.

For a long time, submarine canyons were believed to represent the remains of dry-land canyons, formed back in the ice ages, covered over when the seas rose again. But they simply cut too far. Impossible quantities of water would have to have been bound as ice to account for the depths to which they extend. It was

Heezen and Ewing of Lamont who really made the first strong case for turbidity currents as the causative agent, though others such as Daly had suggested it before them; and I believe it was Heezen who once said that no one would ever see a turbidity current and survive. Of course, he had had in mind the state of the art at that time, several decades back. Still, I felt extremely fortunate that I had been in a position to take full advantage of the shock in this fashion, to register the forces with which the canyon walls were being hammered and abraded, the density and the velocity of the particles, the temperature shifts . . . I clucked with excitement.

Then, somewhere, plunging, that split again, a troubled dual-consciousness, as though everything were slightly out of focus, to each thought itself and a running shadow. This slippage increased, the off-thoughts merged into something entire, something which moved apart from me, dimmed, was gone. With its passing, I too, felt somehow more entire, a sufficiency within an aloneness which granted me a measure of control I had never realized I possessed. I extended my awareness along wavelengths I had not essayed before, exploring far, farther yet . . .

Carefully, I strove for stability, realizing that even I could be destroyed if I did not achieve it. How clumsy I had been! It should not be that difficult to ride the current all the way down to the abyssal plains. I continued to test my awareness as I went, clucking over each new discovery.

"Ease up, Dan! It's running the show now. Let it!"

"I guess you're right, Tom."

He leaned back, removing the stereovisual helmet, detaching himself from the telefactor harness. Out of the gauntlets, where microminiaturized air-jet transducers had conveyed the tactile information; strap after sensitive strap undone, force and motion feedback disconnected. Tom moved to assist him.

When they had finished, the teleoperator exoskel hung like a gutted crustacean within the U-shaped recess of the console. Dan dragged the back of his hand over his forehead, ran his fingers through his hair. Tom steered him across the cabin toward a chair facing the viewscreen.

"You're sweating like a pig. Sit down. Can I get you something?"

"Any coffee left?"

"Yeah. Just a minute."

Tom filled a mug and passed it to him. He seated himself in a nearby chair. Both men regarded the screen. It showed the same turbulence, the mud and rock passage Dan had regarded through the helmet's eyepiece. But now these things were only objects. Away from the remote manipulator system, he was no longer a part of them. He sipped his coffee and studied the flow.

". . . Really lucky," he said, "to run into something like this first time out."

Tom nodded. The boat rocked gently. The console hummed.

"Yes," Tom said, glancing at the indicators, "it's a bonus, all right. Look at that slop flow, will you! If the unit holds up through this, we've scored all the way around."

"I think it will. It seems to have stabilized itself. That brain is actually functioning. I could almost feel those little tunnel junction neuristors working, forming their own interconnections as I operated it. Apparently, I fed it sufficient activity, it took in sufficient data . . . It formed its own paths. It did—learn. When the quake started, it took independent action. It almost doesn't really need me now."

"Except to teach it something new, for whatever we want it to do next."

Dan nodded, slowly.

"Yes . . . Still, you wonder what it's teaching itself, now that it's in control for a time. That was a peculiar feeling—when I realized it had finally come into its equivalent of awareness. When it made its own decision to adjust to that first tiny shock. Now, watching it control its own situation . . . It *knows* what it's doing."

"Look! You can actually see those damn eddies! It's doing around fifty-five miles an hour, and that slop is still going faster. —Yeah, that must really have been something, feeling it take over that way."

"It was quite strange. Just when it happened, I felt as if I were—touching another awareness, I guess that's the best way to put it. It was as if a genuine consciousness had suddenly flickered into being beside my own, down there, and as if it were aware of me, just for a second. Then we went our own ways. I think the neuropsych boys and the cyberneticists were right. I think we've really produced an artificial intelligence."

"That's really frosting on my turbidity cake," Tom said, taking notes. "It was actually a Swiss guy, back in the nineteenth century, who first guessed at turbidity currents, to explain how mud from the Rhone got way out in Lake Geneva— Did you see that! Tore a hunk right off the side! Yeah, that's a great little gimmick you've got. If it makes it down to the plains, I want some cores right away. We've got plenty of recent samples, so it ought to be able to give us the depth of sediment deposit from this slide. Then maybe you could send it back up to where it was, for some comparison cores with the ones it was just taking. I—"

"I wonder what it thinks about itself—and us?"

"How could it know about us? It only knows what you taught it, and whatever it's learning now."

"It felt me there, right at the end. I'm sure of it."

Tom chuckled.

"Call that part of its religious upbringing, then. If it ever gets balky, you can thunder and lightning at it. —Must be doing close to sixty now!"

Dan finished his coffee.

"I just had a bizarre thought," he said, moments later. "What if something were doing the same thing to us—controlling us, watching the world through our senses—without our being aware of it?"

Tom shrugged.

"Why should they?"

"Why are we doing it with the unit? Maybe they'd be interested in turbidity currents on this sort of a planet—or of our experiments with devices of this sort. That's the point. It could be anything. How could we tell?"

"Let me get you another cup of coffee, Dan."

"All right, all right! Forgive the metaphysics. I was just so close to that feeling with the unit ... I started picturing myself on the teleslave end of things. The feeling's gone now, anyhow."

"Voic, what is it?"

Voic released the querocube and lufted toward Doman.

"That one I was just fiding—it came closer than any of them ever did before to recognizing my presence!"

"Doubtless because of the analogous experience with its own fide. Interesting, though. Let it alone for awhile."

"Yes. A most peculiar cause-field, though. It gives me pause to wonder, could something be fiding us?"

Doman perigrated.

"Why would anything want to fide us?"

"I do not know. How could I?"

"Let me get you a B-charge."

"All right."

Voic took up the querocube once again.

"What are you doing?"

"Just a small adjustment I neglected. There. —Let's have that B-charge."

They settled back and began to feculate.

"What are you doing, Dan?"

"I forgot to turn it loose."

"To what?"

"Give it total autonomy, to let it go. I had to overload the slave-circuits to burn them out."

"You— You— Yes. Of course. Here's your coffee. —Look at that mud slide, will you!"

"That's really something, Tom."

Clucking, I toss another chunk of anything handy into my chopper.

Deathrights Deferred
by Doris Piserchia

Doris Piserchia raised five children before finding time to do any writing. She has published two successful and critically applauded science-fiction novels, Mr. Justice *and* Star Rider. *Her third novel,* A Billion Days of Earth, *will appear shortly.*

A VETERINARIAN AND AN OWNER discussed Spot, newly from surgery.

"I fixed it so the leg will lift automatically."

"How is that going to help his weak kidneys?"

"They have to be kept open and clean. Every time his leg goes up, he'll feel the urge."

"Why?"

"He just will. I've been a vet for forty years and I know what I'm talking about. The little motor I put in his thigh will pop that leg up and he'll sprinkle like a pup. That'll be fifty dollars."

Eastcoast suburb—two women chatted over the back fence; the conversation eventually led to their dead husbands.

"By the way, the children said they saw Billy the other day."

"Where?"

"Down by the barn."

"They told me they shut off all those motors inside him. If he's walking around, I'm going to sue somebody."

Atomic motors required a long passage of time to wear out and it seemed that the least little disruption inside the corpse could set the machines in motion— an earth tremor, too much worm activity, gas, etcetera. It was an unpleasant experience to visit the family plot and hear noises coming from beneath grave markers, stones or monuments, or from within tombs or from inside caskets that lay in tombs. Steps had to be taken to alleviate the situation.

At first, the dead were cremated. Religious groups objected. Then the dead were pulverized. Everyone objected to that. Transparent tombs were built above-ground, and relatives were supposed to report undue activity to the authorities. This step didn't work because people didn't want to see the dearly departed turn to dust. Then the dead were laid to rest on top of the ground in caskets made with special lids. Any substantial pressure on the undersides of the lids made them open.

The dead started walking around. Since they had been buried nude, they were easily identifiable, and special squads cruised the streets and picked them up.

The company that manufactured the body motors was sued a thousand times over until the government declared it impervious to lawsuits. The motors were a necessary part of life and if the company went bankrupt there would be no more motors. In the meantime, the government ordered the company to do some research and find out how to turn its products off.

✵ ✵ ✵

The most remarkable thing about Huston Adler was that he was neurotic.

"Welcome to the company," said his superior. "Right up into the third floor lab with you and don't come out until you turn off all the dead meat in there."

Huston didn't completely accomplish what he set out to do, which was to turn off the corpses in the third-floor laboratory of the company building. He failed not because he wasn't proficient at electronics but because of his neurosis and because of a natural disaster in the form of a fire that burned down the building. But the fire came later. At the moment, Huston wandered through his third-floor domain and felt important. This was a lot of expensive property for him to oversee.

His living quarters adjoined the worklab and were ample for his comfort. The kitchen was stocked with food, the stereo came complete with a batch of records, there was a color TV, everything he could possibly want was available. The company wished him to be content when he wasn't working on dead bodies.

The worklab—eighty by sixty feet, unusually low ceiling, fluorescent lights, some of which were brightly lit and some dimly lit, walls pale green, lots of tables and benches, a couple of railed racks on which things could be suspended, a big desk with Huston's electronic equipment on it, the experimental bodies that sprawled about in various states of disarray—except for Billy.

A big meat hook between Billy's shoulder blades kept him in a vertical position on one of the railed racks. His thyroid had never functioned properly, which made his blue eyes large and bulging. Once upon a time, when he was alive, Billy developed serious bone abscesses. He lost his arms and legs to amputation and had to live in a basket for a while and then medics implanted a small antigravity unit in his pelvis. Wires ran from the unit to his thigh joints and all he had to do in order to rise in the air was tense his lower stomach muscles. By keeping the tension equal, Billy could float in a vertical position about three and a half feet aboveground. This odd power of mobility kept him sane and relatively happy until his surgical wounds healed completely. Then he received four fine prosthetic limbs that enabled him to walk and reach, pick up and grip almost normally. The antigravity unit was left in place because his body tissue had grown around it. Now the unit was out of kilter, so Billy was impaled on the meathook, to keep him down to earth. His artificial arms occasionally raised, his legs sometimes swung or made walking motions. When the corpsecatchers originally picked him up, down by the barn, they found him with a terrible bloody wound in his back. He was interesting to the company because of his many motors, so he wasn't returned to his relatives. His circulation was stopped by severing the heart arteries. Little motors were implanted to keep the heart and lungs pumping. The operating technician didn't have a good reason for doing this other than that he needed the practice. Elements were introduced into Billy's veins and arteries to enhance the non-decomposing process. He would rot, but not before some technician worked on him for a while. In this case, Huston Adler.

Buck was burned to death. He used to be a fireman. When he was alive, varicose veins had made his legs weak. A little motor helped him walk. After he died, he wandered about, whenever the motor in his spine became confused by the signals coming from his heart prodder. In his blood was a special enzyme that thickened the fluid in his superficial veins and capillaries. His wounds didn't bleed. They simply oozed.

Miss Sonia was born an imbecile. Her lover shot her through the liver. She looked like a doll. Many of her organs had been defective and so in addition to the brain and spinal motors, there were others in various places. She even had one that stimulated her genitals. It hadn't been an entirely good idea, overstimulated her so that she spent much of her life in amorous pastimes. She made an attractive corpse, small and fragile-looking, tiny facial features, large brown eyes, a dimpled chin that trembled when the motor in her brain created miniscule vibrations.

Tamara had been a compulsive tourist. She drowned in the Grand Canal when her gondola tipped over. Before she took up traveling, she played football. A severe injury destroyed part of her brain. Later, cancer canceled out her throat. She had been a great talker because of the machine in her neck. The cancer had left nothing at all and so an amplifier would have done no good. Her brain impulses had activated the recorder and since she traveled to foreign countries the recordings were multilingual. Now, her inner motors disturbed, Tamara still talked and she sometimes said things in French or German or Swahili when English would have been appropriate. Most of the things she said were defensive. She had always regretted her appearance.

Spot—little dappled canine; his eyes stayed alive after the rest of him died; so big, those eyes, so glistening, and then there were the alert ears that were too large. Each time his leg lifted, he barked. There was a little motor in his throat that connected with the one in his thigh. His owner had been concerned about the weak kidneys; wanted to keep a close watch on what happened. Toward the end, Spot had needed a motor to help him walk.

Huston Adler—alive, neurotic, young, a hard worker; he soon began to sleep badly, suffered from indigestion, had facial tics, wet palms, heart palpitations, red eyes, listened too much for sounds that never occurred. His was such a complete laboratory that there was even a closet full of clothing. Naked Miss Sonia embarrassed him so he made her dress in a red dinner gown. Tamara also caused him to grow hot under the collar and he urged her to choose jeans and sweatshirt. As for Buck, he got tie and tails and Billy decked himself out in a business suit. But that was after Huston succeeded in turning his clients on.

Huston's experience with atomic motors had been confined to plain machines that had been implanted in living persons. He had found a chair that first day, had sat in it and looked, really looked, at the five people he was going to work with. (He already classified Spot as a person.) He hadn't seen many dead people. There had been a few tranquil corpses, in coffins, not up and sitting or standing with their eyes open.

He was supposed to turn off everything in the five. The world wanted the dead to be dead—stiff and silent, with no phony symptoms of life remaining. Well, what would he do first? Turn them all on, of course, otherwise he wouldn't know where to start the job.

The most important of his machines was the integrator. It told him what kind of motors were contained in the bodies. A touch of a wire on Spot's chest and a number of lights on the reading board lit up. He touched the other four with the wire and watched the lights flicker. Green, blue, red, yellow, Huston knew what they meant.

What was death? No heartbeat? Every human being had a heart prodder placed in his chest at birth. Odd that Spot had one of these. His owner must have had money to play with. So the five in Huston's lab had pulses.

What about brain waves? Huston had no EEKG machine, but if he had, at least half his clients would have showed a reading. Two and a half people: Miss Sonia, Tamara and Spot.

Poor Buck and poor Billy; Buck far poorer because his looks were ruined. This was one of Huston's thoughts, and he owned up to the fact that it was weird. He was to have more.

Respiration? The lungs of the five functioned. As

they had been in life, so they were active in death. Circulation? At death, a body received an intravenous injection that inhibited decomposition. Everything flowed because of the operative heart.

Huston set to work turning on his clients.

Buck paced back and forth, slowly, almost haltingly. His expression was startled, as if he were seeing the flames for the first time and hadn't yet arrived at a state of fear. He had been a conscientious fireman. Now he bumped into the laboratory wall, turned and went the other way, bumped into another wall, turned . . .

Billy hung on the meathook and yelled without making a sound. His face was frightened. The hook was heavy and short and prevented him from rising more than a few inches. Each time he went up, he hit his head on the rail with a gentle thud.

Miss Sonia was staring at Buck who was plowing his way between a row of benches near her. "You're like all the rest," she said. "You're not really interested in me as a person."

"Please, which way to the restroom? Damen? Herren? Toilet? Oui. Ach, so." Tamara said it, scowled at nothing, turned her head and glared down at Spot who raised his leg as if to urinate on her shin. He barked as he did it.

Miss Sonia got in Buck's way and he walked into her and knocked her down. "It isn't my fault," she said, picking herself up. "You don't know what it's like not being able to control it. It stands to reason that some men would be just plain unattractive. I mean, they can't all be desirable. It isn't my fault at all. I can't be arrested or anything. I'm a ward of the government. Innocent. Besides, it isn't serious. Men are certainly able to take care of themselves where I'm concerned."

"Will you stop following me around?" Tamara said to Spot. "Just tell me where the bus depot is. That's all I want from you. If you don't leave me alone, I'll call a bobby."

Billy bumped the rail once too often. The meathook had been driving inward through his ribs with each movement, but now it slipped the other way, back and up, and after removing a few inches of his back, it left him altogether and he dropped on his feet. He began to waltz, airily and gracefully. At the same time his hands probed space until they found Buck, gripped, sought to take the fireman in his arms for one last dance. Buck repeated the last conscious movement of his life, took the burning beam in his two hands, lifted it from his shoulder where it had fallen and heaved it away. Billy stumbled backward but instead of falling he raised into the air and sailed toward the ceiling. He bumped it hard and descended to the floor. Again he danced and this time his probing hands found Miss Sonia.

"Oh, God, no," she said. Her arms slipped around his neck and she kissed him. Together they waltzed and kissed.

Tamara: "Mother, I don't care whether you like it or not, I don't care if the world hates the idea of a female football player. What the hell am I supposed to do, sit around and wait for some boy to ask me to the prom? You know damned well nobody's going to do that. It's your fault. Why did you make me look like dad? He's ugly and so am I. Notice how my legs bow the same way his do? Hell, I'm even hairy like him. I'm not crying. I haven't since I was twelve. I'm simply going to find something interesting to do with my life."

Huston slept badly, forgot to dream, worked too hard, absorbed himself in unreality.

Spot barked, urinated on Buck's leg, Buck paced back and forth, Billy waltzed with Miss Sonia, Tamara stopped a pedestrian and asked him the way to the egress, Spot raised his leg and sprayed a fireplug, Buck walked through the burning building and listened while the flesh of his left thigh made sounds like bacon in a frying pan, Billy tried out his artificial legs for the first time by doing a slow waltz around the living room with his wife in his arms, Miss Sonia gave herself over to sensation because that was all there was in her life, just as it was all there was in anyone's life when they happened to be a dimwit who couldn't think their way out of a cloakroom without a machine in their brain to do most of the work. Huston slept badly, forgot to dream, worked too hard and absorbed himself in unreality. He had power over death and power always meant life.

Tamara: "If you really want to know what I think about women's lib, well, it's okay for women who can get a little action. Sure. Why not? It's like eating. You have to, but you prefer to pick and choose. Me? I just want a guy. What's wrong with that? Listen, when I was in my teens and twenties I nearly died. The sex urge is the most important thing in the world then. I mean, it really pushes you. So what did I do? I loned it while my friends took their fellows whenever they pleased. Don't tell me this is an equal world. Youth, looks and money are what count and people who don't have them are at the poverty level."

Miss Sonia: "What do you know about suffering? I was born a pretty dummy. Not only that, my pancreas and pituitary were defective. They put that dingus in my dingus so I could enjoy life. They gave me hell."

Tamara: "Did you ever have a guy flinch when you touched him? Don't tell me your troubles, tramp."

The machines were God, for a little while. No, the manipulator was God. So many motors to be sparked and guided, so much power over life, a wire here, a button there—walk, little puppet, talk like a man, show me what I think you would have said, behave for me, dance, prance. I'm doing it. No, they're doing it. So tired, eyes sore, mouth dry, can't think straight, if only I could sleep.

Buck laid a red and black and blistered hand on Tamara's shoulder.

"What are you doing?"

He touched a finger to her cheek.

"Please, don't," she said softly.

He kept stroking her.

"You're supposed to go away now," she said. "It happens that way every time. Look at me. Do you know what you're doing?"

He stood very close to her.

"But I'm ugly. I'm so damned ugly. I'm built like a meatball, my hair is stringy and I've never been able to make it look right. I'll bet I've used every kind of shampoo there is. Why are you looking at me that way? Are you blind? See my face? Tell me about my mustache. At fourteen I grew a mustache, at sixteen my shoulders were broader than my dad's. I look like him, except I'm uglier."

Buck leaned down, kissed the pouting lips.

"You make me sick," she said, as he straightened up. "I don't want your pity. That's all this is. I once knew a boy like you. He wanted my bicycle so he pretended to care for me. Then one day I kissed him. Do you know what he did? He hit me. And he screamed at me. And he ran away. I parked the bike in front of his house and I left a note on it that said, 'I love you.'"

"Look, just fifty cents," said Miss Sonia to Billy. "You can spare that much."

Billy shook his head.

"What are you, some kind of frigid man? Maybe you don't like girls? Maybe you're dead broke? Then I'll give you fifty cents, okay? Come on over here to the couch. I'll turn the lights down low and put on some music."

Huston found a fifth of bourbon in a desk drawer.

A third of it was gone before he fell asleep in his chair. He needed the rest. He woke up with a stiff neck.

"Stop it," he said to Billy and Miss Sonia. "Stop it," he said to Tamara and Buck.

They kept it up, kept it up, and soon he began to scream at them. He hadn't meant to go this far. But he wasn't really doing it to them. They were doing it to him.

All the bourbon was gone, He would have to find another bottle somewhere. He might even go outside to a store. He hadn't been out once, not once.

"No more of that sex junk," he said. They sat around him, quietly, attentively, demurely, innocently, intelligently.

"Tamara, why did you do what you did?"

"Buck asked me. Nobody ever asked me. Don't you understand?"

"Yes, but it mustn't happen again."

"We'll see."

"Miss Sonia, you're not to do anything like that with Billy again."

"Sure. I didn't enjoy it anyway. Billy's an old man. Which gives me an idea. You're a nice looking young—"

"Don't ever, ever, ever say—"

"I'll give you fifty cents."

He stumbled away to hunt for another bottle.

The next day, he had them again sit around him in a circle. "I'm going to kill you," he said. "That's why we're in this laboratory. My job is to turn you off and once I do that you'll be dead and your miserable problems will die with you."

He smiled at Buck. "You look like a big slab of scorched hamburger. How can you sit there as if you deserved a place in the world? For God's sake, hide your hideousness. Looking at you makes me want to vomit."

141

Buck staggered away to a closet, concealed himself in it.

"And you, Billy Ford," said Huston. "A human name for Frankenstein. All you are is head, thorax and can. They should have let you die. You're an abomination. When I think of how you had the gall to pretend to be a normal man. No arms, no legs, just a can with a lid. You lived with your wife, ate with her, slept with her, slept with her!"

Billy floated away and quietly beat his head against a wall.

"Don't hide your face, Tamara," said Huston. "Ugly little Tamara. Or I should say, ugly big Tamara. Do you know that a man wants his women to look like women? We don't want muscles and mustaches, can't abide the damned things." As Tamara hid her face and sobbed, Huston turned to the next member of the group.

"And last and definitely least, here sits Miss Sonia, the walking dingus—"

"Which you can enjoy for fifty cents right this minute."

He leaped to his feet, face livid, body rigid. Foam from his mouth sprayed the air. "Don't speak to me like that! Bitch! I'll kill you!"

He forgot about dividing lines, reality, sanity.

"Play your damned cards and stop watching the girls," he said to Buck. They played poker in the living room of his quarters.

"Stop flirting!" he roared at Miss Sonia. She kibitzed nearby.

"Go neck with Billy," he said to Tamara. "And get your feet off my stereo." To Miss Sonia, he said, "Go wash your face in the bathroom." He said to Buck, "I don't want to catch you smoking my cigars." Or, "Tamara, why don't you give up being a tourist and settle down with one of these fellows? Either one of them will have you. Spot, quit wetting on the furniture."

They made a mess of his apartment so he herded them back into the lab. "You're not fit to live in a decent place," he said to them.

With a yawn, Billy grabbed Miss Sonia by the arm. "What say we relax on the couch, kiddo?"

"Get your lousy hands off my property," said Huston.

Too much of the company building was made of plastic. A shortcircuit in a dehumidifier on the fifth floor caused some sparks and a plastic cup dispenser caught fire. A wall thermometer caught fire. Curtains took the flames and tossed them to plastic light fixtures. The fire became a conflagration that rapidly spread.

Huston smelled smoke. He couldn't get the lab door open. It had been locked from the inside to prevent Miss Sonia from going outside to solicit. He couldn't find the key.

The last thing he remembered was holding onto the back of a straight chair to keep from falling. The room became dim with smoke. His chest hurt. He coughed, fell across the back of the chair, remained draped in that position.

A long while later, an ax smashed against the door and splintered it. A few more blows made an opening big enough for five men in heavy suits to follow one another inside. They were in a hurry.

Unnoticed through the smoke, Buck walked out of the room and down the hall to pause beside a burning door. His motors momentarily faltered and he sat on the floor, laid his elbows on his knees and held his head in his hands.

The firemen exchanged ideas through the walkie-talkies built into their helmets.

"This guy looks pretty far gone," said one. He lifted

Billy onto his shoulder. "I'm taking him out to the ambulance."

"I can't help myself!" cried Miss Sonia. She stood in the middle of the room, dazed-looking and disheveled.

A fireman took her by the arms. "I'm taking this one," he yelled to the others, and hauling Miss Sonia across his shoulder, he took her away.

Tamara sat in a chair and said, over and over again, "Please, please, please—" She kept saying it as a fireman picked her up and hurried toward the broken door. Behind them walked a little barking dog. Spot followed them onto a ramp outside a window, descended to the ground with them, wandered across a yard to a driveway, paused beside a lamppost and raised his leg. A boy who had come to watch the fire heard the barking, scooped Spot up and took him home.

Inside the lab, the last two firemen came across Huston.

"The ceiling is getting hot! Let's get out of here."

"What about this guy?"

Huston looked so odd, lying across the back of the chair, so unnatural, and they knew there were experimental corpses in the building. Still . . .

"Let's take a minute to check him out."

They lifted him and placed him on his back on the floor. They could tell right away when a man was dead, but how did they do it the other way—tell if somebody was alive?

"His heart is beating."

"Don't be stupid!"

"Oh, yeah, everyone's heart beats."

"Is he breathing?"

"Yeah."

"Well, never mind that, either. All lungs work automatically."

"Right."

"Let's get out of here. He's one of those corpses."

"How can we be sure."

"Because he looks like one! Wait a minute, there's somebody."

They had discovered Buck, gently sizzling in the oven of the doorframe.

"Let's get him out of here! Leave the other one, he's done for."

And so Huston was—permanently. By morning salvagers sifting through the hot coals of the lab could not distinguish his ashes from those of the walls or carpets; but Buck and Sonia, Tamara and Billy and even Spot, they kept on.

Error Hurled
by Babette Rosmond

Babette Rosmond, under another name, is one of the most famous and successful of magazine editors. Under still another name she is the wife of a well-known attorney. As Rosamond Campion she is best known for her nonfiction book, The Invisible Worm, *a sensitively written and explosively iconoclastic account of her own ordeal by surgery.*

NOTE: The sections of this book about Jane Baillie Welsh Carlyle are based on her own journals and are historically accurate; however, the presumptuous surmise made here about the sex life of Thomas and Jane Carlyle was first suggested and then published by Frank Harris. It is likely—at least in this particular instance—that he was telling the truth.

The unexplained, seemingly extraterrestrial events noted here did occur. They were documented first by Charles Fort, an American science-sceptic (1874–1932) who had a large following: among the members of the Fortean Society were Theodore Dreiser, Ben Hecht, Alexander Woollcott, Clarence Darrow, Oliver Wendell Holmes, Havelock Ellis and Lincoln Steffens. Their basic philosophy was that we know very little about the universe and it is reasonable to suspect that we are wrong about the little we do know.

"Let me have one more chance," urged Dix. "I will concentrate. I will try very hard."

"All right," said the Teacher. "One more chance."

For a while things improved. Then, although the Teacher did not mention it, the project once more began to show lack of care and attention. The creatures fought and starved and the rivers and seas grew foul and the small spark that Dix, hardly a firstrate intelligence, had been able to instill in some of the creatures began to flicker out.

Dix grew so innattentive that his small brother worried. Little Brother was not yet ready for school, but he had watched Dix caring for his pets, watering them, heating them, cooling them; he had also watched with interest the way Dix made new creatures from less new ones. His spirit was kind as he determined to help his brother, for it would be a disgrace if Dix failed in his project. Dix was clearly at the mercy of his own tiny attention-span. Too many times he became bored, as all children do, with his pets. Little Brother decided to help. He knew the way to put the creatures together, and there were many pretty designs and textures in Dix's equipment box. Little Brother began to build two glorious persons who would impress Dix's Teacher with their beauty and intelligence and spirit and of course their "love," the word that was so often picked up on Dix's receiver. Little Brother was in stage Pi, but he was small for his age and not as gifted as many of the other children.

PART I

It was easier not to think much at all. People were usually kind, but John guessed that this was so because he was so pretty and so clever and so rich. Sometimes he heard the same people who were so nice to him being very rude to each other as well as to uglier, poorer people. He was about thirty years old.

He was six feet four inches tall, with golden hair and blue eyes and long eyelashes; his body was strong and lean and of a shade somewhat bronzer than his hair.

He did not remember his parents, only that they were dead and that he had a great deal of money and was now the president of a large American chain of retail stores. He was an unusually beautiful creature and a highly respected one, but he had necessarily the intellectual capacities of a child of six, which would have been the earth-age of his creator. It did not make much difference. It was easy to run a huge industrial complex and to control the destinies of thousands of workers; certainly there had been very little time for mischief or evil to descend upon him, and at the age of six there is a boundless amount of energy available providing one gets the sleep to balance it.

That was one reason why it had become so chic in America to copy the continental custom of after-lunch siestas. He had started it, simply by falling asleep in his huge leather chair after lunch; his directors had picked it up, and then their associates, and some newspaper columnists had got hold of it. Suddenly everyone who followed trends was napping after lunch. In the same way, his straightforward opinions of art, books, plays, music and particularly matters of business were widely quoted. "No" and "Yes" took on many shades of meaning. One metropolitan magazine ran a black-bordered box each month containing his current opinions of what was going on in the city, and people read them, exclaimed over them and copied them. "If we didn't know that John Sun had a perpetual tongue in that damask cheek, he would seem somewhat like the truth-spouting child in 'The Emperor's New Clothes,'" wrote an interviewer in *The New York Times*, after John had said, "That is rubbish," about a new book by a popular novelist. (He really thought most novelists, playwrights, TV writers and critics were the same person; he didn't care for the person.)

He lived in a penthouse in a big apartment building. There was a huge garden, tended by two men who at his request put in daisies and buttercups and primroses, and his garden was written up in *Vogue* and *Fortune*. There were also some odd flowers no one had ever seen. These seeds had been in a little box that had been there the first morning he woke up, along with some memories, scattered and inchoate. The closest he came to knowing anything true about himself was when he heard something on a news broadcast about Brigitte Bardot. "*Suis* bébé," he had whispered. That was all.

He was sometimes rather awkward and often completely graceful, as a child is graceful. He would move swiftly and surely through a room and then trip over a wastebasket, catching his foot inside it as he tried to go through a door. Sometimes when he did things like that he wanted to cry. Controlling tears was one of the most difficult things he had to do. So many small sadnesses, so many frustrations. Yet, because of his beauty and charm, and most of all because of his wealth and position, no one was really ever unkind to him.

His office was on the thirty-eighth floor of a glass and steel building. When he got off the elevator there was a long, mirrored wall and a woman sitting at a desk, who said, "Good morning, Mr. Sun," and he always sang back, "Good morning," which the receptionist appreciated very much and told her co-workers that you didn't find many executives who took the time to be *personal* with people.

His office was furnished with chairs and carpets and pictures, but there were no bookshelves or books. This was considered one of his eccentricities. When *Forbes* Magazine wrote him up they said, "It's all there in his head; he won't rely on what somebody else has written." There was a refrigerator in the office, concealed behind a row of statues. It contained milk and butter and soft drinks. He did not drink alcohol and he did not smoke; his directors and officers passed down the word: no one connected with the Sun Stores drank or smoked in public, which is to say, with each other, for each man had the well-based conviction that his long-time associate would be all too ready to report the matter.

He didn't care much for conferences because they went on too long. He tried to shorten them as much as possible, which strengthened the image of a fine-honed, waste-cutting mentality. The conference room was big and bare, with a long table and eleven chairs—there had to be an odd number, he'd been told, because otherwise there could be six on one side and six on the other if they voted. Today they were going to talk about a stock split. It was one of the phrases he learned to accept-and-ignore.

The treasurer was a gray-haired stout man in his forties named Augustus Wanger. He mistrusted everyone, particularly John Sun, because he felt more at home with people who spoke interminably and who were full of malice.

When the meeting was brought to order, Wanger said, "Now I think you all know what the plan is ... we want to split the stock three for one." Wanger was also a director, and he held stock options.

"Three and one make four," said John suddenly, coming out of a daydream of being on a boat on a river with laughing people.

Wanger couldn't help uttering a grudging little "hmph." Goddamn it, the man had a way of being sarcastic, of ridiculing the average stockholder. How did the little guy with ten shares have any idea that a three-for-one split didn't mean three extra shares? Three for one meant, of course, two extra shares for each one held at present; instead of one share the stockholder will have three.

"Good point," he said. "John, you see *through* things."

"Yes," said John, trying to return to the river.

"Why split at all?" asked the merchandise manager. "What's in it for us?"

Wanger pointed a finger at him. Wanger always pointed a finger at anybody he was talking to, until one day when John had pushed Wanger's finger aside. Wanger got the message. John was the boss; Wanger wasn't to treat him like an underling. But it was safe enough to stick out his index finger at the merchandise manager who lived in Garden City and had a fat, shrill wife.

"For the same reason," Wanger said, jabbing the finger hard, "that we did it ten years ago. We have that many more shares held by the public, wider distribution of shares at that price—*and*—" winking at John, who stared for a second and then carefully winked back—"less earnings per share when we talk with union leaders!"

The evening before John had seen a western on television, and a man with a beard had said, "In union there is str—" Str— something. What?

"In union there is strength," John said now, clearly.

Wanger grinned. "You bet. That's their thing. They're damned strong."

"Union," said John.

"Sure," said Wanger. "We have to keep fighting them so much I'm afraid we'll have to close our warehouse in the city. If they struck that we couldn't move a thing to the stores."

"But they're strong," said John, with an image of strong men moving large toys to stores, and chairs and tables and beds and things.

"That's the point," said Wanger.

They all voted to split the stock.

"What about increasing the dividend?" asked another director.

"That sounds good," said John, "but what does that really mean?"

"It means we're increasing the dividend by twenty-five cents," said Wanger.

"That's a lot of money," said John.

The ten men at his right and left nodded and felt refreshed. Most of them, during these meetings, always wanted to be someplace else, but there was no getting away from the fact that Sun always put his finger right on the heart of the matter. Twenty-five cents *was* a lot of money for a dividend increase.

Whenever there was a meeting at which this kind of increase was approved, no one was allowed to leave the room until the secretary of the company telephoned the New York Stock Exchange, so no one could be accused of rushing out to buy new shares under the new plan.

John had once been gravely curious about why no one was allowed to leave the room (suppose they had to go to the bathroom?) and had been told that stocks often tend to increase in price because of such action.

"Why do stocks increase in price?" John had asked. They had all laughed, convinced that this was another example of making each director search his own dreary middleaged soul to determine what he had done to make the stock go up.

"Avoid taking advantage of inside information," John said now, and the others nodded. That was the nub of the matter.

His financial acumen had also been widely appreciated by the various social clubs to which he belonged. When one of the oldest and most respectable in the city had a problem about whether or not they should admit several wealthy South American families, John had said to the club president, "Well, they pay, don't they?" and the president went around quoting that epigram to everyone he talked to, not a long list.

At the office, the secretaries had been amused by John's signature. His personal secretary, Miss Stanch, said, "You can always tell how smart a man is by his signature. Like doctors. You can't read their handwriting."

John's signature was this:

gmm

and was generally admired and imitated by lesser lights of the corporation who wrote too clearly.

John did not know of these opinions. He really could write only simple block letters. When a well-known writer met him once at a party, where John was carrying the well-known glass of milk that had become a trademark, the writer had cornered him. The writer was losing his hair but had had it teased and dressed into a horizontal thicket. His name was Taylor and he was rather fat and ugly and his mind, usually dominated by visions of himself in glory, was occupied with envious admiration of John's youth and beauty.

"What do you think of contemporary writing," asked Taylor. "For example, do you know my stuff?"

John thought a minute, took a sip of milk and nodded. He knew Taylor's writing because he had just seen Taylor write a note on the back of an envelope. Taylor had written it in a hasty, illegible scribble.

"I know about your writing," said John, in his deep, pleasant, serious voice. Taylor snapped to attention. The words "your writing" to him were like "Ten-shun!" to an army private. Taylor put his fat head to one side and tried to look patient.

"The thing is," said John, "it's not good."

Taylor couldn't believe his ears. "Not good," he mumbled.

John smiled his sweet smile. "Because nobody can understand it," he said.

Taylor had had just enough to drink to put him in

a blurry state of almost-contentment, but this got to him. Nobody can understand it. God, that's exactly what the book editor of a New York paper had said the year before, and that's what a professor of English literature had told him during a pot party a few weeks ago ... Taylor, you're overdoing the mythic-obfuscation-shtick. You're writing yourself into a corner. Nobody is going to be able to understand you if you don't watch out ...

Taylor had been accused of being homosexual, bisexual, ambisexual, antesexual, antisexual and post-sexual. At the moment all he knew was that he cared very much about what this gorgeous creature had to say.

"Do *you* understand my writing," he mumbled, looking up at John's golden head.

"No," said John. "I don't. Make it plainer."

When Taylor got home that night he punched his wife and tore up 30 pages of manuscript that had been lying on the typewriter table. It was late, but he turned on all the lights and stuck a new piece of paper into the machine. He began to type: "It was a pleasant day. The sun was shining. The children were ..." And there came over him a newfound sense of peace and fulfillment.

There was another writer who was influenced by John Sun. She was a brisk, tall woman named Alice Bloover who was in charge of Public Relations at the Sun Stores New York office.

Until fairly recently, Alice would have sworn that her job was difficult, that she had to put up with a lot of nonsense, and that she was sick of writing speeches that high-salaried men couldn't pronounce properly. Then her work seemed to become easier. Any information she needed about the stores, the merchandise or the personnel seemed to be close at hand. Part of her job was writing newsy items for the Sun Stores *In-the-Sun Journal;* these began to seem readymade as she approached her typewriter, particularly items about John Sun. No one, if interrogated by Communists or government agencies, could have said exactly when it was that John Sun became chairman of the board and president.

She decided to get a new line on John, apart from his tremendous beauty, charm, brilliance and integrity (none of which sold hard-or-soft goods), and she asked him after the directors' meeting what it was he liked to do best.

"Sing," said John.

"Do you like to sing? Did you ever take voice lessons? Are you tenor? Baritone? Bass? Do you sing at—?"

"Jesus wants me for a sunbeam, to brighten up the day," sang John suddenly in a clear, surprisingly high sweet voice, a choirboy's voice.

"Well, that has a nice lilt to it," said Alice Bloover, frowning. She didn't want to get into any religious stuff.

"I like that song," said John. By three in the afternoon word got around. Several VP's bought pitchpipes and it was decided informally to conduct simple services each morning. Start the day with a double-meaning hymn! Then, in an hour, there would be the usual milk and cookie break.

At noon John lunched with his directors, or his buyers, or sometimes a merchandise man. They always went to the same restaurant, the dining room of a big, unfriendly hotel with call girls tapping their clog-shod feet against the plastic lobby floor. John learned that his colleagues were very fond of bouillon. They would wink at the waitress, and the soup would be brought in the thick cup with handles on each side. At first the men would use their spoons to sip it, and then they would lift the cup by both handles and drink it down. Sometimes they had two or three cups of soup. John was glad to see how talkative it made them, because they stopped looking at him all the time after the soup. He hated to be stared at, but it didn't make him cry.

"Hello, there, Sunbeam," said the elderly waitress with sprayed, teased, ecru cotton-candy for hair. "No soup for you today?"

John liked juice, and had two or three glasses of orange or tomato to keep his friends company.

"You ought to try some soup some time," said the waitress, giggling at Mr. Wanger. Mr Wanger waggled his pointing finger at her. "Now, now," he said. "Soup isn't good for everybody."

John smiled. He had just recalled something else heard on the television. "Problem drinkers are dead?" He put it as a question because he wasn't sure that was exactly the way he'd heard it. It seemed to be a good thing to say because of the way he said it; everybody put down his soup.

"What do you mean, John," asked the merchandise manager, frowning.

"Problem drinkers are a problem," said John.

Later that afternoon the directors and officers got together while John was on siesta-time and decided to lay off the soup for a bit.

It wasn't only Miss Bloover whose job had become easier. Everyone in the company was aware, or, probably, dimly conscious of John having been placed there, but not of the actual means of his arrival. It was taken for granted that he was the son of the founder; no one had any reason to question this. There was an all-over sense of improvement at the store offices. John seemed to have made very successful speeches, so fine that the President of the United States had sent him a citation naming John as America's ideal businessman because of his simplicity. The President indicated that John was very much after his own heart—stating the facts clearly and virtually unblurred.

John's office communications were necessarily dictated (he loved to dictate, and the girls loved to take down his sweet statements) in the way that other everyday routine matters adjusted well to his limited capacities. He knew how to ride in taxicabs but was a little put off by the final exchange of money—like most rich men he carried very little cash and preferred to walk, even for six or seven miles. His financial economies became legendary (here again no one could say precisely when it all began); he loved to turn out lights. Interviewers put this down as a welcome return to traditional American values—the prudence of Benjamin Franklin, the ingenuity of Jefferson, but it was really because John enjoyed moving the switches.

Martin Branch, a vice president of the Sun Corporation, was the only person who was not immediately totally programmed into John's regime. To call Branch a visionary would be like calling Jack the Ripper a surgeon, but he was perhaps more in tune with his own unconscious mind than the others. He knew that lately he had been having dreams, and he knew that the dreams were disturbing. One morning at about three o'clock he turned on his bedside lamp and scribbled some notes. During his REM sleep he had become aware that something quite extraordinary was happening to him and to the entire company. He determined to ask questions the following morning, to find out what happened to a nonexistent person once called J. C. Young who was—yes, he *was*—the president of the company not so long ago.

Mrs. Branch, a grimly pretty woman who still referred to individuals of her sex as "gal," had been bothering Martin for a long time (or what seemed to her re-formed memory a long time) to invite John to the Branches' lovelyhomeinLarchhaven, a word not a phrase. The Branches had three children: nine years old, seven years old and three years old. John seldom went out unless people in the company asked him, and Branch said he would take John to his lovelyhomeinLarchhaven in his automobile, which gave John no reason to refuse.

Martin Branch kept his eyes on John. Handsome sonofabitch, yes, but how . . . why . . . ?

The Branch children (it seemed extremely silly to John that they were called The Twigs by their mother) took to John at once. Most of his conversation was with them.

"Honey, don't make him talk shop today," Mrs. Branch had urged her husband. "Let him see what a wonderful relationship we all have together, and as contributing members of a family unit."

After lunch, which was hot dogs roasted on an outdoor grill, the children surrounded John.

"Are you going to smoke?" asked Sara, the middle child.

"No," said John. "I don't like to smoke."

"How do you know?" asked Janet, the older girl. Have you ever tried?" She glanced around to make sure her parents were safely bickering over the dessert. "We have. We had a lot of cigarettes. They taste like yuch."

"They taste like the sidewalk," said Brett, the little boy. He was violently attracted to John and was now sitting on his lap, stroking his face and rubbing noses.

"The only cigarettes I like are the chocolate ones," said John. "They're quite good. It's hard to get the paper off sometimes."

"I ate the paper once," said Brett.

"You did not," said both his sisters. Sara added, "You're not only a baby, you're a big liar."

"I once smoked a chocolate cigar," said Brett. "That was nice. Did you ever have one of those?"

"No. Real cigars smell," said John.

"They smell like duty," said Brett. Then he and John sat quietly for a while, staring into the fine blue afternoon air.

"Mommy was sick last week," said Janet. "We took

care of her. We made her breakfast. We were good to her."

"Not that I like sick people," said Sara. "They get boring."

"I was never sick," said John, trying to remember if he had only heard the word or whether he had ever had anything to do with it.

"That's a lie," said Sara. "All children get sick. I had mumps and my face was like this." She showed him. John laughed.

"No, look at me," yelled Brett. "Mine was like this!" He puffed out his pink cheeks until John stuck his finger into one of them. They both laughed out loud.

Martin Branch was watching all this from behind the barbeque grill. His first thought was that John seemed extraordinarily fond of children; then he realized that John was very much like his own children. In fact . . .

At this moment, fortunately for the project, Little Brother was paying attention. He disposed of the entire day and removed the infected areas of Martin Branch's mind.

Next morning, at the store, Martin Branch saw John in the corridor and said, "Hi, there, John. Have a good weekend?"

"I think so," said John, frowning a little.

Like most large retail stores, the Sun Company had a perennial problem about shoplifters. Some of them were trained, skillful thieves, some were kids, some were the well-to-do women whose husbands brought lawsuits. John's favorite shoplifter at the New York City Sun Store was Mrs. Messenger. Her compulsion to steal small, unnecessary objects was in conflict with her Dutch Reform Church background. She invariably mailed back the loot, in neatly-wrapped parcels. The difficulty was that she mailed back other stores' merchandise as well (after all, she couldn't remember to a given string of beads just which thing she had lifted from which stores). She seemed to accept as natural law the pleasing concept that whoever received the parcels would remail them to the correct place. John looked forward to receiving Mrs. Messenger's packages. The brown paper wrappings were beautifully printed in clear letters he could read without difficulty.

The store wasn't so lucky with the two Misses Messenger. They were fifteen and seventeen, lithe, quick, efficient as locusts. If there had never been an Abbie Hoffman they would have invented an effigy of somebody like him. Their father had plenty of money and gave them generous allowances, but from the time they were tots they had followed their mother into stores and watched her work. Mr. Messenger, who felt often that the mantle of Job sat on his stooped shoulders, had taken particular care to instruct his daughters in the proper outlook of their mother's "trouble." The girls had listened and dutifully reported after each shopping excursion the stuff Mother had ripped off, but the more physically coordinated they became, the swifter were their movements, the higher their goals. They took full advantage of the fact that department stores looked with indulgence upon their family history, but the store detectives and the entire security system was shaken when the unattractive forms of the two Messenger girls were reflected in the closed-circuit TV.

Once John had been walking aimlessly near scarves-and-handkerchiefs when he had seen the younger Miss Messenger loading up. He put his hand on her shoulder. Without turning around she shook off the hand and went about her business. Sorrowfully, John told her that she was doing something wrong and that she would have to come to his office.

The first thing she saw in his large, light room was a paper bag on his desk. It was magenta-colored and bore his initials in white. He had made the initials himself.

"Hey, that's neat," said Miss Messenger.

John smiled with pleasure.

"Why do you take so many of my things," he asked gently.

Miss Messenger shrugged. "It's something to do," she said.

"But the things don't belong to you," said John. He looked at her, his eyes genuinely puzzled.

Miss Messenger burst into tears. "Oh, for Christ's sake," she said. "That's not fair. Stop *look*ing at me like that."

The girls confined their profession to Macy, Altman, Lord & Taylor, Bonwit, Bloomingdale, and other places after that. Never the Sun stores.

Augustus Wanger had a sleepless night, as he usually did after a meeting with John and the directors. He didn't know exactly what he disliked most about John; there was so much to dislike: John's beauty, charm, forthrightness, honesty. Why couldn't John be more like Augustus Wanger: cruel, shrewd, self-seeking, stout and self-despising?

At three in the morning Augustus began to worry on a grander scale, not so much about the store or his job or the way everybody tried to take advantage of him, but about the planets and the sun. How could planets revolve around the sun? How could we send people into space, to the moon? Who made the whole messy arrangement in the first place? Was there a God? No, because if there were a God, Augustus Wanger would be John Sun and vice versa.

What made a boat stay up? How did the gasoline engine work? What about electricity, the telephone, the effect of alcohol on the bloodstream? Why should he have to lie here worrying about all those things when everybody else was sleeping softly, gathering up energy for the next day to attack Augustus Wanger?

If John were dead, there would be less trouble and conflict in the corporation and in Wanger's mind. Wanger had read a good many mystery stories and was aware of how fruitlessly villains had worked through the centuries to achieve a perfect crime. A crime was perfect only if no crime was suspected. If he could get John to die a perfectly natural death . . .

Old age was out, since John wasn't more than thirty. A heart attack would be unconvincing (the company doctor had gone around telling everybody that he'd never examined a healthier body than John's, every organ functioned like a beautiful machine) and most poisons were detectable. Suppose he and John were crossing the street together, and just as a traffic light changed, John would be given a sure, swift push and his body would fall under the wheels of a speeding car. Augustus Wanger would deliver the funeral eulogy—something about this handsome young whatever being struck down in the flower of whatever whatever. He would wear a sober black suit to the chapel, and tears would flood his eyes as he spoke.

That was too uncertain. You never knew just when traffic was going to be heavy, and it would be suspicious if he pushed John only to have John get up and say, "Why did you push me?" which, God knows, he was perfectly capable of asking.

What about poisons from plants? He'd been reading in a gardening book about America's many toxic plants, some with poison berries, some with poison leaves, some fatal in all parts. Perhaps he could get John to try a new health-drink . . . something Augustus would brew himself out of deadly nightshade, oleander leaves, lily of the valley berries, foxglove, and some angel-of-death mushrooms. How could you make somebody try a health brew . . . ? "John, you've been looking a little peaked lately . . ." Absolutely not. Fellow looked like a risen angel. Maybe distract his attention at the restaurant and carry the stuff in an envelope and slip it into his tomato juice ... but how could you get the brew into powder form? Ask John to do him a favor across the room ... no, have the waiter tell John he was wanted on the telephone. But that would mean taking the waiter into his confidence, and the waiter could spend the rest of his life getting fat on the payola he, Wanger, would have to part with. No, no one else could be in on it.

What about a very sharp stiletto in the gut? Get him in a crowded place, keep the old eyes elsewhere, and let him have it—pssst—right in the belly? The knife would have to be extremely sharp, and he would have to know the exact right spot ... and then what would he do with the weapon? Just drop it (he would be wearing gloves, so there would be no fingerprints)? Try to conceal it or lose it on the floor? No, too much element of doubt there.

What about a simple injection of deadly bacilli? Deadly bacilli, that had a good ring to it. He would get hold of a hypodermic needle—what with all the people under fifty in America on drugs, the Sun stores probably stocked needles. Ha ha. He allowed himself a brief moment of congratulation at being able to amuse himself at a time like this. No, he'd have to be alone with John in a situation where John's arm would be bare. Ask to see his muscle? Show him a new idea for the store, little self-tattoo kits; and he would illustrate on John how to apply the tattoo, every boy would want one, etc., etc. But John would see that the needle wasn't a tattoo needle, and wouldn't sit still for a full injection of bacilli. Don't bacilli, he told himself, digressing for a moment into wondering if he shouldn't become a TV comedian instead of a store director. He certainly had a good sense of humor and could laugh at himself ...

Why was the world so unfair? Life was unfair. If there were a modicum of fairness in the universe,

God would be telling him right now how to bump off John Sun without getting caught. Lie still ... relax ... let it come as an inspiration ... if you just lie still the word will come, the idea will flower ... Augustus Wanger lay perfectly still for a few minutes and fell asleep.

Lydia Stanch was John's secretary. There were two lesser secretaries who worked for her and did all the typing while she thought about John. She was a medium-looking girl, about five feet five, with brown hair and a decent figure and unmemorable features, but that was all changed in her fantasies about herself and her employer; she became Helen of Troy, he stayed as he was. Lydia supplied flowers for his office vases from her parents' home in Westchester. She loved to see the light suffusing his face when he noticed the flowers. It was Lydia who told him about church:

"People think we're Catholic, but it isn't that. It's high Episcopalian, and we go to confession and—"

"Confession?"

"You know. Confession."

John had learned not to go on asking questions when he didn't understand something, which was most of the time, because people went off in even more puzzling directions. "It does everybody good to talk about—well, sins, and like that," said Lydia. "I suppose most Protestants think it's silly, but I know it's very helpful for me to talk about something that went wrong ..."

"Is there a church like that near here where I could go?" asked John.

"Oh, yes." She mentioned one several blocks from the Sun offices. "The priest there would be glad to listen to your confession."

"Thank you, Lydia."

"You're welcome, Mr. Sun. Do you want me to fix your In and Out boxes?"

"Oh, no. I'm going to do that now." John liked playing with the two boxes, just alike, except that one said IN and the other said OUT: easy to read. The boxes could be fitted together neatly, and he kept eight papers in each.

A sign on the main floor of the Sun Building mentioned the Star Security Service. John did not read this, but he had heard one of the words, the second one; it sounded like "skirty."

The skirty man came into John's office that morning and, as usual, said "Have a nice day." John had been told that the building needed a skirty guard for each floor because there were always so many robberies.

The guard used to wait until people replied to haveaniceday; at first John had liked him, but then he noticed that the skirty guard wasn't really paying attention and even if John answered, "Go jump in the lake," with his sweet smile, the man didn't seem to care. It was a good game, and John looked forward to it. Just before lunch, he had a nice conversation with the elevator starter, a much older man who paid attention. He used words and phrases nobody else used, and John would always ask patiently what they meant. "P.D.Q." was one, and John had laughed when the man said it meant pretty damn quick.

"Going out to lunch by yourself?" said the starter. "You're with Number One. Have a good lunch. Make sure you don't take anything that isn't right there on the bill of fare. Then they charge double."

John nodded and thanked him. He walked along a side street thinking about confession, when he felt an arm against his throat. He was being held tight. He looked around, startled, and saw a thin black boy, several inches smaller than John.

"You gimme your money," said the boy, terrified.

"I don't have any money," said John. He'd thought everybody knew that. "And if I did I wouldn't carry it in this street. The skirty man said it was a bad one."

"What do you mean, a bad one?" The boy took his arm away and looked offended. "Nothin' wrong with this street. I used to work on this street. What kind of a thing is that to say?"

"I didn't mean to hurt your feelings," said John. "I'm sorry I don't have any money. The others always pay for my lunch ... after we read the bill of fare," he added softly to himself.

The boy shrugged. "Forget it," he said. "Somebody else'll turn up. 'S okay."

A man in a long beige dress came up to John and gave him a leaflet. John thanked him; just then a policeman came up and told the man in the beige dress to run along or he'd take him in. John was pleased with the uniform and the badge. "Hello," he said. The cop eyed him. "You watch it, too," he said. "I'm going to confess," said John. "Yeah, I guess you pulled all the bank jobs in town," said the cop. "If it isn't one kind of nut it's another. Get lost."

"No, I'll be careful, I know the way," said John.

A girl—no, a woman—wearing a very short skirt and shoes with blocks at the bottom and big hoops in her ears came over to John.

"Going out?" she asked.

"Yes," said John, smiling in pleased surprise. So few people really ever asked him things about himself.

"Well, okay," said the woman. "Come on."

"No, I'm going this way," said John. She was holding his arm. "Where did I meet you," John asked.

The woman laughed. "Oh, here and there," she said.

"Was it at the Branches'? The Wangers' house? Are you a friend of the people who live in Massachusetts?"

"Yeah," said the woman, frowning. "What's the matter with you?"

"Nothing," said John. "I feel fine. But I'm going to church."

"To church," repeated the woman. "What are you, some kind of religious nut?"

"Goodbye," said John. "I hope to see you again." He walked on.

The church had a sign outside. John could read part of it, but not all. He asked a boy playing the violin on the steps what the sign said.

The boy looked around. "It says, 'Watch your purse. Beware of the dog. All welcome. Come in and meditate. Sermon Sunday by Bishop Halstead . . . Don't you read English?"

"I can read some things," said John.

The church was dim and pretty. John told a pleasant gray-haired man what he wanted to do. He was told that his confession would be heard, and he was taken to a quiet, curtained place.

For a few seconds John didn't know where to start, but then he cleared his throat and began.

"Yesterday Gus Wanger pushed me when we were standing near the elevator, he does that a lot, like bumping into me and not really hurting me but I can tell he wants to hurt me. Martin Branch stole two white pencils from my desk. I really like the white pencils best. Last night when I went to see the Ratigans and they were playing cards and I was watching, Mr. Ratigan showed his cards to me and said 'What about that?', so I showed him which was a spade. Harold McBain said something bad about me to Lydia, she started to tell me but then she stopped. I just know it was something bad."

"Is that what you wanted to confess, my son? Is there something you want to tell me that is weighing on your soul?"

John was silent for a moment. Then he said, "Lydia likes me a lot. She brings me flowers and touches my hand. She likes me." He was still for a while, then added, "I didn't cry at all yesterday."

The priest said nothing and John left the still twi-

light of the church for the sun-filled crowded street.
Just as Lydia had promised, he felt a lot better.

On his way back to the office, John passed a
middleaged woman wearing a sandwich board. The
printing on it was hard to read, so he asked someone
what she wanted. He had learned that on most of the
streets in New York, people who walked up and
down wanted something in varying degrees of dedi-
cation.

"Oh, it says like her mother is in this home and
they don't feed the old people right and nobody
wants you when you're old and gray," said the person
he asked, a well-dressed woman with three dogs attached to a leash held with her left hand and four
dogs attached to a leash held by her right hand. She
was trying to use both hands—and therefore both
leashes and seven dogs—to hold down her floppy felt
hat.

John thought about that. When he got back to the
Sun Company he buzzed for Lydia. First he thanked
her for sending him to such a pleasant church, then
he asked her what she knew about old people and the
treatment they received in nursing homes.

"Why would you care about that?" asked Lydia. "I
mean, well, if there's one thing you don't have to
worry about—I mean, well—do you have a relative in
one of them or something?"

"No," said John. "It's just that if they are in trouble
I would like to help them, maybe pay for their food
or something like that. I didn't know that there were
so many old people that other people have to carry
signs about them."

"There sure are," said Lydia. "My grandmother is
in one of those homes. We visit her every couple of
weeks, but half the time she doesn't even know us.
It's like visiting a six-year-old."

John stared. This sounded like a situation he
needed to know more about.

"Could you take me to see your grandmother? Today?"

"Well—why?" asked Lydia.

"Because I want to see," said John.

They took a taxi since John was sure Lydia would take care of all the petty cash transactions. As they were riding he felt an odd sense of urgency. Grown-ups who were like six-year-olds . . . the words meant something to him and he knew it was something important.

The Clara Barton Residence for Dignified Primogenitors was in a decayed street in upper Manhattan. There was a horseshoe driveway bordered with plastic flowers and a lobby containing a smelly marble-veined vinyl floor. Behind a central desk was a short, stout woman with black hair worn at least a foot above her head; she was chewing gum and smoking and talking all at the same time.

"Stanch," she greeted Lydia, with no emotion. It was as though the use of a surname meant to New Yorkers what "Aloha" does to Hawaiians.

Lydia and John entered an elevator that had the same unpleasant smell as the lobby. Neither John nor Lydia could really understand that its core, amid the confusion of disinfectant, urine, sweat and cigar ashes, was senescence.

They got out of the elevator into a corridor where people were milling. John looked around him, puzzled. "Where are the children?" he whispered. Lydia didn't hear him. "Hello, Miss Gorfickel," she called. She turned to John. "I always tip Miss Gorfickel a dollar to take extra good care of Granny," she said.

Miss Gorfickel eyed them with active hostility. (John made a face at her when she wasn't looking.) "Granny's acting up again today," she said in a voice infinitely weary. "She's peeing in the wrong toilets again. She's making trouble."

"Oh, I'm *so* sorry," said Lydia. She handed two dollar bills to Miss Gorfickel. "I'm so sorry. We'll go in and talk to her now."

They turned down a long corridor, peopled with strange, bent forms and steel walkers and wheelchairs.

"No use in that," called Miss Gorfickel, interrupting a conversation about the state lottery that was causing a lot of merriment at the desk. "She's not in her own room. She's in Fun 'n' Rec."

Lydia sighed and turned John around. They went to a large, sunny room with a TV set in one corner. It showed a blurry, oddly-colored picture and tremendous sound volume, for the set was tuned to a channel not received in this city. Most of the old people were sitting in immeasurably dense invisible cases, built out of disassociation and individual mysteries. Some stared ahead of them, others beat aimlessly on chair arms, some banged on a long table.

"Here comes that old woman's uncle," shouted a very old man. He was looking at John.

"Hello, Granny," said Lydia.

Mrs. Stanch was small and odd, like a sea creature outside its own shell. She was in a wheelchair.

"Do you know me?" shouted Lydia.

Granny nodded impatiently. John, too, considered that a strange question.

A woman sitting near Mrs. Stanch hobbled over. "Get rid of her," she yelled, pointing to Mrs. Stanch and putting her face next to Lydia's. "She does everything stupid. She can't even button her dress."

A man with a natty striped blazer and faded cotton pajama pants came to whisper to John. "How about a game of croquet?" he asked, with serious good-fellowship.

"How are you, Granny?" asked Lydia. "Everything all right?"

"What time have you got?" asked Granny, looking at her bony, bare arm. "I lost my watch."

"She's not wearing the bracelet," said Lydia in a
171

low tone to John. "That's because she's a private patient. My parents have to pay for her, and it's an awful lot of money. Most of them here are on Medicaid, because they swear they don't have any money. But my parents both have jobs and so do I, so we have to pay for Granny."

"I'm supposed to be privileged," said Granny suddenly. "I ought to get better food and better care, but I don't. What time is it?"

John felt like crying. He turned his back and faced a fat old lady who was singing a Gospel hymn. She peered at him. "The Lord gave me back my sight this morning," she told him. "I was blind, blind, blind and then He gave me back my sight."

"I was at church this morning," John began, but nobody was listening.

A man was putting money into a pay telephone. He held the receiver and talked, but the receiver was simply clicking and buzzing.

"I want my lunch," said Mrs. Stanch.

A nurse, fat and young, came by. "You know, you know, you *had* your lunch," she called. She went over to join some other nurses at a round table in the corner where a poker game was in session.

"I have to go to the toilet, I have to go to the toilet," whimpered a woman in a chair with a tray in front. She beat on the tray. "Please. I have to go so badly."

John touched one of the nurses. "That lady has to go to the toilet," he said.

"Dealer's choice," said the nurse, and then turned around, laughing. "She don't have to go to the toilet. She just wants some attention."

"I have to make attention," said the woman in the chair. "Please. Somebody. Help me."

John swallowed. He had never seen anything like this. A nice-looking woman who might have been a telephone operator at the Sun Company smiled at him.

"You look troubled," she said, in a low, sweet voice. "Don't feel troubled. There's nothing you can do. They're all so sad."

John brightened. "Are you living here?" he asked.

The woman nodded. "Yes, in a way. Temporarily, that is, until my daughter and her husband return from abroad."

"Oh?" asked John, not sure what this meant, but glad that there was somebody in this dreadful, shrill room who didn't seem either crazy or vicious.

"Yes. They've gone to the court at St. Petersburg to get the papers. There is really nothing to be done until the papers are sent to Washington."

"What papers?" asked John. He saw Lydia shouting in her grandmother's ear; Mrs. Stanch was shrugging and fiddling with the buttons on her dress.

"The *papers*," said the nice lady, with quiet amusement. "The papers that show who I am and when the proper time will be to return to the court."

"Court," repeated John.

She patted his hand. "Of course, you're too young to know about it, but I'm sure that someone older could tell you all about it. I am the Princess Anastasia. My parents were the Czar and Czarina of Russia. It's been written up extensively."

John was glad to hear there was someone who knew what she was doing. A woman with wild, blue-streaked hair called from the end of the long table, "Come here, you." John walked over to her.

"Can I help you?" he said.

The woman's eyes filled with tears. She wiped them with both hands. "Help me get out," she whispered. "My mother is waiting for me at home. She used to depend on me to help with dinner. Yesterday she came and brought me my doll, but it was the wrong doll. But I must get home in time for dinner."

John nodded. This seemed entirely clear. He went over to the table where the nurses were playing cards. "Is it all right," he asked one of them, who was gathering in a pile of colored discs, "if I take Mrs. This-Lady for a walk?" The nurse, counting her chips, nodded carelessly.

John started to help his friend out of the room. Immediately three more people joined them. "I want to go for a little walk to the corner," said an old man. "I have a friend there who'll tell me how the printing plant operates."

"My son is waiting for me in the car," said an old lady.

Lydia had taken her grandmother off to the bathroom. John took four patients with him to the bank of elevators. As they waited for the car going down the patients quarreled and made hostile passes at each other. Then they hustled somehow into the elevator.

At the main floor the short woman with the tall hair was talking on the reception-desk phone. She glanced up at John and went on with her conversation.

For a moment, at the front door, John hesitated.

"How would *you* like to be locked up, way up there?" snapped an old lady, successfully reading his mind.

"I wouldn't," said John, and let them all out into the street.

Several hours later, after Lydia and John had returned to the Sun Company, the tired, middleaged woman who was in charge of the twentieth-floor desk returned from a trip to a funeral home. She made many such trips during her work week. She looked around the room. "Where are—?" she asked, naming names.

Nobody knew at the moment. Eventually the tired woman called the police. She was the only one at the Clara Barton Residence for Dignified Primogenitors who cared anything at all about the patients, but naturally she was discharged for incompetence after the runaways were corraled and shipped back in one prowl car.

"That's a terrible place," said John to Lydia, as they were leaving for the day. "Does your granny really have to stay there?"

"Well, sure," said Lydia. "Where else? All those places are the same. It's okay for the ones on Medicaid, but it's hard on people like us. My parents had put away some money for a trip to Europe, but forget it. The doctor there says Granny's strong as an ox. She's good for another six, seven years. So? What do we do?"

"Would I ever be ... there?" John spoke very low. He didn't really want Lydia to hear him.

She wasn't listening. "Oh, well," she said. "Everybody's got something, right? Except you, Mr. Sun. You're the exception that proves the rule."

John looked a little happier. That probably meant he didn't ever have to live in a place like that where no one tuned in the TV right or could remember if he had been given lunch.

And yet he was saddened all that evening, watching a western at home, because there was something he felt he understood about those people. He could tell what most of them had been thinking, which was certainly odd. They were all so very old, and he was so very young.

Mrs. Wanger's parties were never given for pleasure. They were based largely on Mr. Wanger's idea of getting people drunk enough so he could have something to blackmail them about at the shop, and on Mrs. Wanger's dying daydreams of being a famous hostess, like those people in Washington who wrote their autobiographies and knew newspaper columnists. The Wangers knew very few people connected with the world of communications, much less the arts, but it was easy for Mrs. Wanger to get them to attend her parties. She subscribed to a service that supplied her with unlisted telephone numbers.

"Hello, Mrs. Onassis," she would say, "this is Helena Wanger. I've heard so much about you from Truman Capote. He's dying to see you, and we'll be together at a tiny dinner party here on the fourteenth. He'll never speak to me again if you don't come."

Then, of course: "Hello, Mr. Capote ..." and the same speech, with the blanks filled in slightly differently, would be delivered. The method worked so often that it surprised Mrs. Wanger. Had she been her fifteen-years-before-self, she would have said, "Oh, people are the same everywhere. There are lots of nice folks in the world." Now she simply approached her profession as a roulette player (or a condemned butterfly) approaches the wheel.

The Wangers lived on Long Island in a house that had been designed by two architects who didn't speak to each other. One of them had given up the job when she said she wanted a mud room. "What the hell is a mud room?" he asked viciously. She tried to tell him, but he interrupted. "Go roll in the mud, you silly old sow." He was still writing abusive letters about the money owed him. The other architect had said yes to everything Mrs. Wanger had suggested and then went ahead with a Victorian overlay on Scandinavian Modern. The house had been photographed everywhere and Mrs. Wanger had achieved some fame as a woman who knew what she wanted and went ahead and got it in spite of Philistine opposition.

On the evening after the stockholders' meeting at the Sun Company, Mrs. Wanger gave a big one. There were about a hundred people, from as far away as Bombay, India or Sioux City. She had read somewhere that a careful hostess never has a casual buffet, always a sit-down dinner, so a special table was moved into the interior of the house (in which the first architect had removed all walls) that seated more than a hundred people. John Sun was of course at Mrs. Wanger's right.

Before they sat down to dinner, at nine-thirty, he had taken a little nap in one of the bedrooms, or at least a room that had a wooden slab and a throw cushion in it; he'd been so tired, after arriving at half-past seven and having to listen to so many people talking so loud, while he held his glass of tomato juice. Once he spilled part of it on his white linen jacket (this is the year of Gatsby, his valet had assured him), but he didn't cry. He accepted the ice cube held out to him by a lady in a red satin fringed dress.

"This will take it right out," she told him. "Go ahead." The ice cube seemed to help. She took a handkerchief out of her red purse to mop up the stain. "See this purse?" she asked. John nodded. "Well," she said, "it's the one out of sixty-two that came in handy. Know what I mean? Get the picture? One out of sixty-two?"

John began humming to himself.

"One out of sixty-two *premiums*. Gifts from banks! Every time they used to give away things I'd put some money in all of them and get a gift. Got a whole set of power tools ..." John had put his head to one side and looked puzzled.

"Power tools!" she shouted. "Electric drill, all that mess. I'm not married any more, so I don't use them, but I got them. And a blender, and a badminton set—with birdie—and tennis rackets and juice squeezers and a camera and an electric scissors and a thermal blanket and an ice bucket and God knows what else. Sixty-two. This purse is the only one I use."

"Why?" said John.

She pushed him with gigantic archness. "You!" she said.

Two tall, blond girls, looking very much alike, their hair hanging straight down, their faces carefully made up to look as if they were not made up at all, were talking about a popular humorist, a man who made his own physical and emotional inadequacies the subject of his one-line jokes. They tried to draw John in on their conversation.

"It isn't right to make fun of yourself if you are ashamed of yourself," John said slowly. "It's different if you make fun of yourself because you make mistakes, but not because you really hate everything about you. Then it is sad, not funny."

The girls stared at him for a moment, then one said to the other in her harsh, nasal voice, "I just resent the time that meathead husband of mine spends with that tramp he sees in Brooklyn, that's *my* time he's wasting, don't forget that!" John thought how sad it was that somebody so pretty sounded so mean-spirited; he'd noticed that about many people.

A man who had been standing near them, a man wearing big round glasses and some kind of makeup all over his face, nudged John, who was getting tired of having people touch him.

"She's so goddam self-oriented," said the man. "She hasn't learned to release herself, to be herself. She hasn't learned the real truth ... everybody is his own best friend."

"That would be lonesome," said John in his slow, careful voice.

The man wasn't paying attention and went on talking for a while. A girl joined them. She was not as young as her hair and her costume indicated: her hair was like a child's, loose and straggly, and she wore a tucked, white Sunday School dress that came to the floor in back and just below her pelvis in front.

"I'm going to tell you something," she yelled into John's ear. He looked alarmed. She grabbed his arm and fanned her hand in front of his face.

"Don't worry. It's no knock, it's a boost. I got this outfit at your store! What do you think of that? Every broad here wearing something cost three, four hundred

dollars. Know how much I paid for this at Sun? Forty-
five bucks! That makes me the cheapest baby here.
Cheapest baby here."

"You bought that at my store," repeated John.

"You bet. I don't see the sense in spending three,
four hundred for something all your friends know you
got it and when you wear it again they say oh she's
wearing *that* again and there goes that bread for a
bummer that you could have spent in a chin-lift or
dermabrasion. So I always buy evening clothes at the
Sun. I'm your best customer. How about that?"

Her drink was spilling down her chin and one eye
had a black aura underneath, a lost half-moon of
damp mascara.

"Forty-five dollars is too much money," said John.
"Don't waste your money. You ought to wear a pretty
dress that looks nice."

The girl burst into wild laughter. "Man, you really
lay it on. That is the funniest thing I ever heard in all
my life. You are *some*thing." She planted a wet nasty
kiss on John's beautiful mouth. He looked at her for a
moment (later, during her usual next-morning re-
morse period, she had a distinct impression of disgust
and horror) and then took out his handkerchief. He
wiped off his lips and then ran his tongue over them.

The editor of a literary journal had been watching
this with what he thought of as amused detachment,
a state he rarely achieved because of his inner and
sensible conviction that he, as editor or person, was
not worth bothering about.

The book editor had been answering people's questions about what makes a best seller. He said nobody
knew the reasons, in a hushed liturgical voice, any
more than anyone knew what made literary reputa-
tions or whether—his eyes shifted because he was
going to tell a joke—the moon was made of green
cheese.

"What makes a book sell is because somebody likes

it, but you don't know what people are going to like the next week," said John.

Two publishers began making notes.

The editor decided he would pay John a compliment. During his own period of next-morning penitence he would realize that he was in love with John, but now he felt completely in tune with everybody and pretty damn intellectual-special.

"Prince Mishkin," he said. "That's you."

John smiled a little. He was beginning to feel very tired indeed.

"The idiot," chuckled the literary editor. "You say 'em as you sees 'em."

"Your wig is crooked," said John.

"See what I mean? You're a genius. Listen, why don't you think about writing a book. You take the best sellers of the last ten years, you got all this crap, yours could be a combination seller and realie. You could *do* a realie. I'd personally see to it that you got good review space. Have you ever thought about it?"

"About what?" asked John.

"Well, not the usual. You're not Jewish, but that's pretty well used up anyway, and you don't have physical problems—so I'd have to think about it. Most of the stuff we've been doing is really by the same guy, but he uses different names—"

"I know," said John, thinking vaguely about what he'd been told about current books, plays, films, music and art.

The editor gasped. He had meant to say that many of the reviews in his influential journal were written by his brother-in-law. It had not occurred to him that a probing mind would have seen through all the pseudonyms and deliberate shifts of opinion.

He backed away from John, into a tall, thin youngish woman who looked like a tall, skinny boy with frizzy curls. "Hi!" said the woman. "Who's worth talking to?" The editor shuddered and looked helplessly at John, who felt sorry for the funny man.

"Robins are more careful than authors," said John. The editor turned up his acne-scarred face reverentially as John said, "A robin builds a nest and lines it with something nice and soft and then sits on the eggs whether it's raining or not and is very careful but when the baby birds are hatched she begins to change, and though she feeds them and brings them worms she is very sure that they get out of the nest on time even though the nest was very beautiful and very right for them."

Why am I always outclassed, sobbed the editor to himself, who was *not* his own best friend; why is there always some handsome sonofabitch who makes me sound the way I feel . . . ? He stumbled to the door and walked to the railway station where he boarded the wrong train.

A small man of gray colors—hair, skin, eyes, T-shirt, beads—took hold of John's arm. (Another person handling John who wasn't really anyone John liked; it was becoming harder to bear each time.)

"That fellow—" The young man nodded in the direction of the doomed, departed editor. "All the influence in the world. But no confidence. But—who am I to tell *you?* *You* know there's no such thing as a mind."

John counted to ten, to himself, because he found that if he did that sometimes the tears wouldn't start.

"By the way, I know who you are, but you don't know who I am. I'm Charlie Blei, I'm in plastics."

"Plastics," repeated John carefully.

"Plastics. Manufacturing end."

"Is that what you do?"

"We make things out of plastic."

John nodded; he had understood part of the conversation.

"That fellow, he thinks he's so great. I know all about him, my firm puts money into the conglomerate that owns the publishing house that subsidizes the paper he writes for. Last year my nephew was writing this column? You know? For a paper out here? So this fellow, he says, that's too commercial, why don't you be yourself? So next thing, this fellow that's so smart, he's superintending adviser on a soap opera, it's on every day, he collects a mint. So anyway, it makes me so tired to—"

"When you're tired why don't you go to sleep," asked John, hoping vaguely that the man would say okay and that somehow everybody in the room would go to sleep.

"Jesus, that's it!" The gray man grinned and caressed John's shoulder, reaching up. "Go to sleep if you're tired. Eat if you're hungry. I expect nothing from nobody. Why? I really like my*self!*"

"That's what that other person said," began John, but had to stop because he couldn't remember what was in his mind when he'd started the sentence.

"You take anybody like me, in analysis for ten, maybe fifteen years," said the gray man. "What the hell does money mean? Zilch. You like your*self*, that's money in the bank. I read books—that is to say, I buy books, I don't read them because they don't relate to me, but what gets to me is a machine that performs a function. You're a machine, you know that? You got these stores, you know how to run them, you're a machine."

"I'm not a machine, I'm a boy," said John very softly, so the gray man, who wasn't listening anyway, didn't hear.

"I never have to prove myself any more, that's the thing. I go out and I do this or I do that and business I can handle with my left foot. Do you swim?"

"No," said John.

"What's swimming? What's any of that Superman crap? Who swims? I'll tell you who swims, a lot of fags trying to prove they're not fags, that's who swims. But I'll tell you something else." He paused, put down his drink and his cigar that he was smoking through a convoluted wire holder attached to the middle finger of his left hand, and jabbed John in the chest. "I'M A HAPPY MAN!"

John was so tired of being touched by strangers that he pushed the gray man. The gray man fell into a deep white velvet sofa and began to vomit a little, murmuring, "I don't have to prove nothing, nothing, nothing."

At dinner John was seated to the left of a man who was too drunk to talk, and two seats away from a lady who leaned across the drunk to shout things at John. She was wearing an ensemble that had nothing on top, showing bare, brown, wrinkled breasts unsuccessfully veiled under chains of beads. "Did you ever taste real vegetables before?" she yelled at John. "They grow their own. The Wangers grow their own vegetables. Nothing frozen! God, I hate frozen food, everything frozen . . ."

The word "frozen" meant ice cream to John, so he smiled.

"S'why taste food at a restaurant, it's not the same. AND THEY CALL IT PROGRESS."

John cleared his throat and spoke in his natural voice, which was clear and resonant. "Then maybe it is better not to have progress if it is wrong," he said.

There was silence at the table. Several people began making notes on their white pants, on the tablecloth and each other's backs.

The woman opposite John leaned across the table. "I know you know me," she said.

"No, I don't," said John.

There was another silence. Everybody knew this woman for her own activities, which were vague but famous. She made a point of maintaining extraordinary press coverage. Someone once asked her if it was true that she was having an affair with a certain art director. She replied, "I *only* sleep with celebrities." When that had been quoted to John, he repeated, "I only sleep with celebrities" (evoking laughter from the three directors with him at the moment, who thought he was being funny). Then John smiled his sweet smile. "I only sleep with Teddy," he added. They roared with laughter.

". . . or in politics," Mrs. Wanger, on John's left, the head of the table. John hadn't heard the first part of what she was saying, so he nodded. His chicken was good and he had finished it and was hoping for a nice dessert.

". . . when they make those speeches," Mrs. Wanger called, because as hostess it was her obligation to herd her hundred guests together in a listeners'-hedgehog as she endeavored a pleasing general conversation.

"Speeches," said John.

"The politicians. They all have the same damn writers, they don't even know what they're talking about and—"

The day before, somebody had told John about Abraham Lincoln writing his most important speech on the back of an envelope.

"Why doesn't the President write his own speeches?" said John.

Mrs. Wanger broke into tears. "Did you hear that?" she yelled down the considerable length of her dining table. "Did you hear that? How about that? How about not letting anybody be a senator or a congressman or a anything unless he is fully capable of writing his own speeches?"

"It won't play," said the topless lady, fiddling with her chains. "What is she, some kind of agitator?"

The note-writing was taken up again, and somebody thirty or forty seats away from John called, "And a little child shall lead them!"

"I'm *not* a child," said John, very low. He was so tired.

After dinner he took his nap. But people kept moving in and out of the room and he heard so many fragments of conversations . . .

". . . my nephew the congressman tells me there's a surprisingly large bloc of blind people, there's a vote

you don't hear much about, like your kikes, your nig-
gers, your pot-heads, and excetra, excetra. He's going
to go after those blindies!"

"... they're killing me." A shrill, high, nasal voice.
"These shoes. I wear them, everybody says clogs are
in, but I keep turning my ankle. They cost fifty dollars. They're ugly. They hurt. So I wear them."

"... he just missed that plane crash, the one from
St. Louis, and—"

"What was he doing in St. Louis on a Thursday?"

"It's the day he tells his wife he has the chiroprac-
tor appointment."

"On a *Thursday?*"

"Well, anyway, there were all these people killed
and he wasn't on it."

"On a *Thursday?*"

*Once, when Dix had tried to prove to the Teacher
that he was indeed paying attention to his project, he
mentioned the use of computers. The Teacher had
smiled wearily. "They are the toys of your toys; doing
only what you have taught your dolls, who then care
for their dolls. It would be a pity if your own mind
were the lodestar of any actual life. It is your inade-
quacy that causes you to fashion your project people
in your own image. Like you, they constantly feel an
unappeasable hunger for an unattainable food. In
your own case, it is simply your small attention-span
making you restless; they think it is the center of
their being. I've noticed that they cherish their tribal
superstitions, as our youngest children do, but you
have given them as well the almost criminal notion
that here is a rational explanation for everything that
occurs in the project. How can they know that their
rational explanation is nothing but you?"*

*Dix sulked. He did not like to be laughed at. He
often wished the Teacher would notice the clever
things he had done: from the start of the project,
when the first three beings were evolved, he had*

caused them to originate society, the basis of any combination of animals, insects, or programmed dolls. He muttered something about the structure of the beehive and the anthill. The Teacher smiled.

"By now you should have done much better with your 'people.' Your dim grasp of ends-and-means results in chaos for them. For example, they are incapable of accepting or even recognizing humor and perception . . . what is worse, they seem to punish the few who possess those faculties. Do you remember one of your few acceptables saying, "Only connect! Live in fragments no longer. Only connect, and the beast and the monk, robbed of the isolation that is life to either, will die." Well . . . it seems to me there is a great deal of disconnection going on in little orb."

Dix nodded, sneering to himself. He decided that when he got home he would beat up his little brother; that always made him feel better.

". . . *Thursday?*" someone else was shouting. "Who was in Spain Thursday?"

". . . he said he was going to Spain, so naturally I told him I had this friend in Spain I can't pronounce his name? he lives somewhere, I didn't remember where? so I said look him up? He said he'd look him up."

". . . He was a great mystery story fan. Read everything." John had wandered into another conversation, and listened again without hope. "So when he died, I couldn't help thinking—now remember, you have to bear in mind he was a mystery fan, you see—well, when I heard he died and everyone knew he was such a police buff—a real mystery fan. Followed police calls. Had his own radio. Well, he died, you know, and I said to Dick—just as a whimsy, not anything serious, you understand—I said, "Undoubtedly he has been called by God to help him in his investigation. Get it?"

At this moment, the city of Paraguay was having a red rain. The streets were deserted as panic-stricken citizens, staring wildly at the crimson stains on their clothing, took to their houses. The Gulf of Paolo looked like a pool of watered blood in the morning. In Pasay, just south of Manila, the air was throbbing with small, sharp stones; Pasoeroean was visited with tiny green bats; Phoenix, Arizona, suffered a temperature change from 54 degrees Fahrenheit to 12 below zero; the ruined castle in Pontrefact, Leeds, collapsed. Little Brother had received his beating and was kicking at a large notebook. The notes were in doll-alphabet order, and the book was open at "P."

The day after the party John felt tired. Lydia asked him if he'd had enough sleep; he said yes and that he'd liked the party a little but not much. "The cherries in the drinks were good, though," he said.

"Oh, don't be sarcastic, Mr. Sun," said Lydia. "That doesn't sound like you."

John blinked at her and then dismissed it. "Shall we read the Gossip Gazette now?" he asked. He and Lydia shared a little secret. Every couple of days she would read to him from a syndicated column based on the doings of celebrities. She thought he had some special way of concentrating, that it helped him to think more clearly when he heard the items rather than reading them to himself.

"Okay," said Lydia. She searched through some papers on his desk and found the sheets she wanted. She mumbled part of the time. None of what she read ever made sense to her but she imagined that all the people mentioned were personal friends of Mr. Sun.

"... let's see ... Singer Blanca Marlow has used thirty-four names during her musical career ... Actor Robert Gray recalled filming seventy-eight takes for a commercial. When he was through somebody handed him an aspirin. 'Thanks,' he said, 'I needed that.' ...

Murray Hill, the actor, was visited by his broker after the show. 'I just broke eighty,' said the broker. 'I know,' said Murray, whose piece on Alexander Hamilton will appear in an upcoming issue of *Flatulence*. 'I am one, too.' ... Oliver Wendell Holmes, former jurist and Washingtonian, watched a pretty girl go by and exclaimed, 'I wish I were eighty!' He didn't know it, but he was one, too! ... Frank Sinatra and Clark Gable once used the same dressing room at different times ... Dan Dooley, the X-rated film producer, plans to make an animated cartoon of the Apocrypha ..."

"What does that mean?" asked John.

"What does *what* mean?" asked Lydia, who hadn't understood any more than John what she'd read.

"What's an X-rated film?"

"You know. The porno films. They're X, and then some are marked Restricted, and some are PG for parental guidance ..."

"Parental Guidance?" John felt sad. The phrase meant something to him. "Can you tell me a film that is marked PG?"

"Sure, wait a minute," said Lydia. She looked at the cinema listings and came up with a film that was playing not far from John's apartment. He decided he would take the afternoon off and see it. Parental Guidance was one of the things he wanted to find out about.

The theater had red velvet seats that would move like a swing when you sat down. The picture began, and a funny-looking little man began talking to himself onscreen. People laughed at him, but he seemed so miserable and lost that John felt tears stinging his eyelids again. He held his breath and thought of something pleasant, which was not always effective in holding the tears back, but he had to be sure no one saw him cry.

Then a man and a woman began holding each other and moving around all over each other. They weren't fighting, and the movie wasn't at all like the Westerns John liked so much on TV. Now the man and the woman were lying in a bed, with no clothes on at all. John sighed and wondered why it took so long for the real picture to start ... this might be some kind of advertisement, a commercial for a mattress company? The Sun Company didn't sell mattresses ... what would the directors say if they knew their president was sneaking out to the movies? John smiled. He liked being naughty; he squirmed uncomfortably, waiting for the dull part to be over, but dozed off for at least half an hour.

When he woke up he felt stiff so he thought he'd better take a walk. The afternoon was fine and almost sunny through the gray, dust-dotted air. He walked several blocks and then he saw a lot of people gathered. Usually, he had learned, this meant only that a crowd was watching a man get robbed or an old lady being hurt, but he noticed a lot of policemen and firemen around. He began to run. He liked anything that attracted police and firemen; their uniforms were the nicest clothes he'd ever seen.

Everyone was looking to the sky. John looked up, too. Sometimes planes were going by (and sometimes he saw bright shimmers that reminded him of confused dreams). But there was nothing in the sky now.

"What happened?" he asked a woman standing near him.

"There's a man going to jump." John didn't know what she meant, but he heard some of the people around him yelling, like the crowds at the stadium, "Go on, jump, go on, jump, jump, jump."

A policeman who looked very young went by. John had learned that some really pretty people looked this way not-on-purpose, as though they had just been born a few minutes ago into a big size. Then there were the opposites—all the people he met at parties or saw on TV, the ones who were supposed to

be young, but looked, in spite of their colorful faces
and bodies, a hundred years old, with makeup all
over their eye-bags and mouth-lines and always
held-in by elastic bands on their rigid figures. This
policeman, although tall, looked about twelve years
old. John liked him a lot.

"Sir, can you tell me what's happened?"

The policeman mopped his forehead. "Some Spic
... he's up there on a two-foot projection outside a
fifteenth-story window. He don't know whether he
wants to jump or what. So we get called out, there's a
priest up there with him, there's Channel Two and
Four and Seven and Eleven—*every*body—for one little
Spic busboy. How do you like that?"

"I like that," said John. "It's very nice of the television people and the police and the firemen to come
out because one person is worried. That's really very
nice."

"Ah, come on," said the policeman, "knock it off. I
hear that enough from the bleeding-heart civilian
police boards. Yeah, so one little guy is worried.
Okay—so it makes a great human interest story. Do you
realize that right here, right here in this city, at this
moment, people are getting shot up and murdered and
set fire to and raped and ripped off and nobody is
there because everybody is here watching this big
four-foot-eleven busboy make up his crummy mind
whether he wants to live or not? And you know why?
It's like take your best sellers or your big shows ...
Moses and the Ten Commandments, Star Trek—all
that stuff. The people down here take some kind of
private vow ... I don't know what they do or how ...
but any time there's a guy on a ledge—Bingo! He's in.
You could go out tomorrow and knock off ten old
men in the park and then maybe rob a bank for lunch
and follow a girl home in this Greenwich Village, and
what would happen? You'd get a nice notice in the
paper if they had the room, if something wasn't going
on with the Washington crowd. Maybe. But you take

anybody—and I mean *anybody*—he goes out on a ledge and he's a four hour wonder. Okay, I grant you, tomorrow he's no news, nobody remembers, but this is one of the big-time situations and don't you forget it."

"I won't forget it. I promise," said John. "But how are they trying to stop him from falling?"

"Oh my God, how are they trying ... how are they trying ... I'll tell you how they're trying ... there's a priest up there, and a lawyer and his wife and his kids, and a doctor and a nurse and some newspaper people and TV people—they all promise him anything he wants if he don't jump. But he won't come in and see, he has these small feet so no one else feels very safe being out here, their feet wouldn't fit. I'm telling you, you try to jump, big man like you, you'd fall right off. He's lucky. He's little."

"He's not lucky," said John. "He's unlucky, or he wouldn't have done that. I feel the same way sometimes. Really, I do. Could I go up and talk to him?"

John had learned which was the right card to show people when he wanted them to know who he was. He handed the policeman his card. "Please, may I go up and talk to him?"

The policeman looked at the card, then at John, then at the card again, then at the crowd, then up in the air to the ledge.

"F'Chrissake," he said, "I *thought* you looked sincere! You're the head of a store. Nice headline ... Sun Store Prez keeps little bastard from the big leap. Go on. Go on up. Nice work."

John was led through a corridor to a hotel room. The room was so full of people that he felt frightened. But a TV newscaster recognized him. "And now," said the newscaster in the same tremulous, excited voice he used to talk about laxatives, when he did voice-overs for commercials, "here comes John Sun, the most eligible bachelor in America, and the most dedicated human being these two eyes have looked upon. John . . ." he turned and faced John Sun, who was being hustled through the crowd . . . "what message do you have for Angel Garcia?"

"I don't have any message," said John. "I want to make him listen to me."

He was allowed to go to the window and stick his head out. Representatives from the Catholic, Jewish, Protestant, Islam, and Ethical Culture blocs were all trying to call encouraging words to Angel Garcia. "Go away," said John. "You frighten him." Before they could do anything, John had gone out on the ledge, which meant having to balance backwards, holding by his fingertips to the tiny stone overhang of the window.

"Angel," called John, as cameras and sound machines recorded the scene and the crowd beneath was yelling, "Jump!"

"Angel, listen to me. Listen. I know how you feel. Usually I feel the same way. But it's different for me. I'm very rich and you are poor. That makes a *big* difference. But you don't have to worry any more. If you come in, I'll promise to get you a good job at my company, and you won't have anything to worry about."

Angel Garcia made no answer.

"Please listen," yelled John. The TV people were beginning to talk about his golden hair in the breeze and the sheer humanity of the man, not to mention the sheer drop, and what a great—really *fantastic*— moment this was in history when a rich, beautiful Anglo-Saxon could take the time off from his important work to save the life of a little man of Hispanic origin.

"Please . . ." yelled John. Without thinking about it, he stretched out his hand and inched forward.

Angel Garcia, who was quite mad and unable to hear anything except certain inner voices, saw a representation of the Christ approaching. In full fear and in the sickness unto death, he leaned forward to meet his Lord, and fell to the sidewalk. A Mrs. Peter Succhi, of Teaneck, New Jersey, suffered a broken arm because she hadn't moved fast enough. Most of the sidewalk crowd were like trained players in a game; they deftly avoided the descendant human missile.

. . . *"That was also the day I dropped my eyeglass,"* *said Dix, fidgeting. The Teacher sighed.*

"And also," he pointed out, "the day in Earth-1853 that Sir David Brewster announced to the members of the British Association that he had discovered an object of so incredible a nature that it could not be explained. It was a 'crystal lens found in the treasure-house at Nineveh.' Incredible indeed. You lose an eyeglass, and let it turn up among your dolls. I believe it is in the British Museum at the moment, and quite forgotten. Not really as clumsy as your constant droppings of food—such as the Worcester Times *reported in May of 1881, when thousands of periwinkles fell from the sky—but much more dangerous. A lens is something personal. You must really remember. . . ."*

Dix folded his arms and waited for the rest of the lecture with half-closed eyes.

Little Brother was tuned in on the conversation. He was upset about Dix always getting the blame for things. He prodded the layers of atmosphere near the project (causing seismographs to panic) but then tried something else . . .

If too many things were dropping into the project, why not take some away? With great care, Little Brother removed a two-year-old baby from a stroller in front of a German supermarket. Then a very old man digging in his garden in China, and a good many documents from their "safety" boxes in various vaults. He fooled around a little with the New York Stock Exchange, but stopped himself just in time. The baby and the old man were never heard of again, but Little Brother was doing his simple best to restore the "balance of nature," one of Dix's silly physical rules.

"The whole rotten mess is getting on my nerves," said Wanger. He rubbed his knuckle against his nose and glared at Branch. "I don't know about you, but I'm sick of all this sweetness crap. Why doesn't somebody kidnap him? Why can't he get a government position ... maybe something nice and cheery in the Cabinet . . . why can't the Republicans run him for President?"

"How do you know he's a Republican?" asked Branch.

Wanger was too smart to let himself get dragged into a net like that. Branch was such a low, conniving rat that he couldn't understand natural, normal processes like bugging; luckily, Wanger knew how to keep his wits about him.

They were having lunch in the hotel dining room on the day John and Lydia were at the nursing home. Both had formed a temporary and retractable state of trust: they openly ordered martinis. So long as each had four, same as the other fellow, there was no danger of security leaks.

"Mind you, it isn't as if I don't appreciate his good qualities," said Branch. "You've got to admit that everybody likes him. He's the best thing that ever happened to us, public relations-wise. Half the time he doesn't even sound real. Only time I ever heard him sound like a regular human being is when he was fooling around with my kids. At my house, that time ..." he peered at Wanger, hoping Wanger knew the difference between having a big man at a party and having a big man visit a lovelyhomeinLarchhaven, getting a firsthand look at a personal life full of significant values.

"How's the wife and kids?" mumbled Wanger. He hated children.

"Oh, just fine. My wife wants to take the kids abroad, so they can soak up some real culture, not just this local stuff. I told her there's no point talking about it now because we still don't know when the

London store will be ready, and naturally all the officers and directors will have to go over when . . ."

Wanger and Branch eyed each other. It was like a
religious ritual. The first meeting of eyes lasted only a
second; each glanced back at his drink. Then another
meeting of eyes—three or four seconds. Back to the
drinks. Then a longer look.

"Do you think?" said Wanger and stopped. He'd be
damned if he was going to say it first.

"Well . . ." said Branch.

"It couldn't come from us. I mean, the minute one
of us said he ought to head the London operation
he'd think something was up. You know, just between
you and me and the lamppost"—Branch looked
around, then realized Wanger was being symbolic—
". . . I don't think the bastard trusts me!"

Branch shook his head in sympathy. "I've had that
same feeling once or twice myself," he admitted.

"How can a big corporation survive if there is a
lack of confidence in the men who guide its detsiny?
Destiny, that is. Why, I wouldn't be surprised if the
New York operation would be much better off—in the
last analysis, that is—if we got back to the old footing.
You take all this sweetness and light, it can only add
up to trouble. Sincerity!"

"Innocence!" laughed Branch.

"Be kind to the public! Look, it may be okay on the
surface, I admit the stock's going up and the figures
are good so far this year, but it's no way to run a railroad."

"No way at all to run a railroad," said Branch. He
frowned and fingered the stem of his martini glass.
"How can we work it?"

They were silent for a while. Each was visualizing
himself as chairman of the board of the New York
store. Branch saw his children in caps and gowns,
making commencement speeches that would be
picked up by the media . . . "everything we've done is
because of our father and mother" . . . "my father is in

the great tradition of the American dream. He was a—" well, no, that could be checked out, they couldn't say poor—"rich boy, who in spite of having to ride to school every morning and live in luxury, surmounted these disadvantages to become what he is today, the inspiration of every *advantaged* minority child in this grand country ..." He saw himself on a weekly TV show, giving words of advice to every decently-brought-up kid ... "Mrs. Branch and I have often had our little disagreements, yes, we have—but because of our meaningful relationship and the example we have tried to set for one and all ..." He saw himself at the White House ... "now, Ted, Harry, Howie, Jack, Louis, Everett, Whatever, I can speak only as a man who has made it in a world of commerce. But that world of commerce is a microcosm, and so I feel it does not behoove" ... no, probably "*un*behoove me to apply the simple set of rules I live by to the situations that arise in a gradually shrinking world. We are all closer together, and—" Tears sprang to Branch's eyes. Damn it, he'd be terrific at it.

Wanger's vision was of a beneficent kingdom (the Constitution was tottering now; everyone needed a kindly despot) where closed-circuit television would work two ways in every home; yes, every home in America would have at least three of these sets; no move would be made that could not be approved or, what was more likely, disapproved by Augustus I. He would rule with an iron hand in an iron glove: send all the Commies and rebels back to where they came from, censor all books and entertainment and art— hell, what did anybody need with art? That would be a popular take-away, and would save millions that were wasted now on museums and crap like that. He would have a staff of loyal Protectors of the Person, and he would establish Enlightened Polygamy and Reasonable Worship of Idols. He felt a surge of strength ... it did a man good to get out of himself and devote his God-given brain to humanity. This was what he was headed for, once they got that psalm-singing nut out of the country.

"Easy way," Wanger said finally. "Easy way is the best way. Just have a meeting. Tell him we can't trust anybody else with a project that big. It's his Christian American duty to go over there and show the Limies how to behave. We can talk him into it."

Branch shook his head. He tossed off the last of his drink. "Nope. He wouldn't listen to us. We have to kind of bring it up real sudden, like, and everybody vote. No speeches. Just tell him what he has to do. Only way to get to him. He's like a kid, you know, in some ways. He *wants* people to tell him what to do. But I guess it better be other people, not us."

"Yeah, okay, but we are agreed? Sun goes to London to be there for the opening of the new store."

"Agreed." Branch signaled for the check and made up his mind that the first official act of his chairmanship would be to fire Wanger.

Wanger was wondering how he could frame Branch for embezzlement. I shouldn't be too hard; he'd put a bug in Branch's office ... and without John Sun around it would be a far better world.

Their judgment was confirmed when the news broadcasts showed John on the ledge with Angel Garcia. "Good God—he's helping some nobody, some nobody who's *dead*, anyway. He probably wasn't even a customer of the Sun stores! What kind of public relations is that? We can't afford to have a nut like that around the premises, endangering people's lives like that."

Lydia and Alice Bloover took John over to the television studio. Wanger managed to arrive a half hour earlier so he could "turn on the charm," which meant asking each receptionist and secretary "*What*'s your name? How do you spell that?" He had once used the phrase about his charm in John's presence, and John had said, "Like turning on the water?" Martin Branch had snickered as John went on: "But if you don't *have* any water, you can't turn it on."

"I'll have to give him credit, he's a damn devious bastard," Wanger had mumbled. He was taking no chances. Within fifteen minutes he had managed to build up an incredible amount of hostility and surliness among the network employees of Channel 18.

"Mr. Wanger is in makeup now," said a young woman when John arrived. "You can go in when he's ..." she looked at John more carefully. "Oh. You *have* your makeup on."

The show was called "Rickie Ronson Raps." Rickie Ronson, like most hosts of television talk shows, was an Instant Mix. His private life had been so carelessly assembled by Dix that photographs of him with his wife and two amorphous babies looked faked; and his own image kept fading on the screens of the nation as he talked to singers, actors, authors, comics: anyone who had something to sell, about nothing at all. Since the shows were packaged and played at different times in different cities, the promotion of the guests' wares often led to confusion. "We're looking forward to next week as the greatest Christmas show in years" might be said in the middle of summer, but no one really paid that much attention. Sometimes Dix had to use his tranquilizer darts, which acted on people much the same as they did on wild animals. A tiger has no way of knowing that a sudden penetration of his body is for his own good, that he is being captured to be let loose in a nicer area; no more did television viewers know that they were subject to a less traumatic stoppage of mental and physical capacities. They tended to think of these spells as "commercials," the times when they stared transfixed at the TV screen with all thought and reason and movement suspended.

Rickie Ronson found John in a dressing room. "Hello," said John.

"Hi, there, you," said Rickie Ronson. He was a small man, with wavy white hair, pink face makeup, and high heels. "I'm crazy about the Sun store. My wife buys everything there. You're doing a really terrific job. Nelson Rockefeller told me last week that . . ."

"Nelson Rockefeller?" said John.

Ronson stared for a moment, then guffawed. "Got me," he said, and patted John's shoulder. "Look, I suppose you've been told what to do . . . just be yourself, be natural, and the whole point is the new London store and why you're going over. Don't try to sell. I mean, hey, I can't tell you anything about personal promotion, you're The Man; but play it like for real, you know? Just be casual."

"Casual," said John.

"I knew you'd get it. Right on! I mean, the truth is, the hardest thing in the world is this natural bit you're so good at. Here we are, we work like dogs . . ."

"Like dogs?" said John. "A dog doesn't work, unless he pulls a sled. A dog has a nice, easy life if he lives with good people and they take care of him. He only works when he's digging up a bone or something like that. He is taken care of and he leads a very nice life. I wish I had a dog."

Augustus Wanger walked by at that moment. He pushed Ronson's elbow. "See what I mean," he muttered. "Watch out for him. Watch out for old Simple here. He'll make a moron out of you. Lay off anything about dogs."

"Now, I'll signal you when it's time for a commercial break," said Ronson, ignoring Wanger. He had enough Wangers on his own staff. "I'll look at any one of you when I want you to talk, but don't interrupt when I'm saying anything. I'll guide the thing. Not to worry, you'll all come off fine. How about a sandwich? Small drink? Everybody got makeup on now?"

"I don't have any makeup on," said John. "Lydia does, though, and so does Alice."

Ronson stared at him for a moment and then broke into a false hearty laugh.

"How about a discount at that London store?" he asked. "My wife and I love London. It's so damn civilized. You don't see all the wheeling and dealing that's around in New York. I'd love to live there—soon as I get it all together."

"I'm going to live in London for three months," said John. "I'm going to open a store there and live in Knightsbridge. Will I be able to see myself on television?"

"Oh, sure, we'll let you know when the show is on. This is just a taping," said Ronson's assistant, a formidable woman with a pale, tired face. "And you can watch yourself on the monitor while we rap."

"Oh, good," said John. "I have to go to the bathroom now."

The formidable tired woman showed him where to go, and watched him walk off. "Think he'll be able to find his way out?" she asked, sighing a little.

Wanger laughed. "He could find his way out of a dungeon, a dungeon in the wilds of—of Brooklyn! I think I will have a small drinkie before we go on. It clears my throat." He poured four fingers of bourbon into a paper cup. The formidable woman watched him and mumbled something. Then the semicircle of chairs was spotlighted and Rickie Ronson took his place behind a block mounted on an invisible block. His chair was five inches higher than the guests' chairs, and he never stood up to greet anyone.

"How do those cameras work," asked John, as he was shown to the chair on Ronson's right. "Why are there so many? Why is it so bright? Why do I have to wear this thing around my neck?"

Ronson fiddled with some papers on his desk. "That's right . . . loosen up . . . talk . . . now . . ."

For most of the program, everyone kept talking at

once. During the first lull John looked up into the bright lights, touching the microphone that was his necklace. He had thought of something no one else appeared to have considered in all the conversation about going to another country and leaving the familiar security of his apartment.

"Who is going to take care of me?" he asked clearly, on mike, but before the question was really out everyone began talking at once all over again.

Part II

Anthea Evan lived in a suburb half an hour away by train from London. Her house was a battered one, standing by itself with an old row of brick cottages many yards behind it. There was a little garden in front and a vegetable patch in back; there was also an ancient shed containing old implements, bicycle parts, pools of permanently stagnant water and mysterious smells. There was a front door and a back door, but since the world had long ago ceased to put a house between a tradesman's entrance and that of a gentleman the doors were used at anyone's convenience.

The cottage was at its best in June, when the lane and road swam with the odors of privet and roses. Anthea had removed some of the nettles and weeds; she had had the house repainted; she had worked in the garden.

She couldn't remember buying the house or when she had come to live in it.

The fault of course lay with Little Brother. He knew after he made his John Sun doll that the brain part was wrong; he had thought himself into his creation. It seemed to cause unhappiness, and he didn't want that to happen because he knew that among these creatures unhappiness led to unkindness, hostility, wars, plagues and bad manners. So he broke into a box labeled "Omnibus" and withdrew at random a lovely bunch of memory-flowers and intelligence-plusses, as well as some minor flaws, which he had learned from Dix were absolutely essential to the well-being of the creatures. Little Brother used the same physical model (Type A-Star) for his female. She resembled John closely, save that her body was a perfect female form. She was a smaller, more rounded edition of John, with the same enormous blue eyes and golden aspect. But instead of having an earth-intelligence of about six years ... which was a touchy matter to Little Brother, who was infinitely more wise than his doll; but the mind of a creature always had to be adjusted to the antennae of the other pets ... Anthea was a mulligatawny of impossible thoughts and memories of all experience past age 16 of a file marked Jane Baillie Welsh Carlyle.

She was about four present-days-old in Earth time when John Sun came to London. She was a collage of bright and sad bits of history centering around England, because Little Brother had learned "English" in pre-play school and found it easier to understand than the other tiny, tinny voices on the receiver. Dix could understand over four hundred languages, but Dix was not the proud Parent of these two exquisite beings. Little Brother had been particularly careful about one thing: there was not an ounce of meanness in either John Sun or Anthea Evan. Soon Dix's teacher would become aware of these two new dolls and would then undoubtedly forgive Dix for all the miseries that had taken over his project.

This was the odd thing. The present small house near Taplow, Berks., contained no memories for Anthea whatever. Then why, *why* was it so easy for her to remember this: going past a churchyard to reach a large comfortable house some eight miles from the station. White painted floors in the nursery, with a willow tree outside the window. Under the window a

row of hedges, high and secret ... waking up mornings because Nurse was shaking Anthea and the
(shadowy) other children ... a mantelpiece with an
ormolu clock in its middle, vases holding spills for
lighting the fire. Four-poster beds in the grownups'
rooms. April with lilacs (followed by a memory of
T. S. Eliot as a young man; how did she know that he
worked in a publishing house?) and greenhouses
from which cuttings would be brought to the house.
Learning French; indeed, having to read aloud from
"La Neuvaine de Colette" or "Pecheur d'Island."
Going to picnics in a horse-drawn wagon and
watching, from the safety of the wagon, the horrors
of the exhibitionist poor. Drunken men, painted
women ... they had just as surely been part of the
country as the town, where they were generally ro-
manticized. Visiting one's own poor, in cottages ...
the paper-thin woman, so old she could not lift the
soup bowl, who kept a quince tree in the garden. She
had once been Anthea's parents' servant, and there
were servants everywhere, whenever they were
needed for comfort and for making one eat rice pudding and for dispensing doses of senna-pods.

The new house had a bathroom, but there was
never a bathroom in the house or houses that Anthea
remembered. Instead, there were pails of heated
water, and outhouses for those who did not insist on a
constantly full smelly chamberpot. Cupboards under
staircases with the same mysterious smell-of-ages that
now pervaded the shed near Anthea's house ... but
the stair cupboard smells were sweeter and more real.

If you went to the kitchen in that old house—and
the kitchen was a perilously long way from the nursery, through a winding corridor lined with dim pictures of ancestors, not the vaunted oil-painting kind
but, simply, dim daguerreotypes, there was a long
walk out to the world. (From the upstairs windows
when there was no mist you could see the world; almost all of England.) The long walk was a rutted lit-

tle lane that led to other lanes, and no one had ever fully explored them. (Later, Anthea would dream or think or half-remember that some of the walks would end in clearings near the Thames or be called the something-or-other View). But none of the children, and there were many other children, some her brothers, her sisters, some visitors, some the relatives' children ... all horrible ... were afraid of the follies, the places that looked like the kind of structure now used for outdated band concerts. There was a garden that contained only topiary work and—yes, parterre. Many open lawns with marble surprises: busts of famous Englishmen pitted and scarred by wind and rain into look-alikes ... a water garden with beautiful pond-lilies, and stones that children could step along if no one caught them. Flower beds that *said* something ... dates and names done in parterre ... Anthea could not visualize the names or the dates. She only knew they did exist in the real place that had been her home. A little structure in a wood was a theater for impromptu performances by children. Christmas pantomimes ... figures of Eros and Psyche—garlands—carvings. A curving walk that in spring was so heavy with rhododendron that it hurt to be there; she had always hurried from the pressure of the scent and the color and the beauty. An orangerie, where sometimes the children would steal blooms or fruit for their own treasure-hideries.

No one shopped in London then. Dressmakers came to the house. The other children stole the fruit from the trees: the medlars, the gooseberries, the apples.

But there was another lane, near another, earlier house in a much earlier time in Scotland, a lane that wound off stubbornly by itself in sinuousities. People were assigned work in the fields near it, bending over newly-plowed furrows and dropping beans into little holes. And violets everywhere, the dark blue-purple and the white; primroses, and cowslips from which

cowslip balls were made. (Peaceful brooks, peaceful
meadows ... the land on the other side of the brooks
reached by throwing planks across) ... to make the
cowslip ball, the tuft of flowerets is nipped off just
below the top of the stalk. Each cluster is balanced
across a bit of ribbon until there is a long garland.
Then the clusters are pressed together and tied.
Sometimes Anthea's full basket of them would be upset and she would start again. Often the children
would be caught by a shower; home they would run
through the winding lane and the glistening fields to
the fireside, then bread-and-milk and bed. The snug-
room was packed with chairs, sofas, tables; on the tables were the truest beauties of the world, lilacs,
roses, peonies, tulips, stock ...

School was dull; nothing was learned except
playing games and whispering about the other girls.
Nothing was learned ... then why did Anthea know
all she knew, and why was she now being offered a
job at a new branch of an American store as Public
Relations Director?

PART III

> Jenny kiss'd me when we met,
> Jumping from the chair she sat in;
> Time, you thief, who love to get
> Sweets into your list, put that in!
> Say I'm weary, say I'm sad,
> Say that health and wealth have miss'd me,
> Say I'm growing old, but add,
> Jenny kiss'd me.

No, there aren't many plain women who have been
so pleasingly celebrated, or, for that matter, many
beautiful women. Leigh Hunt was one of our best
friends, and his lovely verse justified a good deal of
the cold gray mornings when my husband and I
would exchange, over the breakfast table at Number
5 Cheyne Row, our daily rota of complaints: insom-

nia, dyspepsia, nervous disorder, irritability and (at least on my part) frustration.

I remember that as a girl I thought of Mr. Carlyle as the very Phoenix of a Friend. Yes, but some mornings, at home *à deux,* the ashes did not produce a bird of prime quality.

My greatest joy now, in the latter part of the twentieth century, is the body I occupy. It is not only beautiful, it works perfectly in every detail, so unlike the shell occupied by Jane Baillie Welsh Carlyle, or by the child I was, before my sixteenth year, when I was suddenly moved backward in time and space as though by some great extraterrestrial phenomenon from a peaceful existence in a country house in the 1890's to London's Chelsea in the 1820's. It has taught me a certain unwilling patience in the twentieth century with stalled commuter trains or telephones out of order. None of it matters, time is a madeup, impractical word.

I was Jane Baillie Welsh. I lived in another corner of the prism (Socrates wrote, "Man is a prisoner who has no right to open the door of his prison ... and take his own life ... [he meant, prism!]), I did marry Thomas Carlyle, and we did decide to live in London.

It was difficult for me to acknowledge, particularly to my finicky self, that I had never really been in a public place until Carlyle took me to the Drury Lane theatre, where we saw a silly play peopled with ugly women. But the house in the play! It is the kind of house I hope to have when we move from Ampton Street to Number 5 Cheyne Row.

I have recently seen Dr. Allan, a Scotsman who has a place for lunatics in the middle of Epping Forest. This seems to me a rather marvelous way to dispose of oneself, lunatic or not, because the place is overhung with roses and grapes, with miles of shrubbery and garden ponds. It is not nearly so much Bedlam as a house we know in London where people "speak in tongues," which is to say shrieking and howling in no tongue. The only person who seems not to speak in tongues is, like my husband, a self-named Mystic. He is John Stuart Mill; yes, I remember now, but did not know then, the part he was to play in our domestic life through an accident of servants. The year we moved into Cheyne Row was the year my husband was writing the History of the French Revolution. In March he lent the manuscript to Mill. At this time a maidservant, a friend of a friend of a friend of the cook, decided it was part of the day's rubbish and deposited all but a few pages of it into the fireplace.

It has amused me to read collections of my letters. They are indeed my letters, but there is no letter describing what happened after this incident:

First, you must try to visualize Mr. Carlyle. Handsome, with light magnetic eyes and a dour cast of perfect feature ... an angel in many ways and the Hound of Heaven, in the least flattering sense of the phrase, when things went wrong. And what, what in all the world, could go more wrong for an author (who has been called "Genius" by people of title!) than to have the only copy of his Great Work destroyed in flames.

Do you know how long it took, in 1835 to copy out a manuscript from fragments of notes? Five months. At least. Mr. Carlyle and I both worked on it, using our pens and our poor fingers and wrists (I think my later, rather famous, bout with a neuralgic arm may have had its birth at this time). It was tedious, tedious, tedious. My husband thinks that the second manuscript is "less vivacious" than the first, burnt version. Perhaps I am less vivacious, perhaps he is, but I think the manuscript fared better than we did.

Luckily, there was a hamper of wine sent us by a dear friend to celebrate the end of our manual labor.

But there is a difference between Mr. Carlyle and me. When the great task is finished, he goes off to Scotland for a holiday. I stay here and, exhausted from the superhuman task of penmanship, do not sleep. One's wit and spirit cannot be used up daily without eventual expense; my payment is that I cannot sleep afterward.

As for John Mill, which started me off on an old score (perhaps in another two hundred years I can forgive everyone concerned; not just yet), he is a rather absurd man. He is so very susceptible to Ladies, as he thinks of anyone dressed in silks and waving a fan—and is confidential—or, as I think of it, *loving* to them. But then he also considers Robespierre the greatest man who ever lived ...

Leigh Hunt lives a few doors away, Dickens visits us often, so does Tennyson. I am in many ways a very fortunate woman for knowing so many spirited people. I do manage to overhear them occasionally, discussing Mr. Carlyle and me ... "It is lucky," said Tennyson, "that Thomas and Jane found each other, or else each would have married another person, and then there would have been four miserable people in this corner of the world."

One of the un-blessings of a mind like mine, thrice-told or eternal, I don't know which, is counterpoint-memories. Much, much later, Mr. Frank Harris, an extremely foolish and vain little man, wrote at length about my marriage. He seemed to have peeped through keyholes, particularly on the night of our wedding, for he wrote in *Saturday Review* that the Carlyle marriage was never consummated.

I wonder what that means. Everybody knows that Frank Harris was preternaturally occupied with the sexual behavior of anything. But from the point of view of the me that was once Jane Welsh Carlyle, I cannot be sure that this is a fair statement. My marriage was devoutly consummated in matters of the spirit; never were husband and wife so close in some ways; never were they so apart in others. For instance, Mr. Carlyle never really understood how important servants were to me. I could not manage without them, and if I seemed to make too much of their nicenesses or villainies, it is because they become part of the life of a woman living in town. I think of them as my friend Geraldine thinks of her lovers, but I think my servants are more necessary to me. Mr. Carlyle could not see this. I have always been so very personal in all my relationships (in all my ages, apparently), that it must have seemed unusual, to say the least, to my maids and footmen. You see, my "dear little nieces," as sometimes I thought of maids, were so very kind—like Ellen, who mislaid no lobsters, or even the wretched Ann, who slept all one night at a stick-woman's—often, indeed, kinder to me than my husband.

No, in the sense that the absurd Mr. Harris meant his phrase, the marriage was *not* consummated. I died as I had lived, a virgin. And yet, no woman was ever more married than I when it came to any other aspect of a shared life: the illnesses, the unkindnesses of others, the small joys, the frequent sorrows, the successes, the tragedies: all Carlyle's and mine together. That is indeed a consummation, and the only true one, Mr. Harris, wherever you are.

Much has been written about my "jealousy" of Lady Ashburton. It is true that Carlyle saw a great deal of her, often, indeed, preferring her company to mine. But my resentment—and that is the proper word, not "jealousy"—was platonic, if it is possible to use this concept when no physical relationship exists to render the situation negative! Do you know, after her death, I was actually offered some of her old clothes by her husband. I was a good deal daintier in figure than she and wouldn't have worn them anywhere!

We saw a good bit of the Darwins, Charles and Erasmus. I was told by Miss Wedgwood that Charles could not summon up any great admiration for me; he considered a woman of wit and spirit "unnatural." Now as far back as Elizabeth's reign, women were beginning to play a part in life aside from that assigned to them: In 1642 some lively petitioners presented a paper to the Commons concerning the great want that was upon them through the decay of trade. "We had rather bring our children and leave them at the Lords' door than have them starve at home," they declared, and prayed that "bishops with their whole who usurped Government ... may be extinguished and abolished ... that popish lords may be sequestered the House ... incendiaries and delinquents brought to tryal and punishment." Cheapside and other large streets had been filled with benches and some waspish members of my sex were said to have poured boiling water on the heads of Royalist marauders. Some women apologized for petitioning, explaining that it was not done out of self-conceit or pride of heart, nor seeking to equal ourselves with men either in Authority or Wisdom. (I reserve comment, as no doubt does Mr. Darwin.) But the women marching to Westminster during this period of civil war were anticipations of the future. Mr. Darwin may have found my own poor health and pale complexion not in keeping with his as yet unpolished ideas of survival of the fittest!

Erasmus Darwin was kinder, I thought. All Darwins were preoccupied with their health; I forget which of them had a woolly gray beard and an equally woolly gray shawl. At best, it was difficult to see just where the beard left off and the shawl began, for the Darwin who wore the shawl was never without it, even through the lovely summers at Cambridge. Or so I have heard. Mr. Charles Darwin heard my cherished friend Mazzini telling me the other day that *I* must really wear a shawl in the house (as I wrote my dear sister Babbie); at the moment Mr. Darwin seemed quite unconcerned as to whether I wore a shawl or just a shift.

But this is the joy of people: they are so unpredictable. In spite of his dislike for women of spirit, and in spite of his announced indifference to my wardrobe, Mr. Darwin actually brought with him, on his next visit to our house, an immense gauze-looking shawl of white lambswool. Now this is what makes life interesting, not shawls but unexpected turns of character. This was supplemented on Friday morning, August 18, when Darwin came after my meal. He was talking about the difficulties of the smells at Newnham Grange, then suddenly switched mid-smell to remark, "Jane, you look as if you need to go to Gunter's and have an ice!" I am still trying to recall what sort of look my rather sedate face could have worn to make him say such a thing. But he was proved absolutely right in at least one of his theories, as I can testify, for we did drive to Gunter's and he did buy me an ice, and I felt much, much better.

It made him feel better, too. He is off to Shrewsbury for three weeks, but insisted on taking me for a drive to Parson's Green yesterday. And he began to talk in a way that made me wonder about the change in his attitude toward me; what gem of wisdom could I have dropped to bring such a reversal of opinion?

"I wonder," said Mr. Darwin, "if Carlyle gives you enough admiration for all you do. Your *needlework*, for example. I fear not. But I have no doubt that Carlyle manages to derive a great deal of comfort from all you do for him." I tried to defend my husband, but Mr. Darwin was expounding, not listening. He is coming close to the heart of things, whether he knows it or not, for I am swamped in sewing. I bought a small sofa, and found out that it needs to be covered (how inanimate things make slaves of all of us!). Carlyle was, I confess, not pleased at the cost. I could see him thinking in illuminated letters, "What? A sofa, now, when there is so much else to pay for! The little woman is falling away from her thrifty character and become extravagant." But he did not understand. This is a sofa I have known about for at least a year and the man who asked nearly five pounds for it was willing to accept two pounds if I took it without mattress or cushion. I had my own mattress and cushion, and even then, found two pounds a great deal of money. I did a stroke of trade with him. The downstairs curtains were dirty and I didn't need them, so he accepted them for thirty shillings, after an hour's lively higgling. What small, small things make up our daily lives and form the core of our existence. Books are written or destroyed or re-copied, nations fall, women petition, lovers quarrel, wars begin and end, but so long as the earth stays the earth, there will always be a woman arguing with a tradesman over the cost of curtains.

I did not see Darwin again until November, when he came to Chelsea with Mr. Wedgwood. They picked an odd day, for a Yankee gentleman had come to call. My maid Helen was nervous, for she had left him alone in the library while my watch was on the table—unguarded. I proceeded to the library to inpect this unauthorised settler: a tall, lean, red-herring looking man. He had actually been sitting at Carlyle's own writing table, peering at all the private papers. "Oh, you are Mrs. Carlyle, are you," he said, when I came in. Do you keep your health pretty well?

"I have come a great way out of my road," he went on, having received no reply from me but two small separate inclinations of my head, "to congratulate Mr. Carlyle on his increasing reputation, and if he does not come while I am still here, I am going to leave him a letter in my own handwriting written at *his* own table." I turned on my heel and left the room to this idiot and bumped straight into Darwin and Wedgwood. We three said not one word to the Yankee. It was necessary that we return to the library in spite of the unwelcome presence, for there was no fire in the room below. After two hours, with none of us addressing the Yankee at all, he kept up a barrage of silly questions to which I made almost no reply.

Then he inquired about my husband's "late hours" ("He does not work by the clock," I said severely in my lengthiest response to him) and about the habits of omnibuses. Off he went, leaving Darwin and Wedgwood ready to expire of laughter. I have met only one Yankee, Dr. Russel, whom I did not feel tempted to take the poker to.

Mr. Darwin was still choking with laughter when I told him that if Mr. Carlyle's "increasing reputation" bore no other fruits but congratulatory lunatic Yankees, I should vote for the diminishing of the reputation with all possible despatch. Carlyle is now, of course, head over ears in Cromwell, and is lost to me and the rest of the world, even to the Yankees: a small blessing.

I have often wished that Carlyle and I could do something about diminishing supplies of money, if not reputation, as Mr. Dickens seems always to do. Every time he is strapped for cash he makes a trip abroad and lectures to the Yankees and other strange beasts about his own work, then comes back refreshed in pocketbook and spirit alike. He is a great one for amateur theatricals. But why does he always choose September? No one is really left in London then, and he and his friend Mr. Willkie Collins need five hundred friends to fill the audience. Collins has indicated that Dickens is envious of the tales of mystery that Collins does so handily. If I know Dickens, he will write one of his own one day, if he dies before it is through. Still, I often wish that we had a way of refreshing our purses and selves as readily as he. Carlyle and I would be a fine pair of travellers ... always ill and unable to speak and no doubt put off by the foreign foods. I have made a list of our expenses, including debts to be cleared: water-rates, church-rates, rent, money for Helen. It comes to more than 24 pounds, which is about twenty more than we have at hand. I am glad Carlyle received a letter from Mr. Ralph W. Emerson admiring our poverty! Poverty is so much more creditable when it is some-one else's. We are better off now than when Mr. Emerson was moved to inspiration by our need, but my income from Craigenputtock is still not enough to keep our noses out of the sea-of-the-poor. Meat din-ners at home are nearly as impossible as can be, and one sleeps ill on tea-dinners. I ate at Verey's today, a beautiful little mutton chop and a glass of bitter ale, for one-and-fivepence. And I know a clean shop in the Strand where a half of roast chicken, a large slice of ham and three new potatoes cost one shilling! It may not be proper for women to dine alone (an outrage, if you will remember Mr. Darwin's words, to "delicate femaleism") but I see many single women like myself at Verey's, and not necessarily improper ... many governesses and the like. Besides, I am beyond all such considerations.

, I have mentioned the constantly rising and falling of our illnesses, Carlyle's and mine, mostly of the dull, listless variety that bear no repetition out of house. My own particular crosses were insomnia and a tendency to blinding headaches, when I could not speak, so cruel was the pain. But there was another disease, more insidious and deadly, which haunted me always: being alone. And alone I was for a good part of the time, for Mr. Carlyle's work came before all else. A friend wrote this little verse; I think it was for me, it must have been:

> How much I loved that way you had
> Of smiling most, when very sad,
> A smile which carried tender hints
> Of sun and spring,
> And yet, more than all other thing,
> Of weariness beyond all words.

This describes me as I must have seemed to some, on days when I could not even summon that small smile. Henry Larkin told us that when he first met me, during the late 1840's, I had "a patiently hopeless look, like a mourner standing by an unclosed grave."

Of course I realized that this was due to a combination of things: first, of course, the eroding loneliness, for Carlyle was not often with me; I would go to the post office and find nothing from him. Why, I wondered, why? Was he so ill that he could not write? *Would* he not write? In the summer of 1846 I recall thinking that being hindered from sleeping is quite another thing from not being able to sleep.

There was a constant fear underlying this melancholy, the fear that comes to most women. It is never discussed, in fact I do not know of one who has mentioned it to me or to her physician; yet it is a community of terror. It is the fear of going mad during that time that occurs to women in their middle years, when nothing but old age and its miseries lies ahead, and the present is a gray painful mist. I suffered from spells of heat, dreadful seizures that filled me with fright and new fright-bred-from-fear. Each day, for how many years I cannot recall, would bring its waves of heat and melancholia, enriched by the ever-present fear of madness. I found it difficult even to write letters to my husband. I could not seem to concentrate on any one thing. My mind splintered and shivered into many ways at once. I could not speak of it but I thought of it constantly, for to be mad was the prospect most appalling, perhaps one day a patient of the very Dr. Allan whose estate I so admired. But it is quite different to look upon lunatics with the mantle of a visitor than to be one so looked upon. The days and weeks and months and years went by in aching fear. There was no one to tell.

Harriet Martineau used to say of me, "Jane Carlyle has eight Influenzas annually. I wonder how she survives it." That was when I was fairly young, when I (the entity that somehow remains "I") became Mrs. Thomas Carlyle. Now it is getting to be *one* influenza lasting all year round. It is worsened by the thought that my little sister, my heart's Babbie, is no longer that, for she is married and has her own life as Mrs. Andrew Chrystal.

I begin to think about God and a possible hereafter. The one thing no one can doubt is Death. One may go a far way in scepticism, may get to disbelieve in God and the devil, or in virtue and vice, in Love, in one's own soul, in the Progress of the Species, in Rights of Women, in the Greatest Happiness of the Greatest Number, in "isms" world without end—everything, in short, that the human mind ever believed in; only not in death. The most outrageous sceptic—myself, after two nights without sleep—cannot let go of that one fact: a cheering one, on the whole. Death will smooth all difficulties, and one shall have a try again at existing under new conditions. This I know as a certainty, for my childhood was at variance with my girlhood and womanhood, and I shall probably have still another set of lives to live. Or perhaps I shall sleep through eternity, which used to be a horrible thought, but no longer. I am weary, weary, weary to a point of moral exhaustion that any anchorage is welcome, even the stillest, coldest, where the wicked cease from troubling and the weary be at rest, understanding, both by the wicked and the weary, myself.

I try to keep from crying. Like a small child, who must cry every day, I devote, each twelve hours, a time in tears.

Sometimes I recognize the hateful self-pity, sometimes I say it is the unbearable heat, but I cannot stop from crying.

Then a little package arrives in the post, a cameo-brooch from Carlyle. I cannot tell why it is, I cannot ask myself such a thing, but his gifts always distress me more than a scold from him would do.

On a Thursday in November 1847, when the heat had stopped and the chill had set in and I was still a wreck of heat spells and fears of lunacy, I was appointed to go to Notting Hill to see a bust of my husband. I could not keep the appointment, unfeeling as it may have seemed to be, for it was more unfeeling—I thought—to risk an inflammation in my husband's wife's chest.

But I cannot put this all to my husband's dark moods, when he is "a fearful, fiend-like creature." Like any man of genius, he is absorbed in his work. I am his sometime-solace.

I wrote to my husband in January about my feeling about Emerson, that he had no ideas except mad ones that *did not derive from Carlyle*. When I mentioned this to our friend Espinasse, he replied, "But, pray, Mrs. Carlyle, who has?"

Feeling somewhat improved, I went to several parties. One of them was a dinner at the Dickenses'. Such getting up of the steam is unbecoming to a literary man, who ought to have his base elsewhere than "ornament and grandeur." The dinner was served up in the new fashion, not placed on the table at all, but handed round! Only the dessert was on the table, and also on the table—dear God—*artificial* flowers. And such an overloaded dessert as it was: pyramids of figs, raisins, oranges. Quite unlike the Ashburton dinner, when the table held just four cowslips in china pots. It reminded me of the cowslips I fashioned into balls when I was a child and yet another person . . .

Mrs. Gaskell, the author, was there, and heard a silly old man ask me if my husband "was as much infatuated as ever with Lady Ashburton." "Of course," I replied, coolly. He got no satisfaction from me. I told Mrs. Gaskell I admired her work so much, as I do. *Cranford* will, I know, outlast much of what is being written.

But still I am weary. I read the new Copperfield, being up to nothing else. Had awakened with a headache (the penalty of all that cleverness), but cold water and coffee staved it off. And a small quantity of laudanum, which I try not to take often, as well as morphia. It creates new evils and does not deal well enough with the existing ones.

We have been visited by a most charming young lady who is to be envied, or, considering the caprices of the lady, pitied, for she is the original of the character "Blanche Amory" in Thackeray's *Pendennis*. It is hard for me to see how anyone prefers Dickens to Thackeray; it is my opinion that *Vanity Fair* surpasses anything Dickens ever wrote. The young lady who stopped here—with lady's maid and infinite fine baggage—has gone, but Thackeray most certainly captured her "manners, the wiles, the larmes." The child is called Theresa Revis, or Tizzy, and a year after she was with us, in January of 1851, I received an account from her about a passage to India at that time, which no one I think can imagine . . .

. . . "the ship was small; we were all together but I did not mind. We played shuffleboard and there was a plentitude of little Pekingese dogs. The ship went as far as Alexandria, after our train to Marseilles, then a tiny paddle-steamer carried us to Cairo.

"I crossed the desert to Suez by camel, which was the least convenient way, but my two male guardians (appointed by Lady Buller, and wishing nothing so much as to wash their hands of me) advised this mode of travel. I would guess that cost had something to do with it. Of course, I saw some friends travelling by waggon, and they told me later it was made for midgets. No one could sit upright in the caravans, much like The Little Ease in which prisoners could not sit, lie or stand with comfort. The horses that drew these caravans of the wealthy were Arabian mongrels. My friends said they were thoroughbreds, but could not restrain their wildness, so that they were not inclined to act as a team, but pulled in individual ways. The people in the waggons, in embarrassing physical contact one moment with their neighbors, would at the next moment be besieged by fantasies of perishing on the hot, white sands with *no other Englishman present,* all countrymen having been pulled in twenty other directions.

"Our sea voyage took many weeks. We were going to visit friends of Lady Buller who had been living for some while in India, and the prospect was dismal for me, with my elegant tastes and my delicate health! There were no trunks, only large crates made up by one's box-man. The cases were lined with tin so that the rats and mice couldn't get to them. Somehow, the rats and mice always did manage to get at the clothes. No one can imagine what it was like to find eternal traces of vermin-droppings upon fine linen.

"We were each allowed one case in the cabins we occupied, but the case was a bit of calculated dash. What really had to be supplied has never been mentioned in romantic stories of passage to India: furniture, washing pitchers, candles, pier glasses, rugs. Many establishments in London provided everything for passengers from corsets to sponge-bags to heavy wooden chairs. Going on board ship—even though so many other means of travel were eventually involved—meant the same thing in a way, as moving house.

"You have never suffered if you have not been aboard a P & O Steamer on the Cape Route. Insects crawled out of every space. We used all sorts of bad smells to frighten them with; it turned out we were much more frightened by those fat black beetles who wallowed in camphorated spirits and sneered. We had brought our own soap and towels, but had to throw all away when we reached our destination. All our clothing, from undergarments to riding clothes, were lined with silk, supposedly to keep the damp out but more likely to keep the sweat in! No sooner was I there than I was ordered by several doctors back to England and arrived with my health perfectly restored. Moreover, to the great relief of Lady Buller, I am engaged to a Capt. Neale from Ayrshire, who came back on the ship with me. I did not know whether to go on the stage, marry him, or drown myself, but I have taken your advice, Mrs. Carlyle, and shall marry the Capt. How lovely it will be to be rich!"

And how lovely for me, and for Lady Buller, to be rid of this troublesome baggage, living or leather.

"... *and on a P & O Steamer on the Cape Route in the middle of your eighteen hundred group of years, or whatever you call something that happened a few moments ago, a shower of stones, perfectly round, fell on board near a young person named Theresa Revis. She had no idea what they were, fortunately for you, and did not mention them as she was being serenaded by a suitor. He was struck by one, thought she had thrown it playfully, and went on singing. May I ask what that occurence was about? It was carried by newspapers in the Northwestern Provinces of India, and corresponds to many other falls of stones and similar objects. I am waiting, Dix."*

"My marbles fell," said Dix sullenly. They had been rather beautiful marbles and he resented very much having them wasted on his pets. "I let them slip through the shield, and they became about ten times smaller than they really are, which shows I was paying attention, because if I hadn't made them so tiny they would have killed everybody near that little ocean."

"I should scarcely call that paying attention," said the Teacher and began to look at some more reports, as Dix fidgeted.

"Of course, the world of your pets is severely limited by your having had to create them in your own flawed image. Dix . . . a deity! Dix, someone's feast, someone's reason, or someone's king! It is unfair to the pets, as they scurry about in their mock-society quite *purposelessly, and it is unfair to you to take them so casually because unless there is marked improvement this project will fail."*

"*Babe Ruth, Shakespeare, Aristotle, Einstein, da Vinci, Beethoven, Jesus Christ and others,*" muttered Dix. *It was his usual defense; sometimes he changed the order—added or subtracted—or chose representative "nationalities."*

The Teacher had stopped listening.

The other evening I met Jane Eyre—Miss Bronte—at Thackeray's. She is not much of a woman for looks. In fact, she is extremely unimpressive to look at. But I am always over-critical when my husband is away for such long periods. Our friend Mrs. Taylor told me my husband was to return shortly; I had no wish to hear it from her, but was glad. Still, I am as clever as she any day of the year. When all is ironed out, Carlyle may someday tell me whether he prefers to be here or to accept Lady Ashburton's invitations. I am going out now to walk off my headache and to cry it away. I have found that giving way to tears—a six year old child with a grown woman's mind, that is what I am these days—is helpful to my aches.

I forgot my own birthday, my fifty-first, for on the 13 of July we are in the middle of thorough house repair. Nobody has any idea of what these London workmen are like. They spend three-fourths of their time consulting how the work should be done, and in going in and out after beer. Even the chimneys at Number 5 Cheyne Row are being altered, and in 82 degrees heat, it is wild work, workmen or no. The builder promised to have it all done in six weeks, painting included; six months will be more like it. Meanwhile I run about in the great heat, carrying my furniture in my arms from one room to another, and sleep wherever I see a cleared space. I know I am needed to keep the workmen from falling into continual mistakes, but it puzzles me why my husband stays on. We are promising ourselves to travel to Germany when this is over, but when, when?

Charles Kingsley came by today to tell me about his wife, "the adorablest wife a man ever had." I went to sleep at eleven, fell asleep at three, then rose at six. Two plumbers were rushing about the kitchen with boiling lead; an additional carpenter was hammering for pleasure somewhere, bricklayers are measuring windows for stone sills, then rush out and are never seen on earth again. I was in the house all day, went out at ten to take a turn or two on Battersea Bridge and managed not to get my throat cut!

To elude the evil smells of paint, Carlyle finally went to Scotland and I took a room in Hemus Terrace. I do insist, though, on coming home for breakfast, and this morning walked in thin silk shoes through a deluge of rain—no umbrella! I looked forward to my Fanny greeting me at my own kitchen fire . . . I am still so dependent on the kindness of servants. They are always there for emergencies; it is the day-to-day petty arguments which wear me out. It usually results in no appetite, and I am a shocking guest, sometimes unable to eat a meal. But this morning Fanny did *not* open the door, but the cleaning person, a Mrs. Heywood. "Oh," she said, "I am so glad you are come. Fanny is in such a way. The house has been broken into during the night and the police are in your kitchen!"

And now I know the real cure for headaches. Mine vanished in a flash at this alarming intelligence.

"What have they taken?" I asked fearfully.

"Oh, Fanny's best things, a silver spoon and a tablecloth."

In the kitchen were two policemen and poor Fanny, but no coffee, no fire: everything had gone to distraction. The thieves had come in the larder window and had opened Fanny's trunk, taking her clothing and drinking the milk for my breakfast. Many little things were left; Fanny's loss amounted to about four sovereigns, which I of course gave her. Dirty naked footprints all over the larder shelf! Policemen coming in and out for three days. Almost every night some house in the immediate neighborhood has been entered, and the police go about "with their fingers in their mouths."

Now I must of course stay here, paint smell or no, and Mr. Piper has given me a pair of pistols. Capital loaded ones they are, at my bedside table. Bars of iron will go on the larder windows, and I will go to Scotland Friday. The happiest moment of the whole shocking affair was when the painter said to Fanny, "Shouldn't like to be a thief within twenty feet of your mistress with one of those pistols in her hand. She has such a devil of a straight eye!" The workmen know this eye too well; it has often proved their foot rules and leads in error.

I shall of course not mention the matter to Carlyle, for it would disturb him greatly.

Frome is without the wickedness of London, but it is a dull, dirty-looking place, full of plumbers. I chose the inn, the George, in which to stay. Cold lamb, dead and better off buried, bread and porter was two shillings sixpence! And one pound eight and sixpence for the train! But the landlord made me look at his fresh vegetables, saying "No agriculture like that in Piccadilly!"

Back to London, house is as well as can be expected, burglars out of sight temporarily. At least we are over the funeral of the weary Duke of Wellington. I saw his lying-in-state, I being crushed by crowds for four hours. But I could not help crying. I had seen the Duke alive in Bath House and remember him so well.

And it was then that Lady Ashburton died, shortly after the death of the Duke, and her husband displeased me with his offer of clothing ... I felt so sick and so like to cry that I am afraid I seemed quite stupid and ungrateful to him, but that cannot be helped. And best of all my husband has been writing touching letters about my dearness to him. This is my happiest pleasure now.

Yes, I believe in Death and now must also believe in birth. I have been asked to be a Godmother to the Simmonds child. There is one fatal objection—I do not belong to the Church of England, and my own Scotch church recognizes no Godfathers and Godmothers. The father takes on all obligation himself, and it serves him right! I am flattered at being asked, but how could I dream of binding myself to look after the spiritual welfare of any earthly baby? I, who have no confidence in my own spiritual welfare! How could I, in cold blood, go through with a ceremony in a church, to which neither the others nor myself attach a grain of veracity? It was a grand performance of the baby to get herself born, so I send this brooch, a talisman for her. Mrs. Simmonds may remove the pin, as I do not advise running a long pin into the creature, and attach the thing to a string in form of a locket. ("But what is it? What does it do?" as a servant of mine once asked me in respect of a Lord.) It must be a potent charm against the devil, for it is an authentic memorial of early Christians.

All things at once. I have also been to a wedding in Scotland. Our old rector, on being told by his wife I was afraid to go to church for the coldness of the place, ordered the fires to be kept up from Sunday over into Tuesday! How kind. I was much pressed afterward to acknowledge how superior the English way of marrying was, but I said my feelings were mixed. "Mixed?" asked the kind rector. "Mixed of what?"

"Well," I said, "it looked to me something betwixt a religious ceremony and a pantomime." And so it all is.

But to return to the one unmixed surety, Death: We were left two thousand pounds by the Ashburtons. Another example of the wished-for come too late.

Money can do nothing for us now. Nevertheless we are off to St. Leonards-on-Sea to find perhaps some surcease from my misery. My husband said my face, seen through the carriage window, was the most pathetic he ever saw. God help me. There is on earth no help.

PART IV

And now, what am I? A young and frighteningly beautiful woman with a face and body of almost unearthly perfection. A strange thing to say about one's self, but understandable when one's memories are of a different self entirely. In London I try to avoid Chelsea. Number 5 Cheyne Row is part of National Trust, now. It is not, I think, any part of the present me. I am suddenly and inexplicably newborn, a monster of nineteenth-century's memories in a contemporary shell. This is not so unlike my own thought after seeing a revival of a film called *Frankenstein*. I do not think the film-makers were entirely faithful to Mary Wollstonecraft Shelley, any more than Percy Shelley was in his own fashion, but there was an episode that amused me and bemused me, both. It is a scene showing the Scientist's dwarf servant rushing out to steal a brain for his master. Two brains are available (is this what happened to me?), and at first the servant steals the one that belonged to a Good Person. Unfortunately he drops it, and has to return for the other brain, which had belonged to a murderer. I could not pay close attention to the rest of the film for wondering what would have happened had the Good Brain not splattered. Would Frankenstein's doll have turned out well, married, raised a little family? And what would happen to the film-maker's sermon at the end: there are Things Men Should Not Meddle With, or something of the sort.

I am something of the sort. But since my memories as Jane are beginning to fade, and my manners and speech and all of me are becoming accustomed to the latter part of the twentieth century, perhaps I shall one day have a film made about me, the story of the Good Little Brain Who Made It. My name is Anthea Evan and I have been to see a man about a job . . .

". . . every reason to think that you will do well in this position," concluded the managing director in his almost-sahib accent.

Anthea smiled. There was no reason in the world to think she would do well at this position or why she had been summoned. But she was becoming used to grotesquery. When asked about her previous experience her first impulse was to talk about the re-copying of the History of the *French Revolution* that John Stuart Mills' maid had thrown into the fire by mistake; she realized this sounded quite unlike the usual twenty-five-year-old female background ("Well, two years working with an educational television show, and then I was a waitress, and then I did this part-time secretarial stuff"); nor was careful and pretty handwriting of many letters and journals a qualification to be offered in return for a high-paid post in Public Relations. Yet, even after she said nothing at all, she was given instructions to report for work a few days before the opening of the London Sun store in Piccadilly.

The person interviewing her wore a badge that read Mr. Sutherland. Anthea stared at it and felt completely lost. The whole idea of the interview had been so upsetting to her that she'd had a whiskey for her breakfast; it did relax her somewhat, but as she was about to leave she felt giddy when she stood up.

She wanted to be in control of the situation, not at the mercy of her own confusion, so suddenly she offered her hand and said in her most authoritative voice.

"Thank you so very much, Mr. Gentleman, you are a sutherland and a squalor."

Later, when she felt a bit more coordinated, she was thankful that Mr. Sutherland was probably left in no smaller state of confusion than herself. She found that she was happy about the new job. On the way to the lift she looked into a long mirror. She stared with unbelieving pleasure. Surely, although a cosmic mistake had occurred and unreality had taken over, this face and body were the best ever born. If in fact, they had been ever born at all.

PART V

The day before the store opening, John Sun had been invited to visit one of the English management team (Wanger called any two people a team), who lived in a little suburb near Brighton. The train ride was one of the things John enjoyed most. He waved to trainmen on the tracks, he waved to people on other trains, and to children in fields. He said very little during his visit because he was looking forward so much to the return trip. And a wonderful thing happened as the train was nearing the station: signs appeared, printed in large clear letters that John could read easily: BEWARE OF TRAINS.

"Beware of trains, beware of trains," he said, over and over. Wanger squinted. What did the cagy lunatic have on his mind now? Was it a cleverly disguised warning to Wanger? Did it have something to do with consecutive thought-patterns?

Wanger had bought cheap tickets, intending to deduct the money for first-class, of course, and they were sharing their compartment with a clean-scrubbed boy in blue jeans. John asked the boy his name, and told him that his own name was John.

"... bruhcawdit," said the boy. A few tries revealed that his brother was also called John.

"Have you been to Bath?" asked the boy in the singing way that John liked in English people; it made questions sound so pleasant.

"No. Perhaps we shall go," said John nicely. "Is it near?"

The boy gave directions and added, "... and if you go to Bath, be sure to get scrumpy."

Wanger looked furious. He disliked clean young people; they were disavowing their image. Damned if *he*'d ask what that meant.

"It's a kind of cider," said the boy, who had obviously been intending all the while to explain it. "Very strong, too. I mean, you think it's a sort of fruit juice, but it really has a kick to it, as you say."

As *I* say, thought Wanger furiously, what the hell does he know about what *I* say. I don't say anything of the kind.

John felt very good. He had learned a new word, scrumpy, and he could read an entire sign by himself. Beware of trains, beware of trains.

As for his other first impressions of a foreign land, he was only confused by the plane trip, the waiting, the ride from the airport, the dressed-up clerks in the hotel and the wine they made him drink. It seemed silly to be thousands of miles away when London, in its sunshiny streets, looked so much like the parts of New York with which he felt familiar.

An American model, whose picture appeared everywhere in the world, had been asked to be hostess at the opening of the Sun store in Piccadilly. The London press had been rather unkind to the Emporium, as it was called: children had wandered in and became lost in the deep carpeting, vandals kept breaking the plate glass windows and stealing silver ornaments; but Kirbye Farmer, the six-foot model with a face more familiar than anybody's own daughter, laughed it all off when she spoke to the reporters in her hotel suite:

"I dread the idea of giving the wrong impression," she had said, with a disarming grin. "Heck, my face isn't perfect—one eye is slightly higher than the other and my mouth is crooked. See? But I'm supposed to be beautiful, so here I am, representing something that is *truly* beautiful: an American dream come true. This store. Like it's the *sharing* of loveliness with another corner of the world. I discussed it with my analyst, and he said that if I hadn't been so well-oriented and essentially liberated, it would damage my psyche to be the surrogate of something so important; yet I feel that like the President has *his* job and the Queen has *her* job, I must be integrated, really willing to represent this dream."

"That's a right knotty one," murmured a representative of a London newspaper to his friend as Kirbye paused to yawn. His friend agreed.

The day of the actual opening was rainy and damp and confused. Kirbye Farmer tried to greet as many customers as possible (*"Try* to smell of heather, can't you?" urged a director. "Anyway, smell English.") but Kirbye looked only squinty due to the three downers she had taken.

Anthea was developing a strange sense of dissociation. Just before noon, when a tremendous luncheon was scheduled at the Churchill, she crept into her own office to sit down for a moment and try to collect her thoughts.

Someone else was there, sitting in her chair.

❋   ❋   ❋

Alice Bloover had sent Anthea reams of material about the store personnel, the American directors, and John Sun. But it was hardly possible for a press release to describe John.

Anthea stared at him. John got up.

"I think I'm lost," he said. "I was supposed to be somewhere else, but the directions weren't straight and I kept missing so much and so much . . ."

(But he wasn't a fat, white woman whom nobody loved, thought Anthea. He was the most beautiful young man she had ever seen, and a familiar-looking young man, at that.)

"You look like me," said John, staring at her. "You're smaller, but you look just the same." He pulled her over to a mirror. "See?"

Anthea saw. She turned to him. "What about missing the luncheon," she asked.

"Say it slower. Say it in American," said John.

Anthea laughed, and repeated it.

They went to a little place where a lot of people were crowded around a bar. There were some round tables near the bar. "There's room here," said Anthea, pointing to an empty one. "We'll creep into the corner and—oh, I'm not hungry. There's the waitress. Let's have some sherry or something."

John could not speak when the waitress came over, so Anthea ordered. Then she smiled and shrugged. "You're the store president," she said, "aren't you?"

"Yes," said John. "I wish I was somewhere else."

"Who doesn't! How long are you going to be in London?"

"I don't know. They'll tell me when it's time to go home."

Anthea was wearing dark glasses, mostly to avoid people in the new store that morning and hide her own feelings.

"Take off your glasses," said John. "I want to see your eyes."

Anthea smiled and took the glasses off. She fluttered her eyelashes and opened her eyes wide.

"Well. What color are they?" she said.

John looked. Then he said simply, "The same."

"... and I really don't know *why* I particularly want this job, or if I want it at all. I'm all in favor of being an independent woman; I must work and not have to rely on someone else for things. Although I hate the idea of not being *sweet* to a man. I mean, I think I want it both ways. Most women really do, I should imagine. A lot depends on the man, of course ..." Anthea was chattering (occasionally alarming herself at the unbridled soliloquy she was providing) and John was listening gravely, not understanding a word.

The three empty chairs at their table were suddenly filled.

"Oh, for Christ's sake," said Augustus Wanger. "Look who's here." He was with Martin Branch and Kirbye Farmer. "We thought we'd ditch the big deal at the Churchill—there's nothing more to be done here, just a lot of merchandise people talking shop ... what about that? Hey, isn't that Miss Evan?"

Martin Branch told a long, involved joke. Kirbye Farmer looked at Anthea and wondered if that bastard Wanger had arranged the whole thing to make Kirbye feel insecure, for Anthea's looks were wonderfully symmetrical and not one thing on her face or body was flawed. "Stupid bitch," mumbled Kirbye. "Probably makes half what I do ..."

"We're all finished," said Anthea. "So we'll leave you the entire table. Come along, John."

"I haven't had my—" John began, but then he understood that Anthea didn't want to sit with Wanger and Branch and Miss Farmer. He smiled delightedly. "Goodbye," he said loudly. "We're all finished. Goodbye!"

At a dinner that evening at the Ritz for the store personnel, John and Anthea sat together and kept quite still. John had been listening to a man on his left going on about wines, something about "second growth" and "bouquet." There were many wine glasses in front of him.

"He's too drunk to know what he's saying about the wine," John said suddenly. Anthea smiled and nodded.

The man next to her was a tennis player, an Englishman who was telling everyone how well he knew America. "It's not only store procedures I'm familiar with in your country," he was saying to Wanger, "but I keep up with my own interests there, too. I often go to Forest Lawn for the tennis."

Wanger stared for a second, then laughed. You never knew when these tightlipped bastards were trying to be funny. Safer to laugh at everything.

"Do you like movies," John asked Anthea softly.

"I haven't seen many," she said. "Do you like them?"

"I like Westerns," said John. "There's a lot of shooting and not much talking."

"Just the way real life should be," said Anthea.

"And even if I *don't* like the movie," said John, "and I know the story is silly and the people are ugly and not worth bothering about, I still sometimes cry."

"Cry?" asked Anthea.

"Yes. I never told anyone before, but I feel like crying a lot of the time. It's better to do it during a movie."

"I used to cry a lot, too," said Anthea. "But it wasn't because people were ugly. It was because . . ."

"Because why?"

"Because it sometimes made me feel better. It made my headaches go away, for one thing."

"I never had a headache," said John. "I hope yours is better."

"I don't have them any more," began Anthea, and then stopped.

Kirbye Farmer had got up to make a speech. Somebody was tapping on his glass with a knife for silence.

"She's silly," said John.

"Yes, she is, rather, but I suppose she's famous enough to do a good job for the store here. I keep wondering about people like her ... women who center their lives around their looks, their strength, their youth ... actresses, athletes, courtesans. No, I don't suppose anyone says 'courtesan' any more. What happens to them in middle age? Do they take dance lessons? Have face-lifts? Write non-books? Yes, I know there are a good many like that. And I suppose many of them settle for a very young lover."

She looked at John, who was staring straight ahead.

"How old are you?" she asked shyly.

"I don't know," said John. "About thirty?"

"About that," said Anthea, feeling she had been tactfully snubbed for being personal.

At least, she thought, if I do take him as a lover he won't be younger than I. Except in spirit. He is so very childlike ... it's so sweet to find that in a man. And when I say lover, what do I think I mean? I am, so far as I know, quite virginal. I believe that is a prisonable offense in a twenty-five-year-old woman these days, but I have the feeling that when the time comes I shall know quite well what to do. My guardian angel will help me.

At the moment, her guardian angel was asleep and allowing a freak flood to occur in China. Little Brother stopped the flood and watched Anthea through the prism, thinking how pretty she was. Of course she would know what to do. That's what Little Brother was there for.

PART VI

PHYSICISTS CLAIM SIBERIAN "METEORITE" WAS BLACK HOLE

The 1908 Tunguska, Siberia, meteorite that leveled 1,200 square miles of forest, has now been identified as a "black hole."

A "black hole" is an object which has collapsed to so tiny a point that its density approaches infinity. They are called by that name since the gravity at their surface is so intense that even light cannot escape.

According to two physicists writing in the British magazine *Nature*, such an object struck the earth on June 30, 1908, knocking down trees for more than 20 miles in each direction and knocking horses off their feet as far as 400 miles away. The scientists, A. A. Jackson IV and Michael P. Ryan, Jr., believe the tiny black hole passed completely through the earth, emerging in the North Atlantic Ocean.

Dix carefully reached for his illuminant and stuck it into a little recess of his outer clothing. He allowed his mouth to curl into one-thousandth of a sneer. The Teacher had been talking again about the evils of smoking, but the fact was that Dix enjoyed smoking and saw no reason to quit for the sake of another million stages or so tacked on to his Presentexistence. Naturally, every once in a while the illuminant he was using would spark and the spark might occasionally fall into the project. He couldn't help laughing when the dolls immediately and predictably rushed to their communications centers with "scientific explanations" of the spark: meteorites, black holes, showers of stones, red rains, rains of frogs ... where did they get these phrases?

When the Teacher had finished, Dix managed to take his leave with an important look on his face. "May I be excused now?" he asked. "There are a thousand new Orientals hatching today and—"

The Teacher frowned.

"No, there's more," he said.

"... On June 20, 1880, a rain of stones struck a house at 180 Oakley Street, Chelsea, England; on February 1, 1888, a piece of iron—or what seemed to be iron but resembled no earthly material—was found in a garden at Brixton ..."

Dix looked surly. "I think that was the day I dropped my ball. I think that was all that was."

"Don't interrupt," the Teacher said. He went on: "... On November 1, 1815, stones were seen rising in a field near Marbleton, Ulster County, New York, then they moved horizontally from thirty to sixty feet; in 1873, water fell in torrents from a dry ceiling in Eccleston, Lancashire. In March 1871, coins fell from a great height into Trafalgar Square, London; on August 30, 1919, at Swanton Novers Rectory, near Melton Constable, Norfolk, England, oil began spurting from the walls and ceilings, quarts of it, followed by gallons of water and methylated spirits. We will not refer to your centuries of silly mistakes with 'holy objects and images'—tears and blood indeed! In October 1883, the Quebec Daily Mercury reported an unknown animal with a head like a horse and jointed fins, twenty feet long, spotted all over.

"It is one thing to be careless in the matter of letting leaks occur, but to show your project-people our beloved tiny pet, the horsefish, is absurd. How you ever let our dear friend and companion, the horsefish, be glimpsed even for a moment by the experiment-dolls is beyond my understanding. It is a most serious offense. So serious that—well, to continue ...

"In October of 1902, vast volumes of smoke obscured all things at sea from the Philippines to Hong Kong and from the Philippines to Australia. There were no fires to explain the smoke. What were you doing, Dix? Were you smoking? ... On December 8, 1931, The New York Times reported that a sailor had received an unaccountable wound, the first of some thirty such occurrences over the next twenty years. On April 2,

1936, four mansions in one county in England were simultaneously burned to the ground, although they were miles apart; people were found for a whole decade suffering mysterious puncture marks that could not be explained; on December 22 through December 30, 1883, a man died in a closed room in a house in Jordan, New York, of stones falling hard upon him.

"I shall not refer to your pompous little tricks that result in devil worship, belief in magic, and all such nonsense. There is something far more serious at stake, Dix, and it is this.

"As expressed in the simple philosophy of some of your 'writers,' there is a wish on the part of a guilty person to be apprehended. You would not have caused such little books to be written if you did not think this to be true yourself, and I have been afraid for some time that one day or another, if this carelessness is allowed to continue, you will reveal yourself, or, of course, some small part of yourself. In that case, you understand quite naturally you would be properly punished and the project dismantled. Do I make myself clear?"

Dix nodded. His thoughts were so clouded that evening that Little Brother on reading them became sad, and resolved to work even harder to help Dix soon . . . or as soon as he could invent the other person who was to complement John Sun.

John was supposed to spend a good part of his days in the London store visiting all Emporium personnel; "Give them the old-cold smile and watch them try to look busy," Wanger had instructed, but since nobody seemed to know or care much about him, John tried to hide out in Anthea's office, following her around as she went to the files or stared out the window, as she used the typewriter or the telephone, interviewed people, yawned or stretched. He liked her so much that he kept up a steady one-sided conversation as he trailed her:

"This is a nice office. I love those fat windows with fat stomachs, you can see so much out of them. The street looks narrower here than in New York. I live in New York. I have some flowers on my terrace but there are more flowers in England. I don't like fake flowers. They're not real. You have nice flowers in this vase. Smell. Don't they smell good? I knew some riddles about a flower but I can't remember them now. Somebody who was a teenager told me. One of the men in the Sun store in New York has two teenage daughters. They laugh a lot and they wear tight pants but one of them's bottom is too big. They go to high school. I said I wanted to go some day, and they said that was typical of so-called-adult-humor, always putting people down, and one of them said 'as far as I'm concerned, high school is the place where you learn not to cry as much as you used to.' Which is why I want to go."

Anthea didn't hear all that John said; most of the time she was talking or being talked to on the telephone. She would catch a few words here and there, and nod at him brightly. Once, when she had a free moment, she said, "Do you always chat people up this way?" and John had made an odd little face. She thought he was teasing her, which pleased her.

Once, when she brought out some sandwiches and sent her secretary out to make coffee, she sighed with relief.

"At last, a moment for an elaborate luncheon."

"May I stay?" asked John.

"Of course," said Anthea. "There are lots of sandwiches. The eminent Public-Relations Director calling herself Anthea Evan always has lots of sandwiches on hand."

John frowned. "But your name *is* Anthea," he said. "Why did you say 'calling herself'?"

Anthea grinned. "Okay. Sorry. I tend to lapse into Cowardese every now and then."

John turned around and looked out of the window.

"Do you play tennis?" Anthea asked him, after the sandwiches had been put on plates on her desk; she swept aside all her papers and made room for their coffee and some tarts.

"I think so," said John.

"What do you mean, you *think* so?"

"Well, I saw some people playing and one of them taught me how to—to serve?"

"Mmm," said Anthea, biting into a smoked salmon sandwich.

"Sandwiches here are smaller and thinner with no crusts," said John. "I like that. I don't like fat on meat, either."

"Oh, cholesterol and all that," said Anthea.

"What?"

"Nothing."

They smiled at each other. "Let's play tennis Saturday," said Anthea. "There are courts not far from my house. I'll tell you about trains later."

"I *know* about trains," said John. "Beware of trains."

"How right you are," said Anthea. "British Railways, please observe. However, it's not too bad a trip, and my house is rather nice."

John said he loved Anthea's cottage. He smelled the privet and the roses, at first walking up and down, then he began to run from bush to bush. Indoors, he had to bend over because he was just a few inches taller than the ceiling, but he thought that was fun. The dining room was to the left as you came in, the parlor to the right, and the stairs right in the middle. The parlor had french windows leading out to a side terrace that Anthea had started work on and was now in semi-permanence, with a few flagstones and a white-painted set of metal garden furniture.

They played tennis before lunch, but it was not a great success. John knew how to serve, and hit the ball hard; but he couldn't remember about where to keep his foot, or where the ball had to land on the other side, so they decided to volley.

After a while Anthea laughed and said they'd better have lunch. She had prepared a salad and some cold meat. "Shall we have some sherry first?" she asked, and John shook his head. He gulped his food and said, "Yum."

"What do you do in America?" asked Anthea, heaping his plate for the second time. "I mean, what sort of thing interests you a lot. Do you go to theater, museums, churches?"

"I go to church," said John, drawing on his single experience. "And I told you about seeing the movies on TV. There isn't much else I watch on the television," said John. "I don't like the shows that have a lot of old people made up like kids, talking and pretending to laugh, and I don't like the stories that keep going on, and somebody told me that the biggest thing on TV is the Western shows anyway. I don't tell everybody about that, because some of the people at the store like the educational programs, but I don't. I'm afraid I just like the Westerns."

"Thus conscience does make cowboys of us all," said Anthea.

"What?"

"Nothing."

"Oh. I thought you said 'thus conscience does make cowboys of us all.'"

"I did."

"Oh. What does it mean?"

"Well, it's a quotation. You know. It's Hamlet, Act Three, I believe ... the one that goes on with 'and thus the native hue of resolution/Is sicklied o'er with the pale cast of thought.' Remember?"

"Yes, now I remember," said John, who had learned to say that in answer to the sly word 'remember?'; no one ever listened to anything for long, so it didn't matter.

He felt sleepy but hid his yawn. "I don't like the

murder stories on television because they make me have bad dreams. I don't like bad dreams."

Anthea had gone into the kitchen and didn't hear him. He followed her.

"The thing I like best about you," he said, as she stood near the sink, rinsing out some glasses, the shadow of her profile purely cast on the white wall behind it, "is that you take good care of me."

"Well, I try," laughed Anthea. "Not much of a cook, but nines for effort."

And they smiled at each other in total sympathy and misunderstanding.

Anthea, not sure that he wasn't playing some mysterious kind of game, went on:

"What do you like to read, then?"

John bent his head toward his plate and took a huge forkful into his mouth.

"Well, I don't read a good deal these days either," said Anthea.

For a while neither of them said anything. Then, when they'd finished lunch, John helped Anthea bring the dishes out to the kitchen.

He picked up a glass, which Anthea had left to rinse by itself. He dried it with a rather soiled tea cloth, rubbing the glass over and over again.

"I dry a glass seven times," he said. "Seven is a lucky number. So I like to try to do things seven times."

Americans like to leer in conversation, thought Anthea. I've noticed that before.

"But I wouldn't like to have the measles seven times," said John thoughtfully. "Or write my name seven times . . ."

"Write your name," said Anthea. "Consider the plight of poor Mrs. Tolstoy. She's said to have copied over the manuscript of *War and Peace* seven times."

"Seven times," repeated John, not quite as a question, not quite as a statement.

"Imagine having to *read* it seven times," murmured Anthea.

"Well," said John, putting down the first glass and picking up another, "maybe she didn't read it. How do you know she read it?"

Anthea laughed. "Right. Daresay she caught the film. Here, let's not stay at the sink all day. How about some coffee?"

"You're beautiful," John said, without any sort of guile.

Anthea laughed. "That's conceit," she said. "We look so much alike, it's as though you were just admiring your own reflection."

"What are you humming?" asked John, who had heard, during the silence at the table, a sort of tune coming from Anthea's direction.

"I don't know. What? This?" She hummed a little tune that she didn't know herself. It was a very old tune.

"Sing it again," said John.

Anthea hummed it as well as she could.

"Again," said John.

"Oh, come on," she said. "Look, it's starting to rain. No tennis this afternoon. Let's see—"

John had found a pack of cards in a cubbyhole. "What are these?" he asked.

Anthea looked at them. For a moment her mind was blank, then a combination of memory and present knowledge supplied the answer: "It's a child's card game," she said slowly. "Children have played it for years and years here. I don't think it is played in America. It's called Happy Families."

They took the cards into the dining room and Anthea spread them out.

"You see," she said, "they're all families, with names and occupations, like this, see? Here's Mr. Bones, the butcher, and—wait—yes, here's his wife, and Master Bones and Miss Bones. Then there's Mr. Bun, the baker ..."

"They're nice," said John. "Let's play with them."

"First I have to show you how," said Anthea gently.

She explained that the object of the game was to collect a complete family, but after a while it became apparent that John was giving away the wrong cards. She asked him why he'd thrown away the baker's daughter; he looked puzzled. Then he smiled.

"I like to collect the messy ones," he said.

"Oh," said Anthea.

After Happy Families, John said he wished Anthea would read to him.

"Do you really like being read aloud to?" asked Anthea. "I mean, I love to read aloud, but most people detest being read to. Are you sure you don't mind?"

John shook his head and smiled. He handed her a book he'd seen in the bookcase, that had a lovely picture on its cover.

"Oh, good," said Anthea. "It's my favorite, too." And for two chapters she read aloud from *The Wind in the Willows*. She'd have read further, but John began to yawn.

After a while the rain stopped and they walked, saying very little.

"What can we do tomorrow?" said John. "Shall I stay here?"

"Well, no, I don't think so," said Anthea. "I'll tell you what. Suppose we meet in town and take the train out to Oxford. It's very beautiful, and—"

"Okay," said John. "Will you call for me at my hotel?"

"Well, yes, if you like," said Anthea.

After tea she drove John to the station and waited until his train came. Then she went back to the cottage and cleared away the cups and poured herself a drink. She tried not to think about the things that were troubling her; she tried to convince herself that John was an eccentric millionaire who played a child's role in some elaborate defense of—of what?

* * *

Anthea brought along sandwiches and fruit for their lunch. It was a lovely Sunday morning, and she knew a place where they could have their picnic. John was wearing the same things he had on the day before. He explained: "I didn't know what else to wear; Peter usually tells me, but he isn't here, but my underwear is clean."

"Oh, good," said Anthea, with a small smile.

Oxford's buildings made John stop and stare. After a long while she steered him toward the gardens at St. John's. The flowers were at their peak, and when John saw them he squeezed Anthea's arm. "Oh. Look!" he said.

The pinks were sending out urgencies of odor, the peonies overwhelmed everything, the lawns were fragrant and striped with mowing.

"I didn't know there was any place like this," said John. "What is it?"

And it was at that moment Anthea understood John to be what her Scottish relatives of long ago would have called a natural.

"Oxford is a very old university," she said slowly. "It is the most famous in the world. It dates way, way back into English history. Many people from many countries have come here. People like us visit it to see its beauty. You do like it, don't you?"

"I love it," said John. "It's as beautiful as you are. Can we have lunch now?"

A bench nearby had only pyracantha petals for its occupant. Anthea brushed some of them off and they sat down as birds began a shy assembly. John threw some crumbs, and a robin came quite close to him.

"Look at that," whispered John. "He likes me!"

Anthea gathered up their leavings, tossing crumbs to the birds and putting papers into bins.

Then she took out her newspaper.

"Do you ever do the puzzles in the *London Times*?" asked Anthea. "I know they're different from *The New York Times* crosswords, but in a way these are more fun. Any time I've done one from the New York paper, I've had to think of things like 'River to Baltic,' or 'Wife of Bragi,' 'Husband of Gudrin' or 'Geologist's Tech. Degree.' No romance at all—anybody could look those things up. Now when you get a real challenge like "Journey on a single ticket to find lead ore in heap, four and five . . ."

"Single ticket is when you ride alone," said John. Anthea blinked. "Of course it is," she said, and wrote it in. "See . . . 'ore' is jumbled in a heap in it—the letters of ore, that is, and—why thank you, John. Ride alone it is."

"You're welcome," said John.

Anthea shut her eyes. "Now let's see. 'Mother goes by automobile on one way to get food.'"

"Automobile is a car," John said. "So—"

"You're absolutely right. Ma—in a car, that's macaroni, a food. You're an old hand at these, aren't you?"

"I don't know," said John pleasantly. "I never saw one before. I never look at the newspaper except the one on Sunday with the color comics. I don't like them very much, though."

"Mmmm," Anthea was not paying attention. "'An evil article surrounded by immortality—sweet!' Seven and three . . ."

"Vanilla ice?" asked John, who had had one that morning at the station.

"Of course. V and ice at the ends and there's our evil article, too. How clever you are."

"I don't think so," said John. "There's so much I don't know that . . ." He stopped, unable to tell even Anthea about his continuing nightmare of being found out as a crybaby.

"Would you," Anthea asked, bent over, her face hidden by her screen of yellow-silk hair, "like to see anything while you're here? There's a very famous museum—"

"Well, I like it *so* much here," said John. "Let's stay here and go to sleep on the bench for a while."

While John slept, Anthea closed her eyes. The sun was sweet and strong on her face. When he woke he smiled at her. She kissed him very quickly and said, "Time to go."

"Please don't go to work tomorrow," said John, his hair rumpled and his eyes clouded with sleep. "Please. Take me some other place like this. They won't know about it at the store, or at least they won't care and even if they do care ..." he frowned. Then he sighed. "It's all right. I'm the president."

"I know," said Anthea.

Anthea watched John's train pull out in the direction of Paddington.

"My God," she thought. "If we ever married and if we ever had a child and if it had *our* looks and my brains, how splendid. But if we ever married and if we had a child with our looks and his brains ... well, there's the new Frankenstein film right there." She frowned as she climbed into her car and started home. Whoever she was, or whatever cosmic error had been committed, she hadn't ever forseen falling in love with an amiable, beautiful moron. She remembered dimly how—in the other life—she had achieved a certain parochial immortality for wit in her chiding of the stupid, the pretentious and the silly. Perhaps this was some sort of recompense. No. This was a new situation with no background and no precedent. It would have to work itself out.

They used her car to drive to Sonning the next day, a town not far from Anthea's cottage. She took him to a beautiful restaurant with a huge garden and a private lake. "It's wickedly expensive," she said, "but you *are* the president."

"I know," said John. "I can go any place I want, but I don't always know exactly where I want to go. One of the directors of my company, Lester Kearns,

says he never knows what to do—no, that isn't what
he said, he said, 'I can't make decisions.' So I asked
him how *he* knew what to wear in the morning or
what train to take, and he said 'Sure, kick me while
I'm down, you All-American rat, and the next thing I
knew Mr. Wanger had fired him and he didn't work
there any more and he was going to a doctor who
told him he wasn't oriented to the right kind of ...
hey, Anthea? You know what?"

"What?" said Anthea.

"Your car has the steering wheel on the wrong side.
It should be on the left side of the car. Didn't you
know that?"

"In England we drive on the left-hand side of the
road," began Anthea, and then thought, what difference does it make? I seem to know these things as
though they had been gathered into a hypodermic
needle and pushed into my veins last week; how can
I explain them to somebody who didn't ever know
*any*thing.

Not much more was said during the ride back to
London. John had fallen asleep.

PART VII

"That nut is planning something sneaky," said
Wanger to Branch on Tuesday morning. "He disappeared with the PR woman all day yesterday. God
knows what he's up to. There's no use putting a bug
in his hotel room because he never talks to anybody.
In fact, I did sort of put just a little bug up there in
the flowers, and all it picks up is 'Jesus wants me for
a sunbeam.' Jesus!"

"Well, then we ought to get somebody to make him
talk," said Branch. They were walking through
Polyester Knits, noting the crowds of women and the
occasional shoplifters, nodding pleasantly and demo-
cratically to all.

"Too bad that PR woman is so damn goodlooking,"

said Wanger. They were pausing to examine some marked-down jeans. Everything in the store was marked down; it said so on the tickets. London stores seldom had sales and it made the customers happy to think of the lovely bargains they were getting in the American Emporium. "She's so goodlooking I don't like her. There's something the matter. I wouldn't be a bit surprised if she was one of these robots you see on TV. No real person looks like that. Personally, it turns me off."

Branch nodded. "Me, too. I like a woman who looks available and has to watch her crow's feet lines. Like Kirbye."

"Kirbye," echoed Wanger. "Hey, why don't we do something nice for Kirbye, like give her a bonus . . .?"

"She's already had two bonuses," said Branch.

"Well, this is important. Because any man with sense who isn't a fag, and I don't think this nut *is* a fag, not that he would be smart enough to know if he was or not, would go for Kirbye. That's the way a woman ought to look. All shiny and glamorous on top and cheap underneath. That's more American—it makes sense."

"Just what do you have in mind?" asked Branch. He changed a pair of yellow double-knit pants into its right size-niche. "Say, these pants are really nice. We're doing something really generous for the average Englishwoman. It makes me sort of glow, you know?"

"Well, why don't we ask John to join Kirbye and you and me for tea, see, because that smug schemer never takes a drink, and then you and I remember we have this appointment . . ."

"That sounds kind of simpleminded," said Branch. "He'd see through it. Remember, he sounds like a kid but he comes out with some real zingers every once in a while."

"Forget that. I'm relying on good old ess ee ex. Let Kirbye really get going on him. I mean, she's really a looker, and we *are sure* he's a redblooded man. And if there's anything in the works we should know about, some plan about this international setup he's going to kick us out of—trust Kirbye."

"I'll trust her *with* her third bonus," said Branch. "Sure. Why not?"

Kirbye's suite at a hotel overlooking Hyde Park was filled with jars and bottles and mirrors and photographs of Kirbye. "I hate the mindless impersonalities of hotel rooms," she had told John. "I bring a little piece of me, a sliver of self, into whatever environment I happen to be a part of. I know I'm a nonconformist, but anyone who has really come to terms with herself in a sense of identity-finding and consciousness-raising has *got* to be aware of hangups versus pressures."

"Where did they go?" asked John. He was watching the door close behind Wanger and Branch, both of whom had drunk briefly out of tea cups and then muttered something that sounded like a foreign language and raced each other to the door.

"Alone at last," said Kirbye. She sat on the sofa next to John and touched his cheek with her index finger.

"Stop that," said John.

"What?"

"Don't touch my face like that. It feels funny."

Kirbye wrinkled her nose, which had been altered by plastic surgery just enough so that when it wrinkled something odd happened to the nostrils.

"Hey," she said. "You know what?"

John stared at her.

"I think you're the best-looking man I've ever seen. But no bull. You *are*. You're gorgeous."

"I know," said John. "Other people say that, too."

"*And* a sense of humor," said Kirbye. "Which is for me. I can't stand people with no sense of humor. They bother me. Hey!" She moved closer and put her cheek next to his. Hers was covered with Moisture-Go

#45 and liquid rouge and pressed powder; it felt sticky. John frowned.

"How do you think of me," she asked.

"How *how?*"

"I mean do you think I'm your type, do you feel we could ever achieve a meaningful relationship?"

"I don't think about that at all," said John. "Yesterday Anthea and I went to a park and we sat on a bench and did a crossword puzzle and we fed the birds. Then I fell asleep and she took me home."

"Anthea Evan? The PR woman?"

"Yes. Do you know her?" For the first time John looked interested.

"Yeah, I know her. The great beauty. The perfect specimen. She doesn't look right to me, she looks like some kind of phony with that complexion and all."

She rubbed her nose against John's.

"John, what *do* you think about me? Be honest."

John pushed her away a bit and considered the world's most photographed face in the models-under-thirty division.

"Your face is full of stuff and it doesn't feel nice. But I'm sure you *are* nice, or you wouldn't be taking so much trouble over me." He got up and walked to the window. "It looks like rain. Anthea doesn't take in her garden furniture when it rains. It can stay right where it is."

"Look, are you trying to con me, or something?" asked Kirbye. She came over to the window and stood next to John. "Do you know how many people, I don't care which sex, would give anything to be in your shoes now? I can't tell you how many really intellectual types, athletic types, all your top-grade recognizables, have wanted to be in your shoes. Doesn't that mean anything to you?"

"Anthea and I played Happy Families." John's eyes opened wide.

Kirbye was silent for a moment, always reluctant to admit not being aware of future-slang. Okay, so he was for plurals. Was that really what he meant, or was it something she didn't know about? That was her ultimate fear, as well as the unacknowledged fear of everyone else in her eccentric social bracket. Whenever anything was said, however bizarre, one's answer had to sound as though previous experience was implicit.

"Do you want to play Happy Families now?" she asked, shrugging.

John stared at her some more.

Then he said he had to go, and he did.

"There's a man out there who wants to interview you for something," said Anthea's secretary, whose North Country accent had become so BBC that it was almost impossible to understand anything she said.

"Who is he?"

"Well, *I* don't know," said the secretary, clearly offended. "He said he wanted to write something about the store for something. *I* really can't say."

The young man, a pale, fat-faced limpet, slid into a chair facing Anthea's desk. He turned out to be connected with a highly reputable paper. He asked for coffee, got it and brought out a pad and pencil.

"Do you like working for Americans?" he asked.

"Well," began Anthea, and the young man immediately told two anecdotes involving himself and famous Americans.

"... feel about liberated woman?" was the conclusion of something; Anthea gathered the question was directed at her.

"Not a very novel idea," she replied. "A spirited woman has always been ruler of her own domain. De Maupassant pointed out how fortunate a woman was, in whatever class, since by beauty, charm and wit she could rise above any social disadvantages. In earlier days, women had definite goals. Some will never be achieved, some already have been." Good Lord, she thought, was that really me talking? How splendid!

The limpet was busy with his pencil. ". . . importance of public relations in today's society?"

"*I* don't know," said Anthea, in imitation of her secretary.

"What are your hobbies?"

"What's that got to do with anything?"

"*I* don't know," said the young man. "Well, do you go to theater or read or any of that?"

"I used to read a great deal," said Anthea, "when there was something to read. There is mainly pretentious nonsense now. I go to theater, but only to *The Mousetrap*. Is it still playing?"

"What *books* do you read?" insisted the young man.

"*The History of the French Revolution*," said Anthea. I am unconscionably familiar with it, as, on a smaller scale, with *Vanity Fair* and Copperfield."

"What about contemporary writing?"

"The wise egg-os? I read them sparingly. A hundred years ago people worked at writing. They may have been overly conscientious and often dull, but they knew what they were doing. If they had any self-pity it was saved for their wives and families, not for their readers. These days, the driving force behind literature, which is in itself a dead word, is self-pity. It is a mistake to display it publicly. The great Victorians often verged on the tedious, but there was a minimum of drivel. These days, it seems, to publish a really good novel would be like dropping a flower petal down the Grand Canyon and waiting for the echo. The difficulty may be rooted in the fact that hard work has gone out of style, and there are no longer in the world the two roots of civilization: taste and style.

The limpet stared and gathered up his belongings. "That's an eerie bit," he mumbled to himself as he backed out the door.

"Oh, blast," thought Anthea as she watched his exit, "I forgot to tell him that at supermarkets I know the value of everything and the price of nothing."

She tapped her pencil against her teeth. "I suppose that outburst was quite inevitable, considering my conversations with John, but perhaps I can make a list of things John is able to talk about. Flowers, houses, weather, colors—what else, I wonder ..."

Then her telephone rang. It was John's secretary, and then John.

"Please, Anthea," he said. "When will I see you? Now?"

"There is quite a bit more," continued the Teacher. "Too much publicity has occurred in connection with some of your mishaps. Do you remember the case of the American brigantine Marie Celeste? *According to the* London Times *of February 14, 1873, the vessel was sighted by a British ship,* Dei Gratia. *She was tacking erratically, her sails set. The Britons boarded her and found everything in perfect order. Dinner was on the table, half-eaten. A bottle of sewing-machine oil stood half-full on a table, indicating there had been no bad weather, there were no indications of mutinous struggles; yet no one was aboard. I demand to know, Dix, how this came about?"*

Dix kept his eyes downcast. "My little brother wanted it for a bathtub toy, so I took it, but the people fell out when they were passing the shield, so I put the ship back. I don't know where the people are. But my brother cried, so I gave him the Rosalie *instead. That was a French ship going to Havana. It had a canary in a cage, but I got rid of the crew first so my brother wouldn't be scared. He likes it in his bathtub."*

"Your brother must be quite a little admiral," said the Teacher. "There are other reports: the Naronic, *in 1893; the* Carol Deering, *the* Waratah—well, that's only part of the trouble. Far more serious are the famous missing persons. For instance, the envoy Benjamin Bathurst, of the court of His Majesty George III, due to return from Vienna to England, went to*

examine the horses in the stable. The ostler was the last person to see him alive. Quite simply, he vanished. There have been hundreds of these cases, often cited by your little Earth presses as 'collective hallucination.' Judge Crater has become the subject of jokes; still he was never found, was he?

"And on the twelfth of December in the year 1910 of their flawed arithmetic, a young girl living in New York went for a walk in Central Park. You seemed to have been concentrating more clearly in that phase. People could still walk through parks without being attacked by vicious persons, an inevitable result of the devolution which is now being enacted in your project. This girl was named Dorothy Arnold. She was looking forward to giving a party for her school mates, and she was seen by several of them on Fifth Avenue. She walked through the Seventy-ninth Street entrance to the park and was never seen again, and I remind you this was in the days when no crime whatever existed in the park. What happened then, Dix?"

Dix tried to remember. "Oh, yes," he said. "It was because I wanted to see if I could turn a person into a bird. Remember, I showed you the little paper in New York, the Sun, that had the story? On the lake near the Seventy-ninth Street entrance to Central Park a swan appeared, and nobody could figure out how it got there. It worked, but the swan died a few days later. I didn't want it to die."

"What about Amelia Earhart?" asked the Teacher.

Dix tried to look innocent and aggrieved at the same time. "But you told me not to collect Dinky Aircraft any more, so hers was the last. I gave up right after that. I tried to send some of them back, but my dolls don't know what they are. They call them unidentified flying objects and write a lot of silly things about them."

"Perhaps the episode that annoyed me most," said the Teacher, "began in—" he consulted a beam of light, "the year 1919. A person named Ambrose Small,

living in Toronto, Canada, was the proprietor of the Toronto Grand Opera House. On the evening of December second he was in his office until six o'clock. No one saw him leave the building, there was no damage in any way to the building, but Small vanished. He left more than a million dollars behind. His secretary was arrested, because bonds of large denomination were found in his sister's house, and eventually the secretary served six years in prison. But no trace of Small was ever found, no clues, no leads to his whereabouts.

"In 1926, in the London paper News of the World, a man called A. Framton, a theater manager, was found dead. His skull was supposedly fractured, but there was no way in which he could have fallen in his carpeted premises; the skull itself showed no wounds. Several days after the body was found it disappeared. It was never seen again.

Shortly before the disappearance of Small and the strange passing of Ambrose Framton, there was another highly publicized mystery, the sort I deplore for the stupid gossip and investigations that result. This was the case of a talented writer named Bierce, who may or may not have been seen in Mexico, New York, California, or a dozen other places where he was supposed to have turned up. But he didn't turn up. He simply wasn't there one minute after he was there. Obviously, there is one unfortunate conclusion to be drawn. You were beginning to lapse into your lack-of-concentration period, and you were motivated by selfish or private requirements. Tell me, Dix, why were you collecting Ambroses?"

"Well, you told me not to collect boats," mumbled Dix.

He remembered the Ambroses vividly; they hadn't been any fun to play with and even Little Brother hadn't been able to use them in his strategy games. They were in his collection case at home now, in the "A" compartment, and needed attention and care; he

254

wouldn't admit it, but he was undeniably sorry that the whole idea of the Ambrose Collection had been undertaken.

"So your little project, a supposedly benign race patterned after your civilization, is failing in the main because of your tiny attention span and your inability to teach the pets how to live amicably together. This tends to reflect your own conflicts, I'm afraid, and that is a decidedly poor method of working. I want you to go home and talk to your little brother and make him see that he is too old for extra-Here toys. Your penchant for failure is worrisome to me; if there is the slightest sign that you have revealed your presence to the dolls, in any way at all, the project will end."

Dix said, "Yes, I see," and planned some punishments for Little Brother.

Little Brother knew what to expect. He had been tuned in to Dix all that period. If Dix ever found out about the two new people Little Brother had impulsively assembled (to help Dix) there would be a miserable punishment. The dolls were usually flawed and unpredictable, clumsy, inexpert copies of true-people, idiotically self-absorbed and almost chauvinistically vicious when frustrated, as though they knew they were only toys and were drawing on imaginary strength and courage to mask their impotence. Briefly, Little Brother allowed himself to wonder what would have happened if a cleverer, less flawed person than Dix had chosen the small universe for a science-project; but this was a disloyal thought, so it was erased. Little Brother hoped still that his beautiful new people, the little golden dolls, would renew the Teacher's faith in Dix's attention-span. But the dolls could only imitate Dix's archetypal behavior; and too often Dix allowed his own frustrations to foment and emerge as aggression. Little Brother hoped for the best and hid inside the project room.

Kirbye Farmer, the girl all young America envied, took her third Valium pill of the day and rehearsed various scenes in which she would be forced to report failure to Wanger and Branch. "Now, look, fellows, you can't win them all ..." or "He's a closet queen. No use trying." Or "He's hooked on his PR woman, and—"

Since the historic week in 1970 that Kenosha, Wisconsin, had loosed a teenage Kirbye on the great world, her true self and her analyst had both become richer and more self-enlightened. What was the use of saying anything at all to those two store clowns that didn't put Kirbye in her customary light of successful, modest radiance? Surely there was another way to eradicate all blame for Kirbye and ...

There was something phony about that PR woman. Nobody looked like that for real.

There was something phony about that gorgeous young man. Nobody looked like that and nobody behaved like that.

Of course, there was always the possibility that still waters ran deep, you couldn't tell a book by its cover, there was more here than met the eye, or that the world was trying to con Kirbye Farmer. All that talk about playing games. The chances were that games were actually being played. What tremendous American business organization wanted to be involved in scandal? Wasn't it up to ruthless crusaders like Theodore Roosevelt and Ralph Nader and Kirbye Farmer to tell the truth as they saw it, never mind if a couple of whited sepulchers got hurt?

Kirbye stretched the skin around her eyes so she could apply liquid eyeliner over the eyelid-base and add pressed eyeshadow in a line just above the first line, then a third line in Apricot Silver above that. It gave the effect of no makeup at all, the photographers had assured her. Her all-over base was so natural that the moisture cream under it and the matte finish over it didn't look like anything more than the slightest tinge of youthful flushed pleasure, and the liquid rouge *over* the base but *under* pressed powder heightened the innocence of the effect. Her lips were coated with pasture-posy honey-bloom (colored vaseline), then touched with Plasma Pink lipstick and sealed by Ecstatic Moment Gloss. Her lashes were applied with special light-navy glue that sparkled under lamplight and were of the same tawny-beige shade that her hairdresser used twice a month on her long, swinging hair, assisted to a certain heft by transplants. Her teeth needed no Perl-Drop #7 whitener because they had all been capped in Kenosha, and her breasts had been enhanced by silicone injection as a fifteenth-birthday present from her parents. Her legs were covered with the same shade of base as her face, and her contact lenses made her eyes a limpid green or blue, or occasionally violet, hue. She wore no fingernail polish; it looked fake.

Kirbye's fame had come about because of this naturalness and her tomboyish stance. She talked to herself in front of the mirror for a while, hands stuck into imaginary pockets just over her hipbones, and tried to remember Late Late Shows in which James Stewart had won out over artificial villains to bring the natural, unaffected American way of life to his admirers. She practiced letting her voice break at the emotional moments of her speech which consisted, so far, of nursery rhymes. No sense doing any thinking until the mannerisms and poses were right.

Only when she was satisfied that she was the Girl Next Door did she allow herself to plot. The trouble was that she didn't think clearly.

"I'll let those smartasses outsmart themselves," she decided, and swung her magnificent mane over one shoulder. She wore no bra, no briefs and no shoes, only faded, recycled velvet jeans and a T-shirt that said "Drink Moxie," picked out in sequins, as she padded along the corridor of the hotel to Wanger's room. She knocked on the door, yelled "It's a bust, look

257

out!" and waited, giggling, for Wanger and Branch to let her in.

"You mean John and this PR are having orgies?" yelled Branch. "Wow. Still waters certainly run deep."

"Can't tell a book by its cover," said Wanger knowingly.

"I wonder if they need a fourth," murmured Branch, mostly to himself.

"We certainly can't have this kind of thing going on in connection with this new store opening," said Wanger. "That's for sure. We've got to put a stop to it. I believe it's up to us to prevent a scandal."

"It sure would be a scandal," said Kirbye, pouring herself a few fingers of vodka and adding a splash of ginger beer. "Gee, I don't know if I'd want my mother and father to shop in a store where the president has orgies."

"*I* certainly wouldn't want my mother and father to shop in a store where the president has orgies if they were alive," said Branch. "It kind of makes us all look—oh, I don't know—cheap." He looked away shyly.

"The Sun stores have never been cheap," said Wanger. "Only in price. Never in morality. I can remember when J. C. Young . . ." he paused. The words had slipped out. For the moment he couldn't remember exactly who J. C. Young was.

Branch picked it up. "He's the real president, J. C. Young! I know he's the real president. But what happened? I mean—who is this impostor? How did he get in? What's been happening, outside of the orgies?"

Wanger poured himself a drink and toasted Kirbye, who was curled up like a kitten in a big armchair, curling her toes. "Listen. There isn't just a question of orgies here. There's something else. You know what I think?"

He put his finger to his lips and ran around the

room running his hand into vases and under picture frames to find bugs. Then he shrugged. "I think . . ."

Kirbye and Branch leaned forward, accidentally bumping heads. "Make a wish," said Kirbye in her little-girl voice.

"I think," said Wanger, "that WE'VE ALL BEEN BRAINWASHED. IT'S A COMMIE PLOT."

Branch fell back on the sofa and rolled up his eyes. "Good God," he said. "Orgies. Commies. What kind of dirty game is this, I'd like to know?"

At that moment, Little Brother was deciding to take no chances. He was in the project room and he was tuned in. He heard everything Wanger and Branch said; it almost made him cry. Now he would have to remove his two beautiful, wonderful persons before Dix got home to set some really bad examples.

PART VIII

Anthea was patient as she told John she couldn't see him that very moment, but that she would see him the following day.

"All day?" asked John.

"Yes, if you like. Do you remember how to get to my house?"

"Yes. I go to Paddington Station and ask for a cheap ticket—"

"You could get a first-class," said Anthea gently.

"—and then I get off the train at Taplow and you'll be there."

"Yes. And if you like we can go on a picnic."

"Really? Can we? That's when you bring your own lunch, isn't it? I'll be there early."

Anthea told him which train to take and sat back. Her desk was covered with papers. Most of them dealt with events in the Piccadilly Sun store in which the press might be interested. She seemed to know

259

vaguely which editor belonged to which newspaper and magazine, but any connection with her own life was completely coincidental.

Her telephone rang. It was a woman she had met a few days before who had attached herself mysteriously to Anthea. Each time she rang up she began, "I know you're shamefully busy, so I wouldn't dream of taking up your time . . ." then on she would chatter about her own woes and infirmities. Anthea thought of her as Mrs. Albatross, which was quite close to the woman's actual name. Mrs. Albatross was the wife of an American lawyer who was very rich and seemed to arrange acquittal for all his dubious criminal clients by passing out millions of dollars to judges. The American press occasionally ran stories about "hints of Albatross investigation," "four judges involved in Albatross scandal," but nothing was really ever done to Mr. Albatross; indeed, he was a leading light of an important American legal body.

Mrs. Albatross had found Anthea at some press party and next morning had initiated daily telephone calls, usually starting with her infirmities-list, then on into:

"You know, I feel that you're a truly sincere person, and that's why I can tell you this: don't you think your aloofness may put some people off, particularly in your job? *I* know you, of course, so it wouldn't bother me, but I can understand why some people might find you remote, so to speak. I'm only mentioning this because it's so important for all of us to know ourselves, and sometimes your friends are the best mirror! Yes, indeed."

Anthea would murmur something while Mrs. Albatross caught her breath.

"And another thing, I find that so many people—not you, of course, which is why I can *talk* to you, it's what makes us close—are phonies! Indeed they are. So many men, some I could mention on the legal staff of your very own store, are so jealous of Mr. Albatross that they say terrible things about him, and about my daughter, too. She's a teacher, you know. She teaches English, and the first thing she did with her students, not that they're really children or anything, but because she believes in fundamentals, is to teach them the terrible burden of orthodoxy. She believes in speaking and writing relevantly. If they try to use 'as' instead of 'like,' she points out the affectation of it, and there are only two authors she will allow them to read for her course—both extremely relevant and violent. Violence is such a good answer to all that's being perpetrated these days when applied in educational techniques, don't you agree?"

"Oh, jolly good," Anthea muttered, looking for something in her desk drawer.

"There! Don't you think it's true that most English people never say 'jolly good' any more? That's something I've made notes about—the true new speech of social dialogue. My daughter tells me I ought to have it published, but one's own relatives are always a bit prejudiced, *I* think. My daughter says when she comes over here next month she wants to meet you. I've told her what firm friends we've become, and she'll be able to help you immeasurably with your press releases and things like that. My husband will be coming over then, too, and I know you'll want to meet him. He likes people who keep busy, like you, which is why I would never dream of disturbing you at work. I've been a good pupil."

"Mmmm," said Anthea, finding her comb and running it through her hair.

"Mr. Albatross would find one fault with you, though. I'll bet you can't guess what it is! You're too polite to strangers, like waiters and things. Now servants are always crazy about me, I always ask for their little girl or their mother if their mother is in the hospital, but Mr. Albatross is much more aware of the hostilities of the working classes, and if his meat isn't done just right he not only sends it back he complains about the waiter to the management. Which I couldn't do, not for a million dollars, because I like to have people like me, but that's one of the faults in our society, and—"

Today Anthea said suddenly, "I must ring off now. Someone has come into my office."

"Oh, of course, I understand completely. I wouldn't dream of keeping you. I'd love to come in and take you out for tea or a drink or something, but my head has been splitting all day. The doctor back home told me it was psychosomatic, but he was being conveniently abrupt, I felt, so—"

Anthea hung up. If educational violence was needed, educational violence would be applied.

She had not the slightest qualms about taking another day off from work. If the president of an organization summoned you, then that was top priority. She spent the early morning at home preparing some sandwiches and eggs, poured coffee into a vacuum jar, and tried not to let her hands tremble, as they tended to do whenever she thought about seeing John.

She took him to picnic near Cliveden Reach. They walked through spectacular rose gardens until they were out of sight of everyone.

"This is beautiful," said John solemnly. "Is it yours?"

"Not any more," she said at first, then; "No. It's part of a great estate. If you look out the upstairs windows of the house itself you can see—well, it looks like half the world. When this property was made over by its owner to the National Trust, he said, 'I have tried to use Cliveden as a place to bring about better understanding between the English-speaking world and various groups of sections of people of other countries. Here have foregathered ministers, MP's, business men, trade unionists, educationists, civil servants ...'" She stopped, because what she was going to add would have meant nothing to John; he did not know the meaning of the world 'scandal'; and a fall from valor was not within his grasp.

They ate their lunch, and then stretched out on the grass.

"There's a pretty cloud," said John. "It looks like a big dog. It was dark at first this morning and I thought we wouldn't be able to go, but then it got to be very nice out, didn't it?"

"Yes," said Anthea, staring up at the sky.

"Anthea, do you think we could be married? A lot of the men who work with me are married, but their wives aren't at all like you. But I like playing with children. I want some of my own so I can play with them all the time. Can we have children?"

"They'd be very beautiful," said Anthea.

"How do people do it?" asked John. "Where do children come from?"

Anthea leaned on one elbow and looked at him as he lay beside her.

"I daresay," she said slowly, "that you'll find out."

She thought about the only adult life she could remember. So far as she knew, she was as virginal as John. There were so many memories, memories of people, places, things, houses, animals, books, illness; but they did not include the physical expression of love.

The purblind leading the blind, she thought. Or perhaps it is better this way. Suppose I'd been Madame Pompadour or Nell Gwynn; I'd feel like a child-molester. At least we're starting this together.

She kissed him on the lips.

He wouldn't let her go. He kept kissing her, and he put his arms around her.

"I didn't know there was any such thing," said John, finally, gazing at her face which was so much like his own face. "I've seen people kiss in the movies, but I didn't know it made you feel so different. Is this the way *they* feel? How can they do it so often? I don't suppose they really love the people they're kissing, though. I really love you."

"I love you, too," said Anthea. She stayed quite still for a while and remembered gratefully that John's mind was a good deal younger than his body. As her mouth stayed on his, his hands moved all along her hair, her face and then her own body, and he didn't seem to require any schooling. Physically he was an unusually strong, healthy thirty-year-old man, and this was how he reacted.

She shut her eyes and didn't try to keep back the tears of gratitude.

The first words between them occurred a long time later when she said, "No, wait. I—I feel a little tired."

"It was only four times," said John simply. "*I'm* not tired."

But he fell asleep and so did she. When they woke it was getting cool; they gathered up the picnic things and went back to her house.

Anthea's bed was large and smelled nicely of the country and the night. Her clothes and John's were all in a heap at the bottom of the bed.

"Tell me about your childhood," said Anthea. The cottage was quite dark except for a theatrical ray of moonshine. John was entwining his left foot with Anthea's right foot.

"What?"

"Tell me about your childhood. Was it happy? Do you have brothers and sisters? Were you rich or poor?"

John turned himself around so that Anthea's foot was under his chin.

"I don't know."

"You don't know what?"

"Are all girls soft? *Little* ones, I suppose. But old women? Are they soft?"

"No. Not really," said Anthea. "Their skin gets dry and full of wrinkles. It hurts them most of the time."

"Oh. Yours is *so* soft."

"Did you have any brothers or sisters?"

"No."

"What were your parents like?"

"Why don't men have breasts?"

"Because they don't need them to feed babies with. Unless, these days, all that's going to be changed. Who knows?"

"Do you—no, I mean, well, do women ever have anything like *this?*"

"No. That's the difference between men and women."

"You mean you'll never have one? Even when you're older?"

"Never."

"Oh. I'm sorry. *No* girl does?"

"No girl."

"And all men? They all have one?"

A confused and unpleasant memory of space and time, in a night of isolated experiment, without sequel, returned to Anthea.

"They all have one, but some are better than others. Now. Answer me. Please, don't you remember anything about your family?"

"No." Then John sensed that he was disappointing her. He thought hard. Then he turned around again and buried his face in her neck.

"I remember something," he whispered.

"What?"

"I remember that I have a brother ... he's older and he's ... that's all."

"Where did you live?"

"Not here," said John, raising himself to shake his head earnestly. "Not here or in America. But I don't know the number."

"You mean," said Anthea slowly, "that sometimes you get the feeling that you were somebody else, that you really don't belong here?"

"I don't belong anywhere," said John. "Anthea, don't talk now."

"I want to go to sleep," said Anthea a little later, stretching. "Good night."

"No," cried John. "I'm *not* sleepy. I won't go to sleep now."

"I'm sleepy," said Anthea. She kissed him. "Really good night."

"Anthea."

"What?"

John spoke very low. "Would you read me a story first?"

"Not now. I'm too sleepy. Last one asleep's a rotten egg."

John laughed. "First asleep," he said proudly.

At about five thirty in the morning John awoke. He couldn't remember where he was at first, then he smiled as he was aware of what was lying not beside, more *inside*, the contours of his body. He shook her.

"Wake up," he said.

She yawned. "Good morning, darling. Did you sleep well?"

"No, I had a lot of dreams," said John. "I kept waking."

"I slept like a baby," said Anthea, and felt vaguely self-conscious for having uttered the word "baby." "Sorry," she murmured.

John made love to her and said, "Anthea, we must get married right away so we can have our children."

"We could have them without being married," said Anthea.

"No, I don't think so," said John, then politely changed the subject to something she'd be more familiar with. "Are we going in to work today?"

"Oh, good Lord, I almost forgot about that." Anthea sat up. John put his arms around her. "No," she said absently, "let me think. Yes, of course, we must go in. People will talk. You'll be impeached or whatever they do to store presidents. How stupid of me to keep you away like this. You may get into trouble. There'll be gossip."

"*Why* don't girls have one?" asked John.

When they got to the store Wanger and Branch hadn't shown up yet. John went reluctantly into his own office and Anthea ran to hers. She immediately picked up the telephone and dialed a number, so she could look busy if anyone passed; as she received the weather forecast she tried to think. Obviously John could not go home with her every night; obviously he would expect to. People would see them, and the slimy directors would do something unpleasant. It was an awkward situation, and John would scarcely be able to think of a way out. Anthea listened to the forecast and tapped her pencil against her perfect teeth. No good blaming John for not thinking straight. There wasn't anybody who could solve this particular problem. It was exciting and wondrous to be in love, but what would she and John talk about on long winter nights? Motor cars? Ice cream? Card tricks?

Of course, this was not as special a hardship for Anthea. In what seemed to be a process of devolution, there soon wouldn't be anybody left on earth, at the rate it was disintegrating, to talk to or to respect. Where were the world leaders, the peacemakers, the artists, the thinkers? The best and brightest had been replaced by the loudest and ugliest, the precious by the cheap. John was no good whatever as a talker, but he wasn't covered with meretricious glitter, which seemed to be the unpleasant aura of most celebrities.

It was splendid to have found out what love was really about. Perhaps in any form, in any lifetime, Anthea would have had to settle for only one firstrate facet of life and skimp on all others. Once she had been surrounded by superb intelligence (and a good deal of poverty), but there had been no warmth, no excitement (and no financial horn of plenty).

There's a lack of attention somewhere, she thought, and replaced her telephone receiver. The most accurate summary of human experience would have to be in the nature of a long and eventually pointless practical joke.

Her telephone rang.

"Anthea, please come to my office now," said John. "I'm really lonesome for you. Please come. There's a couch here."

"John, this is your grown-up life. We can't—"

"Well then, just come and talk to me. Please." He sounded as though he was on the verge of tears, and of course he was.

Anthea walked along the corridor that looked like any corporate empire's office setup in any city of the world. In New York, London, Tokyo, Paris, Copenhagen, Moscow, and probably Dubrovnik, the total anonymity of conglomerates had replaced character.

John was waiting at the door. He grabbed her hand and pulled her in. He began kissing her wildly. She pushed him.

"Now, look," she said. "You've simply got to learn something. Whatever we do at home is our business and it's all right, but that's personal. This concerns other people."

John smiled and raised his eyebrows questioningly.

"It's nicer this way," he said, touching her breast. "Anyway, most of the people here, the directors and all, are too old."

"Ho, ho," said Anthea.

John looked amazed. They sat on the edge of the black leather couch together and he took both her hands as he asked, "Do you mean that the men who work for me, those men in their forty-years-old and their fifty-years-old, DO IT, TOO?"

"I should imagine so."

"That's nasty," said John. "They shouldn't. They're ugly. Why would they want to?"

"That's the way most of the world is, and in that respect always has been," said Anthea. "Sex has—"

"What is sex?"

"That's what you were asking me about. The difference between our bodies. Everybody doesn't look like us, but it doesn't stop them from wanting each other, and—"

"Sex," repeated John. "Sex." He walked over to the window. "That's a little word, it's a *baby* word. It doesn't explain at all how we feel when—"

He came back to where she was sitting. He touched her hair.

"I so much like to touch you," he said.

"Well, I like to touch you, too, but I've told you, it isn't possible to do it here."

John pushed her a little so that she was leaning back against the arm of the sofa. He drew himself against her. The door to his office opened.

Branch and Wanger had been arguing most of the morning.

"First it's the goddam gummint making our lives miserable, playing dirty tricks on each other so it's good old private enterprise keeps the gummint going, then . . ." Branch stopped.

Wanger grabbed his arm.

"What did I tell you?" he said. "Orgies! Right there, right in front of you, at eleven o'clock in the *morning!* Orgies!"

. . ."*I want to go home," thought Dix. "Why does he keep thinking of things to say just as I'm leaving. I know I'm going to fail. He doesn't have to go into long speeches about it. He's being conceited."*

"*. . . some of your pets have come closer than they know in their phrase 'runs of luck.' Of course, that's the only hope they have. When they have a run of luck it means simply that you are paying attention. When a bird flashes by you or a song is sung their* luck 'runs out,' or, more accurately, you have forgotten them for the moment. Moment ... a curious word. However, the experiment is a failure. It is difficult for me to see how you could be given a passing mark. There have been on occasion suggestions that might have worked. Christianity, for example, or communism. As that intelligent Irishman said, what a pity neither of them was ever really tried. But—"

Dix felt a buzzing against his side. His signal was going bee-bee-wee very softly. Little Brother's signature. It had been a terrible day. Now something was very likely going wrong at home. On days like this it really seemed probable that somewhere, in another civilization, on another plane in spacetime, at another dimension, a race of giants was manipulating Teachers and pupils here, much as Dix was manipulating his Earth dolls. (A foolish concept, he told himself, and quite heretical.)

But the Teacher was not quite through. "Since we are nearing the inevitable failure of the project, I wanted to point out some of the idiocies going on in your globe at—let us use that meaningless word 'moment' once more. Aside from the large disasters and wars, in large cities, at this moment, there are four thousand several hundred rapes and assaults ... many fires, some floods, countless burglaries, and innumerable private offenses. No spot on your project is free of crime, corruption and stupidity. Children are either abused or made too much of, the young are not trained to anything that will benefit their fellows, the middleaged are insulated in greed and self-pity, the old are neglected and derided. As you know, in any structure, from amoebae to our very selves, a social pattern always manifests itself. The social pattern of 'Earth' has entered a final stage of rot.

"Your project must receive a grade of 'Inferior.' I'm sorry. Next semester you must start a new program."

Dix walked home. The signal was becoming stronger. The reason for it became apparent. Little Brother was in the project room. Beside him were two dolls, two pretty little things the size of Dix's seventh finger.

"Dix, I wanted to help you, I didn't do anything wrong, I wanted to help, so I got them away. If I hadn't pulled them up right this minute they would really have got into a lot of trouble. Somebody was going to find out about them . . ."

"Anthea, where are we? Are we in heaven?"

"I'm sure I don't know. It's probably a tandem dream."

"What?"

"Nothing. It's not a very reassuring dream."

Little Brother pressed a button. Now he could hear the amplification of their tiny voices. The female one was doing the talking.

"It wouldn't have been any use." Little Brother picked Anthea up and spoke to her. "John would have had to stay six years old for a billion years of your time, and that wouldn't have been any good to you."

"Where are we, what are you going to do?" asked Anthea. She was sitting in Little Brother's hand.

"Well, I'm going to put your memory-bank back where it belongs—quick, before Dix sees me—and I'll put John near you. Then when I get to be in Dix's stage I'm going to ask the Teacher if I can start the project again. I don't have as many Deficiency Ratings as Dix, so he'll probably let me. I think more clearly and I'm much kinder."

Before Dix could absorb what was happening, Little Brother disassembled the dolls and put their files in the proper places.

The Earth itself was traveling its little path around Sun.

"Why, you—you—" Dix slapped his brother. "How dare you fool with my pets? How did you get these

271

two up here? Do you know I've failed? *That I was marked* Inferior?"

Little Brother looked downward. There was nothing to say.

Dix took the rotating globe out of its little universe. He held the dripping, pulsating thing in both hands.

Then, with a savage and timeless older-brother gesture, he hurled it straight at Little Brother. It hit Little Brother in the stomach and made him gasp.

"Oof," said Little Brother, as

THE END

ABOUT THE EDITORS

CAROL and FREDERIK POHL are the editors of *Jupiter* and the *SF: The Golden Years* anthologies. Carol Pohl is primarily an artist, who has done covers and interior illustrations for science-fiction magazines. Frederik Pohl is the only person to have won science fiction's top award, the Hugo, both as writer and as editor. In addition to anthologies, their joint production includes four children: Ann, Karen, Kathy and Frederik IV.

OUT OF THIS WORLD!

That's the only way to describe Bantam's great series of science-fiction classics. These space-age thrillers are filled with terror, fancy and adventure and written by America's most renowned writers of science fiction. Welcome to outer space and have a good trip!

☐	FANTASTIC VOYAGE by Isaac Asimov	2477	$1.25
☐	STAR TREK: THE NEW VOYAGES by Culbreath & Marshak	2719	$1.75
☐	THE MYSTERIOUS ISLAND by Jules Verne	2872	$1.25
☐	ALAS, BABYLON by Pat Frank	2923	$1.75
☐	A CANTICLE FOR LEBOWITZ by Walter Miller, Jr.	2973	$1.75
☐	RAGA SIX by Frank Lauria	7249	$1.25
☐	THE MARTIAN CHRONICLES by Ray Bradbury	7900	$1.25
☐	HELLSTROM'S HIVE by Frank Herbert	8276	$1.50
☐	HIERO'S JOURNEY by Sterling Lanier	8534	$1.25
☐	DHALGREN by Samuel R. Delany	8554	$1.95
☐	20,000 LEAGUES UNDER THE SEA by Jules Verne	8569	95¢
☐	STAR TREK XI by James Blish	8717	$1.75
☐	THE DAY OF THE DRONES by A. M. Lightner	10057	$1.25
☐	THE TOMBS OF ATUAN by Ursula LeGuin	10132	$1.75

Buy them at your local bookstore or use this handy coupon for ordering:

Bantam Books, Inc., Dept. SF, 414 East Golf Road, Des Plaines, Ill. 60016

Please send me the books I have checked above. I am enclosing $_____ (please add 35¢ to cover postage and handling). Send check or money order—no cash or C.O.D.'s please.

Mr/Mrs/Miss_____

Address_____

City_____State/Zip_____

SF—8/76

Please allow three weeks for delivery. This offer expires 8/77.

Bantam Book Catalog

It lists over a thousand money-saving best-sellers originally priced from $3.75 to $15.00 —bestsellers that are yours now for as little as 60¢ to $2.95!

The catalog gives you a great opportunity to build your own private library at huge savings!

So don't delay any longer—send us your name and address and 25¢ (to help defray postage and handling costs).